# JEWELS
## OF THE
# DRAGON

## ALLEN L. WOLD

**POPULAR LIBRARY**

An Imprint of Warner Books, Inc.

A Warner Communications Company

This story is fiction. It relates to nothing in real life whatsoever. Resemblances between characters, places, or events and anything in the real world are purely spurious and coincidental.

**POPULAR LIBRARY EDITION**

Popular Library® and Questar® are registered trademarks of Warner Books, Inc.

Popular Library books are published by
Warner Books, Inc.
666 Fifth Avenue
New York, N.Y. 10103

 A Warner Communications Company

Printed in the United States of America

First Printing: August, 1986

10  9  8  7  6  5  4  3  2  1

# DANGER AT EVERY TURN...

Rikard passed a door and a man came out and fell into step beside him. The man didn't say anything for a while. He was wearing a gun—Rikard didn't know what kind—and a knife.

"Whatcher hurry?" the man said at last, his voice slurred.

"I'm trying to make an appointment."

"Zat so? Think you'll make it?"

Rikard tensed himself inwardly, in case the man decided to jump him. But he never found out the man's intentions. Without warning, a tall glittery thing flowed around the corner, half a block away, and everybody on the street came to a startled stop.

It was twelve meters tall, serpentine, transparent, shining. Rikard wanted to run, but he couldn't make his legs work. The glittering, transparent monster swung its head—if that was what it was—from side to side, as if watching the fleeing pedestrians.

Rikard found his legs at last, and took a hesitant, leaden step backwards. The thing swung to stare at him. He froze...

---

**Critical Raves for Allen L. Wold's Previous Novels:**

"Unique and lively...hair-raising and thought-provoking...absorbing."

*—Fantasy Newsletter*

"A remarkably expansive imagination...highly recommended."

*—Library Journal*

"Engrossing...gives your wonderbone a good tingle."
*—Milwaukee Journal*

"Plenty of excitement...entertaining...offers escapist, wish fulfillment adventure."

*—Publishers Weekly*

As always, for Diane, my best critic,
but especially in memory of my father.

# PART ONE

## 1.

Kohltri was a lonely planet, the only one orbiting its sun, and far from the rest of the Federation, of which it was a member.

Across the Federation from Kohltri were the Crescent Cluster, the Anarchy of Raas, the Abogarn Hegemony, and other political entities spanning dozens or hundreds of inhabited star systems. But on this side there were only the great reaches between this spiral arm of the galaxy and the next. Not truly empty, but there were too few stars and those too far apart to entice expansion.

Kohltri Station, as a consequence, was small. It circled the planet in geostationary orbit 33,000 kilometers above the surface. Its hundred thousand people administered the planet and its commerce, or provided services for the administrators. Station time was set to the surface immediately below it. When the station passed into Kohltri's shadow, it was night.

Now it was nearly noon. Rikard Braeth, twenty-six in Earth years, stood at the door to the station director's office. He was very tall, very slender, and moved with a grace that sometimes made him seem lazy. His skin was dark, his hair black and rather unruly. He was not handsome, and his clothes, once good, were now old.

After the briefest of pauses, he reached out and touched the latch plate beside the door. The door slid open and he went in.

The office was not large. In the middle stood a small, immaculate desk behind which sat the Director, head bent over the several screens embedded in the desk's surface. According to the brass plate at the front of the desk, the Director's name was Anton Solvay.

On the wall behind Solvay were framed credentials and certificates. The entire left wall of the office was a huge window, showing the deeps of space outside the station. The

1

limb of the galaxy cut a messy diagonal across one corner. On the right wall communications equipment and reference shelves bracketed a private door.

Solvay punched a few buttons, some screens cleared, and only then did he look up. He was a compact man, slightly balding, and somewhere in his fifties—still young, given a life span of about two hundred years. He rose to his feet and extended his right hand. He was fully a head shorter than Rikard.

"Msr. Braeth," he said as he shook Rikard's hand. "Welcome to Kohltri Station." He waved his hand toward one of the two chairs in front of his desk, an invitation to sit. "What can I do for you?"

"It's just a small matter," Rikard said, taking a seat. "I'm sorry to trouble you about it, but I don't know who else to ask. I need to go down to the surface of Kohltri, and I haven't been able to find out how to do that."

Solvay sat back, a look of mild surprise on his face. "Why in heaven's name would you want to go down to the surface?"

"I'm looking for my father. I've traced his movements all the way from Pelgrane to here. It's taken me two years."

"And you think he went to the surface?"

"I do. My father was very methodical. On every one of the sixty or so worlds I've tracked him through, his pattern was always the same. He'd come to a world, visit the University Central if there was one, the major museums, and so on, and always the Mines and Minerals Reclamation office. And since the Mines office is on the surface, that's where my father would have gone after he'd finished up here."

Solvay drummed his fingers lightly on the desk. "Exactly when was this?" he asked.

"Rather a long time ago, I'm afraid. My father left home thirteen years ago. Your records show he arrived here about two years later."

"And you were able to follow him here after waiting eleven years? Remarkable. But records like that are not generally available for public inspection. What authority do you have to search them?"

"I'm a Local Historian, accredited by the University of Pelgrane. Getting my degree was part of the reason that it took me so long to start looking for my father."

"I see. And you found a record of your father on a shuttle list?"

"No, but then I haven't found any record of his departure, death, or naturalization either. And he always visited the Mines offices. The surface is the only place he could have gone."

"I see." For some reason Solvay did not seem very pleased. "That is certainly a reasonable conclusion. I wish I could help you, but I can't."

"In that case," Rikard said, "could you tell me who can? I'm willing to pay for a special shuttle trip, if that's necessary."

"No," Solvay said, "I mean you can't go to the surface."

"Why not?" Rikard made sure his voice revealed no emotion other than simple curiosity.

"You don't have the proper clearances."

Rikard sighed. This was not the first time he'd had to deal with the vagaries of a bureaucracy. He took his wallet from his inside jacket pocket, took out his Historian's Accreditization Card, and handed it to the Director. That card had gotten him into a lot of places other people didn't think he had any right to. Solvay looked over the card, examined the holographic representations, dropped it on the ID plate on his desk to check the readout.

"I hope," Rikard said, "that that will prove satisfactory."

"I'm sure that it would almost anywhere but here." Solvay handed back the card. "You are free, of course, to examine any records that are not restricted by law, but I cannot let you go down."

"I don't understand," Rikard said as he put his card away. "Kohltri is not on any of the military registers. Why can't I go to the surface?"

"I am not at liberty to tell you that. The very fact that you don't know why you can't go down is proof that you have no business on Kohltri. If you want to go to the surface, you'll have to get authorization elsewhere."

"Ah, all right. I think I can still afford a round trip. Where should I go, and what kind of clearances do I need?"

"Again, if you don't already know, then I'm not at liberty to tell you. I'm sorry."

"Msr. Solvay, this doesn't make any sense. I know that a lot of people come here—"

"Not a lot, only a couple hundred a year."

"Close to a thousand, according to your own records. And most of those people go to the surface, as far as I can tell."

"If they go down, that's only because they have proper clearance."

"I didn't see anything about any clearance in the records."

"Of course you didn't; you weren't supposed to. It's not good security to label secret things as secret."

Rikard felt his frustration rise. This conversation wasn't getting him anywhere. He decided to try another track.

"Kohltri," he said, "is a mining world, as I understand it."

"Yes, it is."

"The records aren't always very clear on just what is mined here."

"That's true. Look, we're a long way off from the next nearest system. That means we're vulnerable to certain kinds of industrial espionage. We keep a low profile, in large part as a matter of self-defense. I can't tell you anything more than that."

"You mean to say that the ores you mine here are classified information?"

"You've see the records, apparently."

"Some of them," Rikard said, "yes. Does it matter that I have absolutely no interest in your mines?"

"None at all. I'm sorry." Solvay got to his feet, indicating that the interview was over.

"I am too," Rikard said, also rising.

"If there's anything else . . ." Solvay suggested, extending his hand again.

"Nothing right now." Rikard shook Solvay's hand out of courtesy. He turned and went out of the office. He went through the outer offices of the administrative section and out into the corridors of the main part of the station.

"Damn," he muttered to himself. He could feel his face getting hot, and the sound of his teeth grating was loud in his ears. He knew about security, what files were classified and what weren't. Nothing he'd looked at had any restrictions at all.

He saw someone staring at him in alarm, and others moving discreetly to the side of the corridor. Very deliberately, he made his face bland and tried to suppress his frustration and anger.

# 2.

Rikard wanted to get as far away from Solvay's office as possible. He walked along the corridors of the station with that intent, heading for the far end. As he walked, he worked to put Solvay from his mind, to make himself feel as calm as he now looked. But as his composure returned, he became aware that the scar on the palm of his right hand was itching. He tried not to scratch.

He ignored the other people in the corridors, and they mostly ignored him, though a person as tall as he was always drew some attention. He managed to ignore his thoughts of Solvay as well, but now the tingling in his palm became stronger. However calm he'd made his surface, he was still suffering from internal stress and tension.

That was when the scar itched. It wasn't much to see, just a slightly irregular line from his ring finger to the base of his thumb. Thinking about it now made the itching almost painful. Gently, he rubbed it with the thumb of his left hand.

He hated to yield, because rubbing or scratching the scar produced a strange secondary effect, bringing a momentary impression of concentric circles swimming in his eyes.

The image never came when he was calm, no matter what work he was doing with his hands. Only when he was angry did the scar itch, and only when he scratched the itch did the rings appear—a visual and mental distraction. They were as hard to see as the motes in his eye, circling the center of his field of vision. If he tried to focus on the rings, they shifted and faded.

This time the circles were so strong that he knew his inner turmoil was only barely controlled. And the visual illusion and the itching scar were not helping him calm himself. After all, the cause of his frustration and the cause of the scar were the same. It was his father he was looking for, and it was his father who had given him the scar with its phantom rings in the first place.

Back on Pelgrane, when he was just ten years old, his father took him to a clinic and paid a lot of money for an unusual operation, then paid a lot more to keep the fact of the operation discreet. The surgeons had implanted a small device in Rikard's palm, a device his father had found somewhere, that was somehow supposed to have given Rikard better than average skills with a gun. Guns had been his father's one indulgence, the only thing, Rikard now knew, that he had retained from his life before Pelgrane.

The device in his palm was connected by artificial nerves running up his arm directly to the visual centers of his brain where it caused the images of circles. But it didn't seem to work otherwise; Rikard had no special advantage as a marksman. The surgeons had checked the medical aspects of the operation, but the device itself was strange to them. Even his father had not fully understood the mechanism and had been sorely disappointed by the apparent failure of the costly operation.

In later years, after his father abandoned his family, Rikard had grown to hate the scar for what it represented. For a while he had contemplated having the device removed, but he hadn't had the money then. Later, when he could afford it, he'd decided he had better things to do with the money. And so the device, the scar, and the circles remained.

Now those circles added to his anger, undermined his attempts to calm himself. He clenched his hand and stuffed it in his pocket. Let it itch; he wouldn't scratch, and then maybe he could calm down.

He walked through the middle levels of the station, the residential levels. Science was "above," industry and service "below." There were more people than when he'd gone to the Director's office. It must be the local lunchtime.

His stomach confirmed that, even as he checked his watch. He could eat at his hostel, but then he would be alone with his thoughts, and he didn't want that. Instead he walked on to the far end of the station, to the clubs, shops and recreation areas.

He wandered off the main ways, looking for something suited to his mood, until he noticed the marquee of a tavern, situated up a side corridor. A couple of beers, he thought, were just what he wanted right now. He went to the tavern door and stepped inside.

It was not as dim as many such places, and fortunately also served sandwiches. Most of the customers were seated at the few small tables between the bar and the booths against the window wall. Through the window Rikard could see the black velvet of space, the stars above and below. From this part of the station he could even see a bit of the planet.

He'd come here for company, so he looked around for someone on whom he could impose, and was pleased to notice a man whom he'd seen several times during the last few days. A familiar face might be more willing to put up with an unexpected lunch partner than a total stranger would be, so Rikard went up to introduce himself.

The man watched Rikard approach. He was a few years older than Rikard but looked as if he'd seen a lot more of the world. He was handsome in the way that Rikard had admired as a kid, the way he'd futilely hoped he'd look. Rikard stopped by the empty chair across from the man and smiled.

"We've not met," Rikard said by way of greeting, "but I've seen you in the records office several times, haven't I?"

"You have indeed," the man said. He seemed rather reserved, but did not object to Rikard's presence.

"Do you mind if I join you?" Rikard asked. "I'm tired of eating alone."

"By all means," the man said, rising to his feet. He was as tall as Rikard but muscular instead of slender. He extended his hand toward the empty chair in a gesture of hospitality. "Please sit down." His tone and words were polite, but there was an underlying tension Rikard had noticed before.

"I'm not intruding, am I?"

"Not at all. I'm Leonid Polski."

"Rikard Braeth," Rikard said, shaking his hand.

When he sat, the table flipped up its menu. Rikard punched in his selection and credit ID, and the menu slid down. Immediately, the service slot in the tabletop slid open and his sandwich and a pitcher of beer came up.

"You must be new to Kohltri Station," Polski said. Though he seemed friendly, Rikard got the impression that he was never truly relaxed.

"I've only been here three days," Rikard admitted. He poured beer into his glass and offered to refill Polski's.

"No thanks," Polski said. "What brings you to an out-of-the-way place like this?"

"I'm trying to find my father. I'm pretty sure he went down to the surface shortly after he got here eleven years ago, but the station director refuses to let me go down to see for myself."

"That's strange. Did he say why?"

"No, and that's what's so infuriating. Here I've come almost all the way across the Federation, and I know the end of the trail is down on the surface, and now I'm blocked."

"That would be rather frustrating, I imagine."

"To say the least. Solvay says I don't have the right clearances, and then won't tell me what those are or how to get them. Would you know anything about that?"

"Sorry," Polski said with a slight smile. "I've only been here nine days myself."

"Are you going to be working here?"

"I'm afraid I can't talk about it," Polski said. He took his wallet out of his jacket pocket, flipped it open, and showed Rikard the badge of a Federal Police Officer. He held the rank of colonel, and an attached emblem identified him as a special investigator.

"Just forget I asked," Rikard said. "But I'll bet Director Solvay doesn't treat you the way he does me."

Polski put the wallet away. "I don't have any problems with him," he said.

Rikard concentrated on his sandwich for a moment. "If it's not prying," he said, "can you tell me anything about these clearances Solvay mentioned?"

"I really don't know anything about them."

"I just thought that as a police officer...Oh, well, I'll figure something out."

"Forgive my curiosity," Polski said, "but are you by any chance related to Arin Braeth?"

Rikard put down his sandwich, suddenly wary. "He's my father," he said. "Are you looking for him too?"

"No," Polski said with another soft smile. "No, it's just that I studied your father at the Academy."

"My father went out of circulation thirty years ago."

"I know, dropped completely out of sight, no clue or word of him since."

"And yet you studied him at the Academy."

"Him and others like him, though Arin Braeth was always my favorite."

Rikard kept his voice calm and even. "You know," he said, "as a kid I never really knew what my father did before he met my mother. It wasn't until I went out exploiting, to pay my way through the university, that I ever heard anything about his past. Since then, I've heard people call him all kinds of things. But to me he was just my father, even if I didn't always understand him."

"You said he left home more than eleven years ago? You must have been quite young then."

"It was my thirteenth birthday."

"Not a very pleasant birthday present, I imagine."

"No." He finished his beer and poured another glass. "The money had run out. And he didn't like being poor. He told my mother he was going to try to make one more score—I didn't know what that meant then—but he never came back."

"And you think he's here now."

"Maybe I don't, after all."

Polski considered him a moment. "Rikard," he said, "I'm not after your father. As far as I know, nobody is any more. And even if they found him here, there's nothing anybody could do about it."

"I guess after thirty years the statute of limitations does run out."

"On most things, yes. Not on someone like the Man Who Killed Banatree, of course. But that's not the point. In spite of all the stories about him, your father was never indicted—for anything. There's no doubt in my mind that he did the things he's credited with, at least most of them. We're also sure he did other things we know nothing about and may be responsible for things with which he's not been connected. But the thing that makes Arin Braeth so special, the reason he's the subject of an entire semester's course, is that there is not one shred of evidence against him. And without that, who's to make an arrest?"

"You almost sound as if you admire him."

"I do. In a way. We're sure he was responsible for some of the most daring crimes and exploits of the last two hundred years. Your father was known as a pirate, among other things, feared through half the Federation. His reputation extended into the Crescent Cluster, and even the Abogarn Hegemony. And yet, there was never any proof. Was he, or wasn't he, the man of the legends? If he was, how did he get away with it? If he wasn't, how did he get such a reputation?"

Rikard smiled sardonically. "Father didn't let me in on any of his secrets."

"To have gotten away as clean as he did, whatever the truth, he couldn't have trusted anybody. Not even your mother, I'll bet."

"He trusted her with everything except the details of his past. As far as I know."

"She knew what kind of man he was?"

"Oh, yes."

"She must be quite a woman to have made him change his ways so radically."

"She was. She died three years after he ran off. It broke her heart."

"I'm sorry. You hate him for that?"

"Not as much as I used to." He picked up his sandwich and had another bite. "I'm older now. I have a better perspective. Whatever anybody says about him, whatever the truth may be, when I knew him he was just a fine man, a fine father. He was well liked on Pelgrane, served several times on our city council, and had lots of friends who stuck with him even after the money ran out. But that wasn't enough for him."

"And now you've come looking for him."

"I want to find out what happened, why he didn't come back. I suspect that he died down there on Kohltri. I just want to know for sure, find his grave if I can. I wish I could make Solvay understand that."

"As I remember the story, just before he disappeared, he

rescued the Lady Sigra Malvrone from one of the most hideous kidnapping and extortion rings in existence."

"The Lady Sigra was my mother. Her father, Lord Malvrone, knew about my father and hired him to get my mother away from the kidnappers. When Father brought her back, Lord Malvrone refused to pay. Just shut Father out completely.

"What he didn't figure on was that my parents had fallen in love, and Mother just decided to hell with her family and went off with my father. They had enough money between them so that my father could retire. Until his investments went wrong, we lived just like any other middle-class family. My mother gave up her past too."

"So what are you going to do now?" Polski asked.

"I'm not sure, but I haven't exhausted the records office yet. Right now I'm going to finish this beer, maybe have another, take a long nap, and then do a little more research, just to see what I can dig up."

"Don't dig up any trouble," Polski said.

## 3.

Kohltri Station, as small as it was, did not have to operate around the clock. Rikard waited until the night shift was two hours old, with only a skeleton staff on duty, before returning to the records office. Though he preferred not to do anything illegal, he didn't want to be observed should the necessity present itself. As a Historian, he had every right to make use of the facilities, even at this hour, but he would not let any mere legality impede him if he found something interesting.

The offices were locked at this hour, but his authorization card unlocked the door without a hitch. The place was half dark, which meant there was no staff present to glance casually over his shoulder at the readout screens.

He walked through the outer offices, past the cubicles used by government workers, and into the hall of regular consoles.

He looked into every room, even the closets and restrooms. That, he now knew, was what his father would have done. When he was sure there really was nobody else in the office complex, he went back to the main hall and took the console farthest from the door. It was in a corner where, by turning his head, he could see the whole room. That, too, was what his father would have done.

Rikard knew very little about Kohltri other than that it was one of those places where all or most of the business was done on the station. The planet itself merely provided raw materials. In this case those were ores rather than woods, fibers, organics, spices, or whatever. He called up the index, scanned it quickly, and chose a recent report on the planet's nature and resources.

There was only one city, just called Kohltri, directly below the station, population not specified. There were mines whose products he did not recognize. There were imports of equipment, much of it unspecified or identified in code. The main export was refined ore. All the references were unusually cryptic, and he wasn't much interested in mines. But this was a good set of files to revert to if someone should come in. He precoded a call so that he could switch in a hurry if he had to.

Once again he examined the records of his father's arrival and residency. This time he compared them with his own similar records and with those of other visitors at various times during the last twenty years. He was looking for any code or sign that distinguished either his father or himself from the people who had gone down to the surface. He could find none, no clue as to who had clearance or what clearance was.

The records of interstellar movement of people and goods were remarkably thorough—if sometimes cryptic, obscured by bureaucracy, blurred by time, and full of jargon. They hinted at unusual things about business transactions between Kohltri Station, the surface, and other worlds, though only a Historian would notice. Every world had its irregularities, but he wasn't interested in them at the moment. He skimmed through the records, then called for the lists of those who had departed Kohltri for other systems.

A message appeared on the screen, asking for his authorization code. He keyed in his Historian's registration and was immediately given access.

The lists up through this very day produced no evidence that his father had ever left the Kohltri system. He closed that file and opened another. It came on-line without a pause.

And it told him that at no time, from the moment of his father's arrival up to this afternoon, had he or anybody Rikard could identify as him applied for or been given permanent residence on the station. That was an unlikely possibility, but it closed another loophole. There was just one other major file to double-check. He called it up.

The death records were similarly complete. Rikard's father had not died on the station. A quick scan of a related file showed also that he had not been arrested. Rikard closed that file too and sat staring at the prompt on the screen.

The records of his father's two-year trip across the Federation had revealed very little about what he had been looking for. That it could make him rich, Rikard had no doubt, and if his father had found it, Rikard wanted his share. His father, alive or dead, owed it to him.

He had only one thing to go on: wherever his father had gone, whatever other offices he might have visited, he had always checked with the Mines and Minerals Reclamation office. Rikard had seen the record of his father's inquiry about the Mines office here, but that was on the surface.

Arin Braeth would not have left Kohltri without going down to the surface to investigate it in person. If Rikard could have followed, he wouldn't have to be doing what he was doing now.

He queried the computer for the records of the shuttle flights; they had to contain the information he needed. Once again he had to post his authorization. As before, access was immediately granted.

At first this list seemed just the same as the others, but as he read through it, he saw that it was in fact quite different. A few of the passengers to the surface were identified as government officials with specified business. A few others were coded, obviously for security reasons. All these showed a cross-reference to a list of people returning from the surface.

But they were the minority. Most of the shuttle passengers appeared to have come from other systems rather than from the station population, but they had no return-entry reference. Neither did their names appear on the list of those who had come from other systems. The two lists did not correspond.

Far more people went down than came up, and those few who did return to the station from the surface, aside from official and coded passengers, were not the same as those who had gone down in the first place.

These anomalies didn't help him with his original problem, though. There was nothing in any of the records to indicate who had clearance or what it was.

Within twenty-four hours after Rikard's father had checked out of his hostel, six people had gone to the surface. None was listed as Arin Braeth. He could have assumed a false identity, but it would have been for the first time since leaving Pelgrane.

Just to see what he might turn up, Rikard made a copy file of those six people, including all codes, abbreviated references, and data keys, then exited the shuttle file and set up a larger search among all the other files he had examined, hoping to shake out a pattern. These six people must have had that mysterious clearance, and if Rikard could learn what it meant in their cases, he might be able to fake clearance for himself. With or without Solvay's knowledge or approval.

Before the search could produce anything, several messages flashed on the screen simultaneously. The search could not continue without entry into other files, restricted files.

He sat back to think for a minute. So far everything he'd done had been perfectly proper and legal. This was as far as his certificate entitled him to go. But he was too close to quit now.

His specialty at the university had been research methods, and his greatest interest was accessing ancient or faulty files— or secured files. He had gone beyond the curriculum, using the questionable methods he developed to discover still others. Now, perhaps, was the time to use his bag of dirty tricks in earnest. If he was careful, if he still had the knack, no one would ever know that he'd broken the station's security.

He keyed in a request to access one of the restricted files, one he hoped would tell him more about those six people eleven years ago. As expected, he got a message asking for his security code. Just to test it, he tried his Historian's registration. It didn't work. Then he started using his unorthodox tricks. It was like sneaking in the back door, finding a path that was bizarre enough to be unguarded. After several sideways movements and subtly off-key requests, he was into the restricted files. That was what he liked.

The list was more or less as he had expected, with entries for his six people, but he could make little sense of the rest of it. There were numerous cross-references, but whether they were to people, places, products, or events he could not tell. Still, in what he could understand, there was nothing to make him believe that any of the six was his father.

He requested a similar file for the following day and was not asked again for a security code. This file was like the first and contained nothing more intelligible or interesting. He checked the next three days and still learned nothing. On a hunch he tried the previous day. Nothing.

He worked his way into one of the other restricted files, one concerning people coming up from the surface. It was just as cryptic, mysterious, and confusing as the first. No clues.

He tried another sequence of files, reporting on shipments of goods from the station to the surface. One of them seemed to list ground transport vehicles, with some references which made little sense, apparently for secondhand vehicles but with price differentials that were completely out of line, even for a government contract. And the credit accounts were not in the form of the government codes he was familiar with.

Something called "balktapline" was mentioned once or twice. The entries, with the transporter given a code instead of a name, the lack of any destination, and price or value being in another code, suggested that it was some kind of contraband, maybe narcotics, black-market items, or locally illegal products.

That was none of his business, but if Solvay's clearances had to do with smuggling, it was no wonder that he didn't want Rikard going down to the surface where he could learn more. Rikard found the thought amusing. Solvay had nothing to fear from him; it was Leonid Polski who was the threat. Was that why Polski was here? Rikard didn't really care.

He skimmed through a few other files, but could make no more sense of any of them. There were shipping lists, passenger lists, and sometimes hints of transport to and from the surface that did not go through the station. The entries were obscure, partly in code, and with the cryptic cross-references that were now becoming familiar. There was plenty of material to look through, but the night shift was running out. He'd have to quit soon and plan to come back later.

He was not so completely absorbed in his work that he did not hear an outer office door opening. He listened for a moment, his fingers above the keyboard. There was a pause, then he heard the door close softly. Whoever was there had not meant him to hear.

He cleared the screen and called up the public files he'd set up for cover, the ones concerning Kohltri's production and shipping of ores. He heard a soft footstep at the door to the console hall. He called up reference material on the kinds of ores Kohltri produced. The door opened, but he did not look up from the screen. Instead he pretended to be absorbed in the document, though the words went right through his consciousness without stopping.

From the corner of his eye, he could see a woman standing in the doorway, watching him. He took his hands from the keyboard, leaned back, and continued to read. When she started to come toward him, he looked up, carefully feigning mild surprise.

The woman was maybe forty, well built, good-looking, dressed in blouse and slacks. But she had a hard face and a stiff tension that reminded Rikard of Leonid Polski, though somehow she was harder and colder.

She walked right toward him. Rikard watched her, not touching the keyboard. She would be able to see clearly that it showed a perfectly innocent file.

"You're Rikard Braeth?" she said, not really a question. Her voice was mellow but emotionless, her face expressionless; her eyes revealed nothing.

"Yes, I am," Rikard said through a long and very real yawn.

"Up kind of late, aren't you?"

"I couldn't sleep. I thought I might as well find out a little more about Kohltri's mines."

"Indeed. Someone's been looking into restricted files. That wouldn't be you, would it?"

Rikard pushed his chair back. "Look for yourself," he said.

She didn't bother to look at the screen, just kept her eyes fixed on him. Rikard affected an expression of puzzlement and offended innocence.

"You switched files," she said, "just as soon as I entered the outer office. You're pretty good."

"I don't know what you're talking about."

"Of course you do. But it doesn't matter. Director Solvay wants to see you, right now."

Rikard fought to control his tension. "What if I don't want to see him?" he asked.

She moved her right hand behind her to the small of her back. "Then I'll have to carry you," she said, and brought her hand back into view. She held the conical spindle shape of a police jolter.

Rikard stared at it for a moment. "I'd rather walk."

# 4.

The corridors of the station were empty. The woman walked a little behind Rikard and to his left, giving him no chance to get away or attack her. She didn't say anything, and Rikard didn't try to question her. Though she wore civilian clothes, she had to be part of the station's police force. Rikard was sure she could be quite dangerous.

She did not signal their arrival at the office, just palmed the door open. Inside were two other officers, in local uniform, one on either side of the desk. Their jolters were prominently displayed on hip holsters. As the door slid shut, the woman put hers away and nudged Rikard forward to stand in front of Solvay's desk, then stepped back out of Rikard's sight.

After a moment the private door opened and Anton Solvay came in. He stared at Rikard as he moved to his desk. His face was grim.

He sat; Rikard remained standing. Solvay said, "You think you're pretty clever, don't you?"

Rikard returned the man's gaze. He kept his anxiety out of his face and said nothing.

"You have to be clever," Solvay went on, "to be able to gain access to restricted files."

"I was looking at Kohltri's history and products files," Rikard said.

"Yes," Solvay said, "when Msr. Zakroyan walked in on you, but not before. When certain restricted files are accessed, even by me, an alarm sounds and subsequent use of the files is tracked for later audit. So we know damn well what you were looking at in there."

Silence was better than a futile denial, but Rikard's palm started to itch.

"What did you think you were going to find out anyway?" Solvay asked.

"Evidence that my father did in fact go down to the surface eleven years ago."

"In those files? That's pretty farfetched."

"If you've tracked my search, you can figure it out for yourself. If my father is on a shuttle list, his name was changed for some reason. I was just trying to identify him."

"Even though you knew you were intruding on restricted files."

"I'm a Historian. I have the right to research whatever I want."

"You do not have the right to go into government files that contain sensitive information." Solvay's voice was tight and controlled. "I want to know why you deliberately overrode our file security system."

"I thought that I might be able to figure out what it would take to get clearance."

"You're evading the issue. But then perhaps I should expect that from someone who uses clever tricks to break into restricted files."

Once again Rikard felt that silence was his best response.

Solvay touched a button on his desk and one of the screens on its surface lit up. He looked at it for a moment.

"Look," Rikard said, hoping to distract him, "I'm not interested in anything in those files. I just want to get down to the surface and find my father. You could easily assign me someone from your office to help me. They would see to it that I didn't get into anything you want kept secret."

"Easier for you, perhaps," Solvay said without looking up.

"Easier for you too, because if you won't do that, I'll be forced to go to Higgins or Kylesplanet and get court orders giving me the power I need to find my father. I have a right to find him, no matter what security you think you need."

Solvay looked up sharply. "You'd do that?"

"Damn right I would. My father is here, and I intend to find him, whether he's alive or dead."

Solvay glanced briefly over Rikard's shoulder to where Zakroyan stood. "I don't think it's a good idea to go quite so far."

"It's your choice," Rikard said. "If you won't help me, then I'll leave tomorrow on the first ship to Higgins."

"No, I don't think you will. You're not going to go to Higgins or anywhere else."

"How are you going to stop me?"

"Very simply. I'm going to file charges of espionage, illegal access to restricted files, improper use of authority, and anything else I can think of."

"You can't prove anything that will delay me for long."

"You forget. You're not in the heart of the Federation now. Here, I'm the court. No, my friend, I think you've just overstepped yourself."

The two police officers started paying more attention, and rested their hands on their jolters.

"I demand to speak to a Federation Police Officer," Rikard said.

"If you can find one," Solvay said, "go right ahead."

"Fine, then please call Colonel Leonid Polski. I don't know his address, but he arrived here about nine days ago."

Rikard's words took Solvay by surprise. The Director stared at him, then beyond him to Zakroyan. "Is he bluffing?" he asked her.

Zakroyan came up to stand beside Rikard. "There is a Leonid Polski registered here," she said to Solvay. "I wasn't aware that he was a Federation officer."

"Well, find out, dammit!"

Zakroyan went to the communicators mounted on the wall beside the desk. She punched a few buttons and a moment later whispered into the wall mike.

There was a pause. The response, when it came, was tuned so that only she could hear it. She listened, her eyes fixed on Solvay. Then her expression changed slightly and she turned to stare at Rikard. "Thanks," she said to the mike, and turned off the communicator.

"Colonel Polski," she said to Solvay, "is here under special orders, with complete security." She turned to Rikard. "Why is he here, do you suppose?"

"I have no idea," Rikard said. "I just met him this afternoon. We had a nice conversation. I'd like to talk to him now, please."

Solvay started to say something to Zakroyan, but she held up her hand to silence him, then leaned across the desk to whisper in his ear. Solvay occasionally glanced at Rikard, and Zakroyan looked over her shoulder at him once. The two police officers were fully alert now. They glanced from Zakroyan to Rikard and back, and kept their hands on their jolters.

Rikard was in far more physical danger than he had expected. He cursed himself silently for his incaution and indiscretion. He had thought of his search as just a bit of slightly irregular snooping, and he'd been too smug about his cleverness in breaking into the files to watch for hidden alarms. It was not the way his father would have handled the situation. The information in those restricted files must be damaging to Solvay; more than a little petty smuggling, more than Rikard had realized.

At last Solvay and Zakroyan finished their whispered consultation, and Zakroyan turned around to sit on the edge of Solvay's desk. They both stared at Rikard.

Solvay cleared his throat and said, "Well, Msr. Braeth, you wanted to go to the surface. You should be pleased to learn that we have decided that you do in fact have adequate clearance after all."

Solvay's words were a surprise and a threat. "I don't understand," Rikard said.

"It's not necessary that you do," Solvay told him. "You do want to go to the surface, don't you?"

"Yes, but . . ."

"Fine. The next shuttle leaves in two hours."

Rikard didn't like being put into a corner, even one of his own making. "I'd like to talk to Colonel Polski first," he said.

"I don't think that can be arranged," Solvay told him. "It is really a most inconvenient hour." He turned to Zakroyan. "Emeth, escort Msr. Braeth to his room. He is not to use the communicator for any reason whatsoever."

As she rose from the desk the two cops came forward. Rikard's palm itched madly, but he just clenched his hands. Zakroyan took his shoulder to turn him around. He shrugged her hand off and walked to the door. The two cops followed.

Outside, Zakroyan fell into step beside him. The two cops took their places immediately behind. They walked toward Rikard's hostel.

He had difficulty keeping his face under control. He wanted to go to the surface on his own terms, not under Solvay's gun. Not much choice now. He was in trouble, and possibly in danger of his life. Best to worry only about getting to the surface alive and in one piece.

As they left the administrative section, Zakroyan smirked, showing emotion for the first time. "It's a one-way ticket, Msr. Braeth."

"You're going to kill me?"

"I don't have to. If you're not tough enough, the surface will take care of that for me."

"I don't understand."

"You will soon enough." She was baiting him and enjoying his discomfiture.

There was absolutely no one in the corridors. Even at this hour there should have been a few people about. Neither was anybody on duty in the lobby of the hostel. It seemed everybody had been warned to stay out of sight.

They reached Rikard's floor, where the cops took up stations on either side of his door. Zakroyan came in with Rikard and stood with her back against the door, her arms folded, watching while he packed.

He had only one suitcase, into which he quickly put his few clothes. There were some files which he packed into his note recorder, a portable word-processing and data-base computer. He was packed within fifteen minutes. He left the suitcase and recorder on the bed and sat in the room's one chair.

He watched Zakroyan, she watched him, neither of them speaking. Rikard's nerves were on edge. At last the two hours passed, and Zakroyan stood away from the door. "We'd better get moving," she said.

Rikard picked up his two cases and, at her silent instruction, preceded her out the door. The two cops outside were alert and ready. All four walked to a part of the station Rikard had not visited before.

It was the shuttle depot, and nobody was on duty there either. Zakroyan worked the controls herself. The door slid open, the shuttle hatch on the other side slid open, and Rikard went in. The other three did not follow. Rikard turned to see Zakroyan, a slight smile on her face, punching the controls again. The hatches closed.

There were twenty seats on the shuttle but no other passengers. Rikard tossed his suitcase on one seat, the recorder on another, and sat down in a third. There were no ports or windows. He felt his stomach clench, his palm itch. He rubbed the scar; the circles floated in his sight.

After a moment he felt a slight jerk. It surprised him. If it was just the shuttle departing the station, it should have moved without any jerk at all. A few seconds later he felt a gentle vibration, also unusual, and a sign that the shuttle was not in good repair.

The planetary drive took the shuttle away from the station and started it down to the surface. You could go from star to star in just a few days on the flicker ships. It took nearly a day to travel the relatively infinitesimal additional distance from a system's jump-slot to planetary orbit. The trip to the surface lasted an hour.

# PART TWO

## 1.

The surface terminal was small by any standards Rikard knew, with facilities for only three shuttle bays, and those for human passengers only. The lifting of ore and the transshipment of other merchandise would all be handled at another part of the facility not directly accessible from here.

It was empty at this hour of the morning—unless orders had been sent down to keep people away. Rikard looked around for a floater for his suitcase and recorder, but saw none. He'd have to carry his luggage himself.

His footsteps on the not-too-clean floor echoed from the faded ceiling. He crossed the embarkation area and followed the signs to a directory located in a glass-enclosed lobby. The seats here were stained, old, and empty.

The directory proved to be less useful than he had hoped. It listed only the Port Authority offices and facilities, nothing outside the building itself. At least there was a Traveler's Aid office. He crossed the foyer to the suite where the TA was located.

Traveler's Aid was a minuscule place, not capable of handling more than a hundred people at a time. There was nobody here either. Rikard dropped into one of the lounge chairs, pulled the screen forward, and punched the arm for general assistance.

There was a long pause, as if he were the last in a line of hundreds. With nobody else in the TA office, that could only mean the equipment was old and run-down, a reasonable assumption considering the state of the rest of the terminal.

At last the screen cleared. "Directory, please," Rikard said. The white blank became the index pattern. "Living accommodations, cheapest possible."

"Temporary or permanent?" the screen asked.

"Temporary, and close to the terminal."

A list of three hostelries came on, each with a brief description. Rikard chose the first and asked for a reservation.

"All transactions are handled at the hostel," the screen told him.

That was unusual. "How do I get there, please?" Rikard asked.

A map came on the screen, showing his present position, the location of the hostel, and a route between, including his route out of the terminal.

"Do you require a printout?" the screen asked.

"No, thank you. What kind of transportation is there?"

"There is none."

"I *walk*?"

"Yes."

For a moment he was nonplussed. Walking through a spaceport terminal was one thing, though uncommon. But walking any distance through a city was unheard of.

"Better let me have a printout after all," he said.

The chair clicked. From a slot at the bottom of the screen came a thin sheet of white foil, a copy of the map he'd seen.

He looked at it more closely and saw that before he left the terminal and port facilities, he'd have to go through an office labeled Immigration. After that it was two blocks one way, one block left, four blocks right, a left, another left.

The hostel was a little farther away than he would have liked, if he was going to carry his own suitcase. "Are there luggage floaters for rent?" he asked.

"There are. What is your form of credit: account, voucher, or currency?"

"Voucher," he said. "Also, I have a credit account on the station." The mention of currency surprised him.

"Do you wish to establish an account here?"

"Since I'll be here for a while, I guess I'd better."

"Please use slot C," the screen said. Rikard found the aperture in the left arm of the chair. "We will transfer your station credit to your local account."

He swung the screen back, pulled his suitcase onto his knees, and opened it. From a flap inside he took out a packet of foil vouchers. It was not as fat as it had once been, and the vouchers remaining were not as richly colored as the ones of larger denomination which he had long since spent. This was all that was left of his life savings.

He put the case back down, pulled the screen into place, and fed the vouchers into slot C. The screen showed a running total. When he was done, a conversion factor increased his credit value slightly. He put the palm of his right hand flat on the arm of the chair, and a moment later an ID card with his credit number came out of the slot below the screen. He put it away in his wallet, started to push the screen back, then let it fall into place again.

"Let me have a guidebook, please."

"There is none."

He sat uncomprehendingly for a moment. Every world had a guidebook. He asked again, got the same answer. He began to appreciate Solvay and Zakroyan's strategy in sending him down here. He pushed the screen back and stood. A luggage floater came up and stopped beside him. He put his suitcase and recorder on it and, map in hand, left the TA office.

He had no difficulty finding Immigration, but met no one on his way there. Even at this hour, Rikard expected a few people to be around. The building didn't feel neglected or abandoned; it was just deserted. And his complete ignorance as to why that should be so meant he would have to be very careful if he didn't want to run afoul of local custom—or any agents Solvay might have sent down separately to check up on him.

At the Immigration office he faced a large screen, was scanned where he stood, had his ID checked, his planet of origin noted, the planet he'd last come from listed.

"How long do you expect to stay?" the Immigration screen asked him when it was through with him.

"I don't know; indefinite." He found the whole process disturbing. The immigration procedure was the most primitive he'd ever endured.

"An approximation, please."

"I really don't know. My business could take a couple of days or as much as a quarter year."

"Do you have a return ticket?"

"Uh, no."

"Permanent visit until further notice."

"How do I get a return ticket?"

"I do not have that information. You may inquire at any phone booth. May we examine your cases, please."

Rikard hefted his suitcase up onto a pedestal that started to rise from the floor in front of the screen. He had a moment's qualm. He didn't know what the local regulations were, but he was sure they did not approve of secret luggage compartments. He'd had no trouble passing this suitcase on any of the other worlds he'd visited. But then, the suitcase had been designed for normal inspection procedures. The system here was very old, and different from what he was used to. It might catch him, the way the records office up on the station had.

There was no alarm, at least none that he could hear. That in itself was not completely reassuring. But the Immigration screen just told him to put the other case on. He put his suitcase back on the floater and put the recorder on to be scanned. Nothing to worry about there. The screen told him he could go, so he put his recorder with his suitcase, and with the floater following him, went out to the street.

It was still night. Streetlights were soft, the sky overhead black. He could see, faintly glowing above the light of the city, the rings that circled the planet.

The street was designed purely for pedestrians; there were no vehicles of any kind. But there wasn't anybody walking either. That made him feel nervous until he thought that maybe the city wasn't as big as he had expected.

The buildings were small—less than ten floors—unimposing, of relatively modern design. The equipment in the terminal might be badly out of date, but this part of the city could be no more than five hundred standard years old. Here, near the shuttleport, would be all the offices and agencies concerned with trade, and the local government. All planetary authorities, embassies, and so on were up on the station.

He walked up the street, away from the port, following his map. The floater followed behind. He came to the first left turn, then the right, and passed out of the area of modern buildings and into the city proper. There were still no pedestrians, but now he knew he was in trouble.

# 2.

It was not that the buildings were old, but that they were primitive and small, built of steel and glass and porcelain, materials that had gone out of favor ages ago elsewhere in the Federation. On other worlds such building materials, along with wood or stone, were found only in neighborhoods that had been preserved or restored. This neighborhood was too lived-in for that to be the case here.

The farther he got from the port, the more the character of the buildings changed. None was more than five stories tall, and many were only two. They had no windows, just smooth, featureless facades with a central door. The streets were different here, too, and designed for vehicular traffic. There were cars of various kinds parked at the sides of the street, many of them actually wheeled. And though by their condition none of them looked to be more than ten years old, the designs were badly out of date.

Following his map, he made his second left, then the third. There was an occasional moving car on the street now, and a few people, dressed in a style he had not seen elsewhere, though he never got close enough to make out the details. The hostel was on the right, on his side of the two-lane street, just two doors from the corner.

He went through the entrance into a courtyard open to the sky. It was dimly lit, with doors on all except the street side. There were plants growing everywhere: grasses, vines, shrubs, flowers, in containers gathered in groups around the courtyard, on wall brackets, hanging from hooks. The walls were covered, one way or another, with living green and purple. There were even plants on the roof, dangling down and reaching up.

An archway across from the entrance was well lit. Rikard went to it. But instead of a registration screen, there was a man sitting behind a counter.

27

He had asked for someplace cheap. On almost every other world that Rikard knew, personal service was available only at the most expensive establishments. Either this hostel would cost far more than he wanted to spend, or else there weren't enough cybernetics to go around. Considering what he had seen of the city so far, he guessed the latter.

Rikard had only once before been on a world like that, when he'd spent a year exploiting on Gorshom with Damia Kalentis. Gorshom had had no spaceport, no interplanetary embassies, no starflight, no Federal contact. That was why Kalentis had taken her crew there. Their job had been to set all that up and, in the process, reap as much profit as possible. Rikard had made enough to live on for the next nine years, get him through school, and bring him to Kohltri.

But Kohltri was a well-established member of the Federation, even if it was way out on the edge. It should have had all the benefits of modern technology. The lack of such technology could not be due to accident or oversight.

The clerk looked up from the flimsy he was reading. He smiled at Rikard and leaned his elbows on the counter.

"I'd like something small and cheap," Rikard said.

"That's all we have. Just in from the port?"

"Yes."

"Not the best world for a holiday." The clerk continued to lean on his elbows.

"I agree. How much are your rooms?"

The clerk told him. They were very cheap. Rikard had visions of a dark cubical with a mattress on a cot and no water. The clerk made no move to get him a key or direct him to a room.

"Do I have to sign something?" Rikard asked.

"Not at all. You in a hurry?"

"No, it's just that I've had what you might call a long day. I'd like to get some rest."

"Okay by me. Soon as I see some cash, you'll see a key."

"You want currency? How about a credit account?"

"Let's see your card."

Rikard showed it to him. It was an ID only; the actual credit was keyed to the palm of his hand.

"This won't do you much good in the city," the clerk said. "*I* can take credit, but a little farther out they don't have the equipment at all. As a matter of fact, only the port zone itself is prepared to handle credit. If you're just here for a visit, you'd be better off going back uptown and paying more."

"It's not exactly a visit," Rikard said.

"You running?"

"Not as far as I know. But I don't think the Director is going to let me back up to the station."

"Look, buddy, are you here just for fun, or do you want to hide out?"

"Neither. I'm looking for my father."

"So what does the Director have to do with that?"

"It's a long story. Can I have a room?"

"Sure. How long are you going to stay?"

"I don't know."

"For God's sake, how am I going to charge you if I don't know for how long? Where's your return ticket?"

"I don't have one."

"No ticket. Look, I don't understand. Couldn't you afford one?"

"I wasn't given one."

"There seems to be a failure to communicate here." The clerk sounded as flustered as Rikard felt. "You aren't *given* a ticket, you *take* one."

"When the Director's agent puts you on an empty shuttle at the end of a jolter?"

"Is that how it happened?" The clerk's opinion of Rikard seemed to go up. "Looks like you're here for a long stay. Do you want your room by the quarter, the tenth, or the year?"

"How about five days to start with."

"Okay by me. You want some cash?"

"If I can't buy anything with credit, I'd better have cash, hadn't I?"

"How much?"

"Enough to buy meals for five days—make that ten, so I'll have a cushion."

The clerk diddled with the counter. "Okay, slap her down."

Rikard looked at him uncomprehendingly for a moment, then got the idea and placed his palm on the counter. Instead of a special pad, the whole surface was a sensor. A display lit up and showed him his balance, and the clerk pushed over a pile of paper currency. It was old-fashioned stuff, elaborately printed on special paper as if to prevent counterfeiting.

"Up the hall to the end," the clerk said as Rikard pocketed his money and ID. "To the right"—he held out a plastic card key—"and to the end again." Rikard took the key. The number 13 was printed on it. "Hope you don't mind," the clerk added.

Rikard looked at him blankly.

"The number thirteen," the clerk said, jabbing at the card key with a finger.

"Why should I?" The clerk stared back. "Will I have any trouble getting the floater back to the port?" Rikard asked.

"I'll let it out."

"Thank you."

Rikard left the desk and followed the clerk's directions to his room. It was not a dark cubicle after all, but a rather pleasant, if small, suite. There was one room which served as a sleeping and living room, another which contained kitchen facilities and a table and chairs. A third room held all the sanitary facilities.

There was no comcon, only a videophone. There was no printer, no computer display, no keyboard, no entertainment channels.

But the bed was comfortable. Rikard didn't bother to unpack, just undressed and got under the covers. His fatigue overwhelmed him, and he fell asleep at once.

# 3.

Next morning Rikard bought a directory and a city map from the day clerk, a woman this time, and took them back to his room. The directory was slender, and even here the inhabitants seemed to have no name for the city other than Kohltri, the same as for the planet and the station.

Many of the residents were listed with only an address and no phone connection. Others had a phone but no address.

Some had neither, only a cross-reference to somebody or someplace else. There was no entry under Arin Braeth.

He was surprised at how hollow he suddenly felt. He had been unconsciously hoping he wouldn't have to visit the city's records office, but it wasn't going to be that easy after all. He was afraid that all he would find there would be a record of his father's death and the location of a grave. That, at least, would bring him to the end of his search. Then he could worry about how to get off Kohltri and back home again.

He unfolded the city map. It showed only major streets, with a more detailed inset for the port area. His hostel was located in the inset, as were the government offices. That left ninety-five percent of the city mapped in only the crudest fashion. He folded the map back up and tucked it in his pocket. He'd have to find a better one if he was going to stay here any length of time.

He left his room and asked the day clerk where he could get breakfast. The woman gave him directions to a place two blocks away, on his route to the government buildings.

There was plenty of traffic on the street now, both pedestrians and vehicles. After walking a couple of blocks, Rikard realized that there were two kinds of people here. There were those who were dressed more or less as he was, in a wide variety of clothing styles, as would be expected in any port city.

The others, whom he took to be the citizens of Kohltri, wore clothes like those he had glimpsed last night. They seemed to be made of leather, or what looked like leather; boots of some kind, pants, shirt or jacket.

And they wore guns.

No one dressed in regular clothes was armed. That was to be expected; nobody on any civilized world carried a gun. Even the police carried only the nonlethal jolters. But all the locals, all those in leather clothes, were armed, men and women both. Rikard wondered about the clerks at the hostel. They had not worn leather; was that because of their jobs? The counter behind which they had sat had prevented him from seeing if they had guns on.

Rikard watched the faces of the leather-clad citizens. They were hard and wary. They looked at the other, more normally dressed people with unconscious contempt. For their part these visitors looked timid and uncertain, a feeling Rikard was ashamed to discover he shared. He suppressed his feeling of being lost and put on a confident front.

The government offices, like his hostel, surrounded a courtyard where every available nook had been filled with living plants. He found the records office easily enough. It, too, like the hostel, was staffed by people rather than by machines.

"Excuse me," he said to the elderly woman who seemed to be in charge. She looked tired beyond enduring. She wasn't dressed in leather, though he was sure she was a permanent resident. "I would like to see the immigration records from twelve years ago." He showed her his Certificate of Authority.

"Whatever you please," she said, not looking up from her work. "Room 4B, far wall." Rikard thanked her and went through the indicated door.

In the middle of room 4B were a table and several chairs, where two people sat reading. The walls were lined with shelves, and the shelves were filled with documents—all on paper. He should have expected as much. He was going to have a long day.

# 4.

He was aroused from the document he was studying by the dimming of the light overhead. The building was shutting down for the night. He'd been alone in room 4B since the middle of the afternoon, when he'd come back from lunch, and had lost track of the time.

He straightened up, his back and shoulder muscles creaking. It had not been an encouraging day's work. It had taken him half the morning just to find the year he wanted. Then he had gone through a whole year's worth of reports before discovering that there was more than one shuttle terminal at the port. That was when he belatedly deciphered the addresses and found he'd been checking on the wrong one.

By then it was midafternoon. When he'd come back from his late lunch, he spent another hour tracking down the identity code of the various terminals and separating out the reports for each one for the day of his father's departure from the hostel up in the station, and for the two days following.

So far he'd drawn a blank. He had, however, begun to get a feel for the system in use here—or rather lack of one—and had some ideas for another search since this one had failed to show any results. But he couldn't start it tonight. The building wanted him to go home.

He put the document copies away and left room 4B. In spite of not getting any specific information, he had accomplished a lot. He'd just never thought that he'd ever have to handle hard copy.

As he reached the courtyard, he had an inspiration and went back inside. There was another set of shelves in room 4B that held credit listings.

It took him another hour, working in the half-light, to find the right file, but when he did he had his answer. The very day his father had checked out of the station, he had registered a credit account down here in the city. It was still active, according to the last hard-copy record.

Rikard sat back with a feeling of elation. He still had a long way to go, but with a copy of the account number he could get to work tomorrow and pull all the answers he wanted. If the documents hadn't been lost or misfiled.

He felt uncomfortable about being in the deserted building so late on such a primitive planet as this. People who carried guns might not care about his Certificate of Authority. He hurried out, through the court, and into the street.

It was evening. The lights had come on, such as they were here. There was a distinct change in the character of the traffic from what it had been that afternoon. There were fewer vehicles of any kind, and all the pedestrians wore leather. He was the only outsider on the street.

He was some ten blocks from the hostel. He needed supper and thought about finding a restaurant. There were no dining facilities at the hostel. He remembered the place where he'd had breakfast, and decided to stop there on the way back, if it was still open.

There were fewer and fewer people abroad, all of them

wearing the leather style of this place, and none of them looked friendly. Nearly everybody he passed in the darkening night looked at him curiously, in a way that made him feel decidedly wary. If the restaurant wasn't open, he'd just have to forget his empty stomach and see if he could send out for something when he got back to the hostel.

As he walked along a particularly dark stretch of street, he picked up an escort. Two figures fell into step with him, one on either side. It was too dark to make out their faces, but he knew by their leather clothes that they were citizens of Kohltri. The fact that he was taller than either didn't seem to bother them any.

"Kind of lonely out, isn't it?" a woman's voice, strangely slurred, said on his right.

"Maybe you need an escort home," a man's voice said on his left. He, too, sounded as if he were drunk or worse.

"I hope I don't," Rikard said. He kept his own voice flat and even.

"I think maybe you do," the woman said as they hurried on. "Even an old-timer can get lost."

"This won't hurt," the man said. "We're just kind of low and you turned up to be the lucky donor. No trouble, no hassle, nobody hurt, just a mike or two and we'll be on our way, okay?"

"What's a mike?" Rikard asked. The next streetlight seemed terribly far away. The faster he walked, the farther it seemed to get.

"You trying to be funny?" the woman snapped.

"Let's not get cute," the man said. Hands grabbed Rikard's arms and jostled him along. When they came into the light, his two escorts stopped suddenly.

"What the hell," the man said. He was a boy, actually, maybe eighteen, the youngest person Rikard had yet seen in the city. His eyes were blurry, and he was obviously under the influence of some drug, perhaps the "mikes" he had asked for.

"You picked us a real winner," the woman sneered. She was easily seventy, not quite into the prime of life, but looked badly worn.

"What are you doing out on the street at night?" the boy asked. He shoved Rikard away from him disgustedly.

"Damn offworlders," the woman muttered. She and her companion vanished into the darkness.

Rikard stared after them for only a moment and then went on. He decided not to bother with the restaurant and hurried on to his hostel. He got there without any further incident. Inside the courtyard he found a bench where he could sit and catch his breath for a moment.

One thing his search during the last two years had taught him was that the stories his father had told him during his childhood had all been true, more or less, not just made-up adventures as he had pretended. Rikard had loved to hear about his father's supposedly imaginary exploits before he and his mother had met. According to those stories—understated if anything, he now knew—his father would have had no problem at all surviving in this city. In fact, the way his father had told it, it would have been the citizens, not his father, who would have had trouble.

But after his father's disappearance, Rikard had done everything he could to forget about all that. After all, he'd been brought up in a quiet, civilized world. His one stab at adventure, exploiting on Gorshom, had convinced him he wasn't the adventurous type. The other members of Kalentis's crew had been violent, uneducated, despising the locals. He'd stuck it out for as long as he could, but after a year, when he'd saved up as much as he wanted, he'd quit. He hadn't liked remembering his father's stories and thinking how much better he would have done on the same job.

Of course, he'd been only sixteen at the time.

And here he was, making comparisons again. When his breathing was more or less normal, he went to the registration desk.

"Out kind of late, aren't you?" the night clerk asked, not unfriendly.

"I lost track of time. Can I send out for something to eat?"

"Sure. You don't want to go out on the street again. It'll cost you extra that way, though."

"How much?"

The clerk told him. It was more than he wanted to pay, but not enough to go hungry for.

"Deal," he said, and slapped the counter to exchange the credit.

The clerk laughed. "You learn fast. If you can manage to stay off the streets at night, you might even live long enough to put your knowledge to some use."

"I wasn't aware it was going to be quite that rough out there."

"Well, now you know. The only place that's worse than the streets at night is the Troishla anytime. Now *last* night, you came in so late *nobody* was out. That's how you got here in one piece. Whoever scheduled your shuttle either didn't know what they were doing—or else they did."

"Probably the latter," Rikard said dryly, and went to his room to wait for his supper.

# 5.

While he waited his thoughts kept returning to the two people who had demanded "mikes" from him—a drug of some kind, he guessed. Though he had not been in any real danger, his experience had been unexpected and had frightened him. But the thought that occupied him now was that he'd also felt a thrill of excitement.

He had never been subjected to personal violence, or even the threat of violence before. Even on Gorshom he'd kept on good terms with the rest of the exploitation crew and hadn't gone looking for trouble among the locals. He didn't like the idea of fighting or violent competition, and found it hard to understand how his father could have willingly exposed himself to that kind of experience, sought it out, lived with it.

And yet, here he was, with some of his father in him after all, if the thrill meant anything. Would he have fought if they'd tried to rob him? He didn't like to think that he might have another opportunity. Right now the thrill, if any, was dissipating. All he wanted—he told himself—was to find his father and then get back to civilization.

Doing the latter would not be easy. Starships could be boarded only from an orbiting station. Even though he still had enough money for passage from Kohltri to Higgins and then the next nearest world, he'd have to get past Solvay at Kohltri Station. He wasn't sure he knew how to do that.

He was still worrying over the problem half an hour later when someone knocked on his door. It was a young man, dressed in leather but without a gun, carrying a white plastic box.

"You Braeth?" the young man asked.

"Yes, what is it?"

"Your supper." He handed Rikard the box. "That'll cost you eight bills."

"I already paid the clerk at the registration desk."

"I don't know about that."

Rikard stared down at him for a second or two. "Shall we go out and talk to him?"

"Ah, no, never mind." The young man grimaced, then walked rapidly away.

Rikard closed the door and took the box into his kitchen. He didn't know whether it was his size or his attitude that had won that little contest, but he felt good about it anyway.

Everything he'd ordered was there in the box, but it was cold. He loaded it all, except the beer, into the kitchen console and turned it on.

Even assuming he could get off Kohltri, he had to decide what he would do then. If his father had made his last score and there was any money left, there would be no problem. Rikard would just demand his share, take what he could, and then leave his father to whatever kind of life he'd made for himself here.

But if the money was gone, or if his father hadn't made his score, or had died trying, Rikard wouldn't have enough money to buy passage all the way home. He'd have to get a job somewhere, probably as a teacher at some university. That was what Historians usually did.

And once he was home, then what?

He opened his first beer and drank half of it. The kitchen console pinged. He took out his dinner, set it on the table, and started eating.

He didn't want to be a teacher. Not any more. Though his two-year search for his father had been frustrating, Rikard had come to enjoy being on his own, completely independent, with no one but himself to answer to.

Maybe he could use his degrees as a Local Historian to set himself up in some kind of private research business. But even that didn't seem very appealing right now. It could hardly provide the same kind of excitement as the hunt for his father had so far. He didn't really have any idea what he wanted to do with himself.

Ever since his mother died, his life had been guided by the desire to be just the opposite of his father, both as he knew him and as he had imagined him to be. He had tried his best to deny everything his father had taught him, to ignore the meaning of the useless operation that had scarred his hand.

Only after he finished at the university had he realized that his revenge was no revenge after all if his father wasn't there to see it. That was when he'd decided to find his father and show him that he was his own person. And take his share of whatever his father had found.

And his father was here on Kohltri somewhere. Rikard wasn't about to let some toughs who had wanted to mess him up a little frighten him away. His father would have laughed.

He finished his meal and opened another beer. He had to make up his mind what he was going to do next. If he stayed here and continued his search, he'd have to accept the fact that he was his father's son after all. That was what his experience of the last two years was building up to.

Now was a turning point. He could give up now, having come this far, try to go home, and just be another normal citizen. Or he could face the challenge, finish the search, and become something like the kind of man his father had once been. He would have to, in order to survive here. Did he want to face his father that badly?

His father . . . But how had his father started out? Just another citizen of the Federation, as far as Rikard knew. He'd *become* an adventurer; he'd not been born one.

If Rikard left Kohltri now, the last two years of his life would be wasted. He would have to reassess his whole attitude about himself. But at least he'd be alive—assuming he could get off Kohltri in the first place.

He fingered the scar on the palm of his right hand. When the impression of concentric circles appeared in front of his eyes, he tried vainly, as he always did, to make them come clear. They flickered and faded.

He cleaned up after his meal, finished a third beer, then went out to the registration desk. Another patron, an off-worlder by his dress, was talking to the night clerk. Rikard waited until their business was finished, then went up to the desk.

"The guy who brought me supper wanted eight bills," he said.

"Did you pay him?"

"No. I suggested we come out and talk to you about it."

"That was smart. Cherep'll take you for anything you've got, if you let him. Otherwise he's trustworthy."

Rikard leaned on the counter and tried to organize his thoughts. "I think I mentioned," he said slowly, "that I have no return ticket to the station."

The clerk just looked at him, but with something in his expression that made Rikard think a return ticket could be had—for the right price.

"I was wondering," Rikard went on, "if it might be possible to book passage from here to Higgins, or Kylesplanet, even so."

"Surely," the clerk said softly, "and nobody up at the station need know about it. Cost extra, of course."

"How much?"

The clerk told him. Not quite double the regular fare. Rikard had that much, but only enough more to live on for about five days after he got there. He'd have to find a job quickly, but he could leave tomorrow.

"Just curious," he said. He left the surprised clerk and went back to his room.

# PART THREE

## 1.

He got to the records office early the next morning, prepared to spend the whole day searching. He found the credit information he wanted almost at once. His father had established an account and had drawn from it for two-thirds of a year. There were no further deposits or withdrawals for the next eleven years, right up to today. There was still credit in the account.

There was an address associated with the account, but it was only a postal drop. That was not uncommon in this city, and was the kind of thing his father probably would have arranged anyway.

The last place to check was the records of deaths. Rikard had been putting that off for as long as possible, hoping he wouldn't have to look there. And besides, there was no sense searching that file until he had a better idea of the probable dates.

The death records were in another room. He found the right year and combed the files. The records were incredibly incomplete. Some entries for multiple deaths—accident? mayhem?—didn't bother to list all the names. Pages were missing or out of order. If his father had died eleven years ago, it could easily have not been recorded. In any event, there was no certificate of death or burial.

There was no more information for him here, but there was still more he could do elsewhere. His father was sure to have made an impression on people over a period of two-thirds of a year. Now all Rikard had to do was find somebody who had known his father back then.

He had no idea how a police investigator or private detective would go about that kind of search, but he felt it couldn't be much different from historical research. One simply questioned people instead of documents. He just hoped the people would be willing to talk to him.

He went back to the main office and found the old woman who had directed him to room 4B the first time he'd come. She still bore the appearance of incredible fatigue, but he had since learned that it was appearance only. He stood in front of the desk where she was working.

"Is there any other source of documents and records?" he asked when she looked up at him at last.

"None that I've ever seen. Run dry?"

"As of eleven years ago."

"End of the line, huh?"

"This part of it anyway. I'm hoping I can find some people here who knew him back then."

"Lots of luck."

"Thanks, I'll need it." He hesitated a moment. "This is only my second day here, and I'd never even heard of Kohltri until about ten days ago. The only thing I know about this place is that my ignorance could be fatal."

"You've hit it," the woman said dryly, but with good humor.

"So I figure before I go on with my research, I'd better learn something about how to survive here."

"You're already beginning to pick it up. What do you want to know?" She held out her hand as if she were feeling a piece of fabric. With only the slightest hesitation, Rikard took out his wallet and handed her a small bill. She smiled, the money disappeared, and she put down the document case she'd been holding.

"Just what *do* you know about Kohltri?" she asked.

"Nothing but what I've seen since I got here—the port zone, my hostel, these offices. Except, of course, that mining has a lot to do with the economy."

"Mining *is* the economy, but I'm not the one to talk to about that. Ask around and you'll find talkers readily enough, even if you are an offworlder."

"I've gathered that laws and regulations are less stringently enforced here than in the rest of the Federation," he went on in obvious understatement.

"You really *don't* know anything about Kohltri, do you? Sonny, whatever law and order exists here does so by virtue of somebody's gun. You've no doubt noticed that every citizen of Kohltri wears a gun." She reached down and brought up a needler. "Everybody—unless they've established a reputation for being both harmless *and* not worth the effort." She put her weapon away.

"Do you know who the citizens of Kohltri are?" she went on. "We're criminals, all of us, one way or another. We managed to get here one step ahead of the law. You might not believe me, but look around you. Everybody here, with the exception of a few Gesta, exploiters, and the offworlders who come here for sport, everybody is here because anywhere else they'd be arrested and sent to prison. At best."

"Even you?"

"Even me. Kohltri is a refuge, kid. It's a place tolerated by the Federation because if we're here, we're not out there causing trouble. It's a prison of our own choosing. We can leave anytime we want, but nobody ever does. So what you have here is a society of rampant individualists. Everybody is a leader, nobody is a follower, and nobody is used to taking orders from anyone unless those orders are backed up with the threat of instant reprisals. Beginning to get the picture?"

"Ah, yeah. But if what you say is true, then I guess I'm surprised anybody bothers to maintain these records or handle any of the other business necessary for the survival of a community."

"Survival *is* the reason. We have to eat, even here. We hold jobs here just like the ones we held out there. I've always been a record keeper. The fact that I killed my husband fifty years ago doesn't alter that. I'm probably one of the nicest people you're likely to meet here." She started laughing softly.

Rikard felt out of place and defenseless. For a moment he wished he'd bought the ticket the clerk had tacitly offered him last night.

"I don't think I belong here," he said, "but I didn't have any choice in the matter, and it's not likely that I'm going to be able to get away very soon."

"Then you'd better learn how to survive."

"What's the best way I can do that?"

"The only way *I* know is to go out on the streets, watch what everybody else does, and do the same. You get a few knocks that way, but if you're observant and bright—and lucky—you'll make it. That's what I did."

She lost interest in him all at once, turned away, and went back to her work.

Rikard left the records office and walked back to his hostel. He felt as though all the citizens were watching him, just waiting their chance to cheat him or mug him. He watched them in return, hoping to learn something, but they did nothing interesting. Except for their clothes, their guns, and their expressions of disdain when they saw an offworlder, they behaved just like pedestrians anywhere.

He watched the offworlders too. Now he knew why they had that frightened, cautious look. He felt frightened himself and did his best not to look that way.

The night clerk had been friendly and helpful, in his own fashion. Rikard hoped the man would give him some advice—for a price, of course. He had to learn a lot more about Kohltri if he was going to go among the citizens and stay in one piece. And he wouldn't be able to find his father if he just hid out in his room.

As he turned into the courtyard of the hostel, he noticed a woman standing across the street, as if waiting for somebody. He stared at her openly for a few moments before her identity sunk in. She was wearing the typical leathers of a citizen, and a machine pistol was holstered on her hip.

The last time he'd seen her, she'd been dressed as any resident of Kohltri Station. She'd worn a jolter then at the small of her back. It was Emeth Zakroyan.

# 2.

He was not prepared to confront her. He entered the courtyard, crossed it quickly, went up to the registration desk, and asked the day clerk if there was a back way out. The woman did not seem at all surprised. She showed him a corridor that exited around the corner from the hostel. Rikard thanked her with a small bill and followed her directions.

He didn't know why Zakroyan was here, but he was sure

she wanted to see him. He had no intention of letting her find
him in his rooms, or anywhere else if he could help it.

Especially not if she was wearing a machine pistol. That
was a much more effective man-slayer than the needler the
woman at the records office had shown him. He doubted
Zakroyan was wearing it just for prestige.

Out on the street he went back toward the front of the
hostel and peered cautiously around the corner. He felt conspicuous, being so openly sneaky, but none of the citizens
paid him any attention.

Zakroyan was not where he'd seen her. Maybe her being
there had just been a coincidence after all. Or had she seen
him and followed him into the hostel? He hoped she'd just
left, but he suspected she was in his rooms. He wondered if
the day clerk would tell her how he'd left the building. She
could be coming out that back entrance right behind him.

He didn't wait to find out. He started walking away from
the hostel as quickly as he could, and turned at the first corner.
After about five blocks, he turned another corner and stopped.
He was still in the central district, but he didn't know exactly
where. He checked the street sign against his map.

He wanted to give Zakroyan time to finish her business
and time to get bored and go away, so now was as good a
time as any to observe the citizens some more and try to learn
how to behave in the city. He walked on, keeping away from
the hostel, changing directions frequently but never straying
from the well-mapped central district.

He watched everybody, both citizen and visitor. There
were far fewer offworlders than he had at first thought; their
varied clothing just made them more noticeable. They almost
invariably had the look of tourists. Rikard couldn't imagine
why anyone who didn't have to would come here.

Maybe they were seeking thrills, he thought, though some,
like him, might have more legitimate business. And perhaps
some of them were newly arrived criminals, almost as ignorant as he.

The more he saw of the offworlders, the more he understood the looks of contempt the citizens gave them. They
were a sorry-looking bunch of intruders, ignorant of the ways
of this world.

As he walked along, he wondered what kind of life the

citizens must lead. Free in their refuge, like primitives on a reservation, they could do what they pleased within their own boundaries. But they were prisoners, nonetheless. Everyone a leader and not a follower among them, the woman at the records office had said. That they were able to cooperate at all and keep their society running was something of a miracle.

He began to take more notice of the buildings he was passing. The modern section near the port looked like anything he'd seen elsewhere, except for being so small. But the rest of the central zone was different.

It was a kind of interface between the civilization of the outside represented by the port itself, and the wilderness of the rest of the city. There were few citizens in the port area; most of the pedestrians were offworlders. The farther from the port he got, the fewer offworlders he saw. At some distance from the center, there would be no offworlders at all.

At first he saw the buildings outside of the modern section as just anonymous blanks. The outer walls which enclosed the courtyards were featureless. After a while he began to notice the subtly executed signs set flush to the walls above the central doors. He entered one door on impulse.

The courtyard, as with the others he'd been in, was filled with plants. Most of them, he guessed, were imported from other worlds. But unlike the hostel and the records office, this courtyard had display windows on the three inside walls, and doors for eight shops. None of the merchandise displayed was of any interest to him. They were just typical stores, like ones he might find anywhere. He left that courtyard and entered another. It was much the same.

The thought struck him that if he were dressed in leather he might be able to pass as a citizen and visit some of the remoter parts of the city. He didn't know how far he could trust the merchants but felt they would be more honest closer to the port.

He went back to the modern section of the city, where the shops and stores opened onto the street instead of into courtyards. There he found what looked like a more or less normal clothing store. The styles and fashions displayed inside were eclectic and, as usual on other worlds, were only samples.

There was an alcove with a selection of leathers as well. These were not display samples but the actual clothing to be bought and worn. Rikard examined the merchandise while the clerk, dressed like an offworlder, was attending to another customer.

The "leather" wasn't made from animal skins, of course, though certain accessories were advertised to be so and accordingly were very expensive. Instead it was a hydrocarbon polymer which looked, felt, and weighed like leather but was far more flexible, rather elastic, and considerably stronger than the real thing. The sales tag also claimed that the pseudo-leather was impervious to normal knife cuts, defended well against needlers, and was nonflammable. That gave him something more to think about.

At last the clerk finished with her other customer and came over to ask if he needed some help.

"I've been thinking about buying some of these," he said, indicating a leather jacket.

"I wouldn't."

"Why not?"

"You'd still look like an offworlder, and somebody would take offense. They'd want to test you, teach you a lesson, and you'd have a good chance of winding up dead."

"I thought if I looked more like a citizen, I'd be less conspicuous and people would leave me alone."

"Not at all. How long have you been here, a couple of days? You want to go out into the rest of the city, right? Go ahead, take your chances, but don't pretend to be a citizen if you're not. They'll never forgive you. If you look like you're just a tourist, you may get rolled or razzled, but they won't shoot you just for the fun of it."

"Would you shoot a tourist in leathers just for the fun of it?"

"If I thought you were trying to get away with something, I would. You're an outsider. You don't belong here. If you put on leathers, I'll make sure you know that—later."

"All right, thanks. But why are you telling me this, when you could make a sale?"

She shrugged. "No need for an innocent to get killed if he's just ignorant. Now if you've got something on your mind like trying to pass, go to another store and buy your leathers, take the consequences, and be damned. But if you just don't know any better, then back off. I don't need the profit that badly."

"Thank you very much. Ah, you aren't wearing leathers."

"Not this close to the port."

"I see." He thanked her again and left the shop.

He had been lucky. Another merchant might not have been so considerate. He felt embarrassed by his ignorance and wanted to get out of sight of the shop as quickly as he could.

He turned the corner and saw, halfway up the block, something that startled him so badly that he stopped cold and stood staring at the apparition until it disappeared almost at once into a narrow alley between two buildings. It could not have been what he thought he had seen, he was sure. It had looked like nothing so much as two people bundled into a single set of slightly garish, oversized clothes.

He hurried to the place where the thing had disappeared. The narrow alley turned a corner just a few steps in. He started to enter, but the alley was dark. What he had seen could have been bait put out by muggers to lure the curious. He backed away from the alley mouth and looked at his map.

He found the street he was on and the intersection he'd just passed, but the map did not show the alley. Now that he looked at it more closely, he realized that it didn't show any alleys at all, and he'd passed several.

He needed some time to think. The nearest courtyard had a sign indicating a fast-food stand within, so he went in, bought himself some lunch, and sat down in the courtyard to eat.

Little impressions had been accumulating during his walk. The affair of the "double person" was another element to add to his understanding—or lack of it. There was more to this city than just the secrets of a criminal society, else why the vagueness of the map? And what was the reason for this city's existence, aside from the mines and as a so-called refuge? And what could the "double person" have been? He was beginning to become intrigued with the place on its own merits.

But he was still too ignorant to take any chances. The offworlders, the "tourists" out on the streets, probably knew more about this place than he did—that was why they had come, for the thrills, the mystery. He had just fallen in by accident. It would probably be better if he went back to his hostel and stayed there until he could talk to the night clerk and buy that ticket to Higgins, where he could learn more and prepare for a return visit. That would be the safe thing, the wise thing to do.

As he finished his lunch, he tried to think what his father would have done in his place. First, he would stay calm. And his father had had no false pride; he would run and hide if circumstances warranted.

Rikard was not being threatened at the moment, but his palm was itching, and he felt his muscles all bunched up with tension nonetheless. He forced himself to relax and went back out to the street. He leaned against a wall to watch the people pass. The simulation of calm made him calm.

Nobody took more than a passing interest in him. That gave him a chance to still his thoughts, drive out both his anxiety and his excitement. He forced himself to think of nothing for a while. Then a sign across the street, at which he happened to be staring, forced itself into his awareness.

It was an advertisement for a tavern called the Troishla. That was the place that was supposed to be more dangerous during the day than the city streets at night.

At first Rikard thought the Troishla was located right across the street. Curious, he crossed over to read the smaller print on the sign. It gave a different location for the Troishla, somewhere at the edge of town.

He turned away from the sign. He felt calm now. That was the first step; now he would be more aware of what was going on around him.

The afternoon was wearing on, the sun sliding down toward the city skyline. He'd seen a lot, and it would take him a while to assimilate it all. He was a long way from his hostel, far on the opposite side of the city center, and he didn't want to be caught out after dark again. Zakroyan had surely given up on him by now. It was time to go back.

On his way he found a grocery store. They would deliver, for an extra fee much less than what he'd paid to have his supper brought to him the night before. He made up an order, gave his address, paid, and went back out into the street.

Emeth Zakroyan stood on the other side, lounging indolently against the wall.

His heart did a flip, and he cursed himself for not having checked outside before leaving the store. But he remained calm. He flipped her a salute that was jauntier than he felt. She smiled slowly and stood away from the wall.

He turned away from her and continued back to the hostel. At first he thought she was going to cross over to him, but she just stood there, watching him. At a corner where he had to turn he looked back. She was behind him now, following half a block away. He didn't try to lose her; he didn't think he could. He walked on, neither hurrying nor delaying.

The sun dropped below the skyline. There were fewer people on the streets. He checked his map, and estimated he'd be back at the hostel well before dark, if he didn't waste any time or get lost. Though it was dusk, he passed through a park, wondering if he was being foolhardy to do so. It was the first park he'd come to, and he was curious to see some native plant life.

But everything growing here was imported, as far as he could tell. At least they were the same kinds of plants that were set out in every courtyard he'd entered so far. There was something off through the trees, however, which glittered and shone.

All of a sudden people were yelling and running away from the shining thing. He could not see what it was; there was too much foliage in the way. What he could see looked transparent and very tall, about four stories if he was not mistaken, and definitely serpentine.

He froze as a sense of unreality came over him, as it had when he'd seen the "double person." The sense was stronger this time, with an added thrill of fear. The running people were all gone now. He was alone in the park with whatever it was.

And then it, too, was gone. With it went the sense of unreality and fear. He looked over his shoulder to see how Emeth Zakroyan was reacting. He felt some satisfaction in seeing that her face was as pale as he knew his own to be. She hadn't run either, however.

He decided it was time to hurry home.

# 3.

There were several people in the hostel courtyard when he came in. He hadn't yet met any of the other tenants, and was surprised to see so many congregating here at the benches and low tables, among the green and purple plants. He went up to the night clerk, told him about the groceries he was expecting, then turned back to the court. Zakroyan did not come in.

There were a dozen people in the court—six offworlders, four citizens, and two others who wore offworld clothes but had the manner of locals. Half were men, half women. One man, an offworlder of middle age, about a hundred or so, was sitting at a small table to one side, drinking coffee, watching the others in the court. Rikard went up to him.

"Hello," he said, and introduced himself.

"Pleased to meet you." The man offered a seat. "I'm Carls Menthes. How long have you been here?"

"Got here two nights ago. And yourself?"

"Ten days. Fascinating place, isn't it?"

"Very. I've got the feeling there's a lot more here than meets the eye."

"There is. Yes, indeed. Are you here on business or pleasure?"

"Business. I'm trying to trace...a relative who disappeared some years ago."

"Aha," Menthes said. "One of those. What is it, a matter of insurance?"

"Exactly." It was easier to lie than to try to explain the truth.

"I'm here for pleasure myself." Menthes went on at some length to describe the kind of pleasures he'd come for. Rikard was appalled, but made no comment.

When he could get a word in, he asked Menthes how he got along in the city, how he survived. Menthes's answer, however, revealed him to be less aware of Kohltri's true nature than Rikard was. As soon as he could tactfully break away, Rikard did so. He needed to talk to someone who could give him useful information.

None of the other offworlders were very helpful. Several had come to buy or sell something illegal in the rest of the Federation. Others were here to enjoy the dubious thrill of being among murderers, thieves, swindlers, and such types. None knew any more about the city than not to go out after dark and not to buy anything without opening the bag first. Rikard was disappointed.

One of those dressed as an offworlder but acting like a local was a new citizen. Rikard did not ask how he had become one or why he was fleeing the police. The man had arrived only three days ago and was already quite at home. The other dubious person, a woman, was just a visitor, but a natural hardcase. She was of no help to him either.

That left him with the four citizens. He approached the first one cautiously.

"Are you staying at the hostel?" he asked.

"You gotta be kidding," the man said, and turned away.

Rikard shrugged off the rebuff and turned to a slender woman.

"Could you give me some advice on how to get along here?" he asked her bluntly.

She appraised him quickly and made the gesture of feeling cloth with her fingers. He gave her a small bill. She looked at it.

"Never talk to strangers," she said, and turned away. There was a light ripple of laughter from the other people nearby.

"Everybody starts out a stranger sometime," Rikard said quietly, and turned to a small man standing near.

"Would you give me some value for my money?" he asked, holding another small bill.

"Not likely, when your business is the same as mine."

"Ah, what is your business?"

"None of your business," the man snarled. He snatched the bill and stepped away, laughing. The others watching joined in heartily.

He didn't bother talking to the last citizen. It would only cost him more money, and though he had learned something from his two encounters, another similar lesson wasn't worth it. He started to go back to his room, but the night clerk stopped him as he passed the desk.

"Don't let them get you down, kid," he said. "But those two had good advice, even if it was expensive. Don't talk to strangers, except as strangers. You try to get friendly, they'll take your shirt. And what anybody does is none of your business, unless your business makes it so."

"Aren't you violating both those rules?"

"Sure, but I'm a hostel clerk, so what do you expect? Look, kid, I know you're not here for the fun of it. You've been out all day, and I hear you've been spending a lot of time at the records office. And I *also* hear you've got one of Solvay's watchdogs at your heels. So if you feel like talking about it, go ahead. I've got nothing better to do."

"How much will it cost me?"

The clerk laughed. "Nothing as long as it amuses me."

"I'll do my best. My father disappeared thirteen and a half years ago. I'm trying to find him. I know that he came here eventually, that he lived in the city for about two-thirds of a year, and then disappeared again. I know he didn't leave the planet. He might be dead, but I don't know that. I can't learn anything more at the records office. What I'd like is to find someone who knew my father back then and who can tell me where he is now, or where he's buried."

"And how long ago was this?"

"The records stop eleven years ago."

"You're not asking much, are you? Things change a lot around here in eleven years. I've been here nine, and nothing's like it was, even a year ago."

"Nothing at all?"

"Oh, well, the port's still there, and Solvay is still looking down on us, and Rodik Bedik still runs the mines, but you know, that's nothing, that's like saying the rings are still in the sky or the sun still rises and sets. It doesn't matter.

"But say, that just might be it. Now, I see a lot of people, but mostly offworlders and such low life. No offense intended. What you want is to talk to somebody like Rodik Bedik, who talks to everybody, including the big guys.

"Now, if your dad was here eleven years ago and did anything to get any attention at all, Bedik would have heard about it. At least he'd know other people you could ask. Of course, it's not easy to get to Bedik. He's a busy man and not known to be overly generous. But it's an idea. He won't shoot you out of hand, that's for sure.

"And here's another idea. There's a place out on the west side of town called the Troishla. I think I mentioned it to you once. It's a tavern, of sorts. I've been there a couple of times. There's lots of things known there."

"You told me it was the only place more dangerous than the streets at night."

"That's right, I did. No question about it."

"So how do I go in there and come out again in one piece?"

"It's a good question. I can't tell you that. If you go in dressed like you are, they'll play with you for a while and take everything but your clothes. But if you buy leathers and they catch you faking it, they'll just shoot your legs off before they blow your brains out."

"You've been there. How do you survive?"

"By being very careful. And besides, I belong here."

"Sure. Look, I appreciate your talking to me."

"Forget it. Oh, by the way, your groceries came a while ago, when you were handing out money. They're in your room."

Rikard thanked him again and went in to fix himself supper.

# 4.

He looked at his map again. He was out of the area that was given in full detail. The street he was on was shown on the map, but the major intersection he'd just passed was not.

That morning he had asked the day clerk for the location of Rodik Bedik's ofices, and for a small sum she had given him directions on how to get there. After breakfast he had gone out into the city, beyond the central section, keeping to the streets shown on the map. There were no other offworlders here.

The buildings in this part of the city were of the same type as in the area of his hostel. They were still made of glass, steel, and porcelain, still two to five stories tall. Some of the wide doors in the blank-faced walls stood open, and in the courtyards beyond he could see more shops and, out here, what he took to be homes.

But the character of the city as a whole was different. The buildings here were dingy, unkempt, neglected. None of them were new. And there were no more easily interpretable signs. Instead, where signs existed, they were heraldic and cryptic. They undoubtedly conveyed meaning to those who knew how to read them. To Rikard they meant nothing.

Through those courtyard doors that were open, Rikard could see that the profusion of plants here was the same as elsewhere. It struck him as odd that a society composed almost exclusively of escaped criminals would have developed such a strong habit of domestic-plant cultivation.

There were few vehicles on the streets, and not many pedestrians either. He had seen no other offworlders at all for the last two hours. He felt conspicuous, dressed as he was. The quiet, reserved, predatory stares of the few leather-clad people on the streets made him nervous. Nobody spoke to him, challenged his presence, or threatened him, but he could feel their animosity, their unspoken warning to take care. While they might tolerate his trespass so far, they would tolerate no more than that.

The map, which he was beginning to actively distrust, indicated that the area of the city was quite large, but the population appeared to be disproportionately small. And it was a quiet city. Rikard had been in slum areas on other worlds, in poorer neighborhoods, in "underground" zones often enough to know that there was always an undercurrent of noise—children, drunks, whatever. But this city was different.

Only once had the general quietness been broken. Someone had screamed, several people started running, then there was the sound of gunshots. But that had lasted only for a moment, and no one near him had paid the least attention. Following their example, Rikard had ignored it too, and had just walked on, more wary than before. The quiet had quickly returned. There had been no police sirens, of course.

He looked at his map again. It showed only the major streets in this part of town, about one in every four or five. It never showed the narrower ways and alleys.

The street he was on was one of those displayed. It was broad, had been relatively straight, and according to the map was supposed to run right out to the north edge of the city, where a cross road would take him to the circles that represented the mining domes. But where the map showed the street making an angle to the right, the actual street he was on swerved left.

He walked to the next major cross street. That was not on the map at all.

He kept walking, staying on the street he had followed out of the central area. At every intersection he tried to locate himself on the map. Nothing corresponded.

The city could have been changed since the map had been printed, but the streets he walked all seemed old. He felt it more likely that the map had been drawn falsely on purpose, though he could not imagine why. He could easily find his way back to the hostel again by simply turning around and following this same street back the way he had come. But whether going forward would take him to the mines, he could not tell.

He needed to ask someone for help. "Don't talk to strangers" was rule one. "Mind your own business" was rule two. He intended to abide by those rules as well as he could. But unless someone gave him directions he would have to go back to the hostel. The day clerk would be amused, he was sure. She had probably sent him out on a wild-goose chase. Maybe the night clerk had fed him a line too, and there was no Rodik Bedik, no mining domes.

It would do him no good to go back in defeat. Though his map wasn't true, he had no other reason to believe the day clerk had actually lied to him. It would be even worse if he gave up prematurely. He kept on walking, wishing he had a car.

He came to a place with the courtyard fully open to the street. It was a service station, or this world's equivalent.

Even here, cars needed to be attended to sometimes, though this was the first such station he'd seen.

It was primitive. There were no robotic lifts, no cybernetic analyzers. The simple machines were operated by a human attendant, a woman, he thought, though it wasn't easy to tell in this case. Rikard waited as a small floater drove in, was fueled, and drove out after an exchange of currency. Then he went up to the attendant.

"Excuse me," he said, "but I'm lost and—"

"You sure are," the woman said, not unkindly.

"I'm trying to find Msr. Bedik's offices. Do you know where they are, and would you tell me how to get there?"

"Boss Bedik? Now how'd you hear about him? Sure, I know where he works. Dome 14 out in Skareem."

"What's Skareem?"

"The sector of town where Dome 14 is. You got a map? Let me see it."

He gave it to her. She looked it over quickly and snorted.

"Somebody's idea of a joke," she said. "Keep the tourists at home. You really ought to *be* at home, you know."

"Yes, I do, but I'd really like to see Msr. Bedik."

"*Boss* Bedik. That's the way he likes it. And since he runs the mines, that's the way he has it. It's not easy to get to see him, you know."

"That's what I've been told, but I don't want to give up before I try."

"Admirable sentiments, I'm sure. Lots of luck. Okay, look here." She pointed to the map. "This street is right here, though it's not shown. It runs this way, with some wiggles in it. Now, out here you'll cross Farjeon. Go three blocks more and take a left. It's an alley with no name. Go on for seven blocks more, and you'll come out on Skareem. Take it north and you'll see the domes, right at the edge of town. It's number fourteen. After that you're on your own."

"Thanks very much." Rikard offered her a small bill. She took it as if she had been expecting it—which could explain why she had been less unfriendly than many of the other people he'd met.

Rikard found Farjeon with no problem and turned into the narrow, nameless alley three blocks farther on. It was crooked, and the streets that intersected it were just as narrow and dark.

He passed the third intersection, and the narrow street turned a corner, opened out into a court, and came to a dead end. Three men and a woman sat on the curb. They were all looking at him as if they had been waiting for him.

Rikard slowed to a stop, a knot of apprehension—mingled with that sense of thrill—growing in his stomach. He had assumed that the service attendant had just been friendly, like the night clerk, and that had been a mistake.

The four people got to their feet and fanned out away from the curb.

"You've made a wrong turn," one of the men said.

"You're way out of your territory," the woman added.

They moved toward him slowly, one of the men sidling around to cut off his retreat.

The attendant at the service station had set him up for a mugging. Rikard, without thinking, spun on the man now blocking the alley behind him, dodged to the right, side-stepped to the left, and lashed out with a fist, striking the man behind the ear. Then he ran, took the first corner and ran to the next, turned it and ran on until he could no longer hear footfalls chasing after him.

# 5.

There were more people here, which probably meant less likelihood of another mugging. The eyes that watched him were not friendly, but nobody approached him. He slowed to a walk and, while the sense of thrill faded, tried to catch his breath.

Now he was really lost. He wished he dared ask somebody for directions, but he'd learned another lesson about talking to strangers—and about muggers—and he couldn't trust anything they might tell him.

Not everybody would lie to him, he was sure, but he would have no way of knowing if they had until it was too late. He hoped he wouldn't be so surprised the next time something like that happened.

He could try to find his way back to the street he'd been following before he'd turned off, but he wasn't sure he would be able to recognize it when he came to it. The best thing he could do would be to go on. He went in the general direction of the domes, following the instructions the clerk at the hostel had told him, not the way the service-station attendant had pointed out.

The name on a street sign at one intersection seemed familiar. He looked at his map and found it. He kept walking, and farther on there was another correlation. All of a sudden, for no reason he could guess, the map and the streets matched each other again.

But if his map was true, he was far off course. He'd gotten turned around somewhere and was going at right angles to the way he wanted to go. He decided to follow the map as long as it corresponded with the actual streets. At least now he thought he could find his way back to the hostel again, though since he'd come this far, he might as well continue. But the morning was more than half gone, and if he didn't hurry, he'd be far from home when night fell.

He walked quickly, keeping alert, staying out of people's way. He passed a door, and a man came out and fell into step beside him. The man didn't say anything for a while. He was wearing a gun—Rikard didn't know what kind—and a knife.

"Whatcher hurry?" the man said at last, his voice slurred.

"I'm trying to make an appointment."

"Zat so? Think you'll make it?"

"I'm beginning to have my doubts." Rikard didn't pause. He tensed himself inwardly, in case the man decided to jump him.

But he never found out the man's intentions. Without warning a tall, glittery thing stepped around the corner they were approaching, half a block away, and everybody on the street came to a startled stop.

It was like the thing Rikard had half seen in the park. It was twelve meters tall, serpentine, transparent, shining.

The man beside him grabbed his arm convulsively. Rikard felt the hair on his head and neck stand up. Then suddenly the man was running away. Everybody else on the street was running too, away from the thing up ahead. They didn't yell; they just ran.

Rikard wanted to run too, but he couldn't make his legs work. The glittering, transparent monster swung its head—if that was what it was—from side to side, as if watching the fleeing pedestrians.

Rikard found his legs at last and took a hesitant, leaden step backward. The thing swung to stare at him. He froze. It looked away. He too another step.

He couldn't see its edges. It was bright and transparent in the middle, but faded to thin air where an outline should have been. It was basically yellow and orange in color, but there were hints of shades Rikard's eyes did not recognize and could not quite see. Deep within what might have been its body were several spots of intense light that slowly tumbled over each other. It seemed to have two small arms, or forelegs, and two larger hind legs. The air rippled behind it.

The thing moved, and the impression of neck and legs faded. It wasn't really serpentine; it had just looked that way. Now it was just a sphere of yellow light, borderless, pulsing, five meters in diameter at least, floating three meters above the pavement. Only the bright spots in its center remained clear, slowly revolving around each other. And the eyes.

A hand grabbed his elbow. He was jerked roughly through a doorway into a plant-filled courtyard, where a man and a woman hustled him through another door into a bar.

"It almost got you," the man said.

"Not even a damned tourist deserves to die that way," the woman added. Then someone shoved a glass in his hands, and without word or hesitation Rikard drank it down.

# 6.

"What the hell was that thing?" Rikard asked as he paid for his second drink.

"I don't know what they really are," the bartender said, "but we call them dragons."

"Good name for them." He gulped half the whiskey. "How come they're allowed to run loose?"

"There's no allowing to it, kid," a patron said, an older man, well into his second century. "The dragons come and the dragons go and the only thing they don't do is come into our houses. Thank God." The close call with the so-called dragon seemed to have made the citizens more tolerant of strangers.

"Can't you kill them?"

"It's been tried," the tender said, "but as far as I know, nothing seems to hurt them much. Bullets make them go away. A blaster will send one off in a hurry, if you've got a blaster. But a freezer or flamer does nothing to them."

"How about electricity?"

"I think they like it. I've seen them dancing around in a thunderstorm, with the lightning striking down on them, and they just come back for more."

"I don't remember ever hearing about an animal like that."

"Hell, kid, that's no animal," said the woman who'd helped drag him in off the street. "It's just a bundle of energy with eyes."

"Is it aware of us?"

"Sure is. If we move *or* stand still too long. You notice how they kind of fade out around the edges? We really can't see them too well. I don't think they can see us too well either. But they sure as hell know we're here."

"Just seeing that thing made my hair stand on end," Rikard said. "How dangerous are they?"

"Let's put it this way," the tender said. "If they touch you,

you fry. On the spot. And if they look at you too long, you freeze up, just like you did. And then they come over and poke around you a little bit, and then up you go, a puff of smoke and a clinker."

"I don't think they do it on purpose," the old man said.

"The hell they don't," the woman snapped back.

"What difference does it make?" the tender asked. "Fried is fried, accidental or on purpose."

Somebody poked his head in the door, announced that the dragon had gone, and popped out again.

"Real close shave you had there," the tender said as Rikard downed the last of his whiskey. "What the hell is a tourist like you doing way out here anyway? If you don't mind my asking."

"Trying to find Boss Bedik."

"Oh, yeah? Aim high, don't you? You don't just knock on his door and walk in, you know."

"That's what I've been told."

"Look, I don't mean to be nosy, but what are bartenders for? I mean, you're a tourist. Bedik was born here. You can't know him from Ephram. You're not from Solvay or you'd be in a big car with a couple of cops for company. So what kind of business could you possibly have with Boss Bedik?"

"I was told that he might be able to help me trace someone who was here eleven years ago, who never left, and who was not reported dead."

"Eleven years. That's a long time. Yeah, Bedik might know. He's got strings out all over the city. But you've got two problems first. One is getting to see him. And the other is getting him to tell you anything."

"There's another problem—just finding out where he is in the first place."

"Hell, everybody knows that. He's in Dome 14 out in Skareem. That's where he does all his business."

"That much I've heard, but look at this." Rikard showed the tender his map.

"One of those," the tender said. "Damn fool things. No two the same. Only the central port area is accurate. Look, here you are. Just follow this street here. Now here the map goes all funny. Turn left, though that's not shown, and follow around to here. This is Skareem Street, just like it says, and Dome 14 is about here."

"The last time I followed directions like that, I wound up in a dead end with four hungry types."

"No kidding. Who'd you ask, the bartender, the service attendant, or the beggar?"

"The service attendant."

"That'll be Saleth. She does that whenever she gets a chance, even to locals. For ten percent of the take. How'd you get out?"

"Clipped one guy up the side of the head and ran like the devil."

The tender laughed. "No kidding? Good for you, kid. Serves them right. If they can't roll without losing the tip, they deserve to be clobbered."

"So I was just wondering, no offense, mind, if I'd have to keep on the lookout for dead ends if I follow the route you've shown me."

"No dead ends, kid, but keep a lookout anyway. You've been lucky so far, you know. You could have gotten killed about eleven times between the port and here. Not counting the dragon."

"Only eleven times?"

The tender laughed again.

"Okay," Rikard said, "I'll take the chance. But I'd like some lunch first. Do you make sandwiches?"

"Sure do. What do you want?"

Rikard told him, then thought of something else.

"If Boss Bedik won't help me," he said, "I've been told to try the Troishla."

"Boy, does somebody want you dead?"

"I don't think so. I know it's supposed to be a rough place, but they're also supposed to have a lot of information there."

"Sure they do. Nothing happens in the city they don't hear about at the Troishla eventually. But kid, listen, if you think you've been having trouble on the streets, you have no idea what it would be like for you in the Troishla. I've been there a couple of times myself, and I know. It's rough. This city's just one jumble of special conventions, but the ones in the Troishla are different, more special, and enforced to the limit. And *they* decide what that limit is."

"Just what is the Troishla?"

"A real joint." The tender gave Rikard his sandwich. "Bar, restaurant, shows downstairs. Sex, drugs, other stuff upstairs. Part of it is a hotel. There are offices there, some club rooms. Lots of stuff. It's a big place. And don't let *anybody* take you into the cellars. People don't come back from there."

"I saw an ad for it downtown."

"Yeah, sure. They've got some good shows there. Great food. The whiskey is the best. If you stay out where casual drop-ins come, you'll have no trouble—no more than on any city street at night. But if you want information, you'll have to go into one of the main rooms, and kid, that's dangerous."

"Let's hope Bedik will tell me what I want to know."

"Yeah, lets."

# 7.

There was no way he could miss the domes when he got to them two hours later. They were right at the north edge of the city, huge, stark hemispheres, separated from the other buildings on either side, and the forests just north of them, by concrete aprons and trimmed lawns. They were windowless, but each had a door, above which was a number. He found number fourteen and went in. Beyond the front entrance was a pleasant lobby, with three people working at desks at the far end.

Rikard had never seen so many people employed in menial tasks. It reflected a level of technology far below that of the average Federal world. The station in orbit had been perfectly up to date. The port of the city was fully functional, if somewhat outmoded. It was almost as if someone were deliberately keeping the city backward.

He approached the three receptionists.

One of them, the man, looked up inquiringly. "How may I help you?" he asked. His tone was perfectly polite, but there was a knife scar that ran from his temple, through his right eye, down past his nose, across the corner of his mouth, and over his chin.

"I would like to see Boss Bedik," Rikard said. He'd seen no other disfigured people in the city.

"May I inquire as to your business?" The man's voice was smooth, his intonation bland. He had gone to the trouble, Rikard saw, to have his right eye replaced.

"I'm trying to locate someone who disappeared here about eleven years ago. I was told that Boss Bedik might have known him, or have known of him, or might know somebody else who could help me."

"I see." The man looked down at his console, shuffled his papers, then looked up again. "The Boss is busy."

"I won't take much of his time, only five minutes or so. It's a long walk from the port."

The man's eyes held Rikard's for a long moment. The color of the right one did not quite match the color of the left. "The Boss is busy."

"All right then, I can come back another time. May I make an appointment?"

"I don't handle that." He pointed to the woman to his left.

Rikard went over to her. She looked up at him pleasantly. "I'd like to make an appointment," he said.

"Who with, please?"

"With Boss Bedik."

"On what business?"

Rikard explained again, though he was sure she must have overheard him talking to the man.

"The Boss is a very busy man," she said. "I'm sure you'll understand that he doesn't have the time to see everyone who wants a favor from him, and many people want favors from the Boss."

"I just want to ask him—"

"So do a lot of other people, all kinds of things. I'm sorry, I can't make the appointment."

"Not even for five minutes?"

"I'm sorry."

Rikard looked helplessly at the other two receptionists. The man's face was expressionless. The other woman was smiling pleasantly.

The eyes of all three were laughing at him. They were

playing a game with him, and he didn't know the rules. He kept his own face bland as he turned away and left the dome.

They had, he realized, never intended to let a mere tourist see the Boss.

He walked away from the domes until he saw a sign which he now knew signified a tavern. He entered the courtyard. The plants were more profuse here than usual, and many were in bloom. There were four other businesses besides the tavern.

He entered the darkened interior of the bar. It was fairly empty at this time of day, still too early for the after-work trade. He sat at the bar, and the tender came over.

"Small whiskey," he told her. She punched the buttons, handed him the glass in exchange for a bill. He gulped half the drink.

"Pretty far afield, aren't you?" she asked him.

"I've just been trying to see Boss Bedik."

"Did you really expect they'd let you in?"

"I didn't know what to expect."

"Boss Bedik's a busy man."

"That's what I understand." He told her what had happened in the dome. "What's he do, anyway?"

"He runs the mines. What do you think, we live on air? Kohltri's got nothing, it's just a refuge, but it does have deposits of balktapline, reserpine, and anthrace. That's the basis of our economy. If we didn't have that, we'd all starve."

"I'm not familiar with those substances," Rikard said, though the name balktapline seemed familiar.

"Artificial stuff, left over from earlier civilizations."

"There were people here before humans?"

"At least a couple. There were the Belshpaer, but they died out thousands of years ago. Balktapline is from whoever was here before the Belshpaer came."

"Right, right." He remembered seeing the name in one of the station's files. "So there's a lot of this stuff here?"

"That's it. You come to Kohltri, chances are you'll wind up working in the mines. If you're lucky, you'll find a place like this instead. Or if you're careful with your money, you can save up and buy one after a few years—or many."

"Isn't balktapline what they use for star drives?"

"Could be. I don't know that much about it."

"But if that's what they're mining here, everybody should
be rich."

"You don't know the operation here." The tender served
him another drink. "First of all, the mines are owned by a
small group of stockholders. Everybody else works for wages."

"That's insane."

"Of course, but that's the way it is. And Boss Bedik runs
the whole match. So you can see he'd not be likely to find
the time to see the likes of you—or of me, for that matter."

"He must be taking in quite a rake-off."

"Not as much as he'd like. He can't sell the stuff on the
market. It has to go through Director Solvay first."

"So that's what he was afraid I was looking for." He told
the tender how he'd been exiled to the surface.

"Stupid of him," the tender said. "He's getting paranoid.
If he suspected you, he should have just killed you. You can
get off Kohltri in spite of him if you want to."

"I found that out. But I think he may try to kill me yet.
One of his agents has been following me around."

"Not Emeth Zakroyan, I hope."

"That very one."

"You're a dead man. She's Solvay's private executioner.
Even Bedik is afraid of her."

"She's only been following me."

"Sure, playing with you, waiting for the sporting moment.
You'll know it when it comes, but nobody else will. And
there'll be no connection with Solvay at all."

"Then I'd better get on with my business while I have the
chance. Except if Bedik's people won't let me in, I'd be
wasting my time going back there."

"Maybe you just didn't ask them the right way." She made
the gesture of feeling cloth.

"How much should I offer?" he asked her, handing her a
bill.

"About ten. But try the one you didn't talk to first. She
hasn't refused you yet."

"Thanks," Rikard said. He gulped the last of his drink and
went back to Dome 14. He thought he must be getting the
hang of things if the bartender's willingness to talk to him
was any indication.

# 8.

He reentered the lobby of Dome 14, remembering his father's easy way: calm, straightforward, unruffled. Rikard had never tried to bribe anybody before, and even though that might not be a criminal act on Kohltri, the thought of it still made him tense. He resisted scratching the scar on his palm and walked right up to the third receptionist, trying to imitate his father's manner as well as he could, and laid a ten on her desk.

The woman looked at the bill, then up at Rikard.

"I'm afraid Boss Bedik really is too busy to see you," she said.

Rikard just smiled softly, as his father would have done, and laid a second bill beside the first.

"Well," she said, "maybe five minutes." She stood, led him to a door, and let him through.

He was at one end of a short corridor, with only one other door at the far end. The walls, floor, and ceiling of the corridor looked perfectly normal, but Rikard knew that he was in danger of his life. There would be detectors and weapons hidden behind those innocent panels.

He hesitated for a moment. He was unarmed, without so much as a pocket knife. But if they just wanted to kill him, they would have done so by now.

He walked up the corridor and reached the other door unharmed. He knocked once, opened the door, and stepped through into a comfortable office, with pictures on the windowless walls, bookcases in the corners, a small couch, two comfortable chairs, a bar on one side. There was a large cluttered desk, behind which sat an elderly gentleman, heavyset but distinguished. The man looked up with mild curiosity.

"Boss Bedik?" Rikard asked.

"Yes, how can I help you?"

Rikard told him what he'd told the first two receptionists.

"I see," Bedik said. "And they let you in for that?"

"No, they let me in for a couple of tens."

Bedik's face split into a grin and he chuckled. "You were lucky. That doesn't always work. Okay, you're here. Who are you looking for?"

"Arin Braeth. He lived in the city for two-thirds of a year and finally disappeared with no trace. . . ."

The humor had gone out of Bedik's eyes.

"Sorry, kid, I never heard of Arin Braeth. I can't help you."

"Uh, then could you refer me to someone else who might have known him, or who would be likely to have kept track of that kind of thing?"

"Don't push. You've got no business asking me or anyone else questions like that. I'd suggest you head back to the port and book passage off Kohltri."

"I don't mean him any harm." Rikard tried hard to sound harmless. "He's my father. I just want to see him again, or find his grave if he's dead."

"Lots of sons kill their fathers. What's your name?"

"Rikard Braeth."

"Indeed. I'll tell you. If you're not out of here in thirty seconds, I'll have you thrown out, and I mean physically."

Rikard hesitated for just a moment, then turned and hurried out of the office and down the corridor.

Bedik's sudden change of manner at the mention of Arin Braeth indicated that the Boss knew something, was concealing something. But Rikard was in no position to get that something from him. It was unlikely that Rikard could bribe him, he had no way to threaten him, and Bedik was not interested in reason.

He passed through the lobby. The receptionist who'd taken his money called after him, "Thanks for the twenty." She chuckled. The other two joined in. Rikard was thankful when the closing of the front door shut off the sound of their laughter.

# 9.

He walked half a block before he realized that the receptionists had known, before they'd let him in, that he would get nothing out of Bedik. The bartender had probably known it too. But Rikard, in spite of warnings, had just thrown away his money.

That didn't bother him so much as the fact that he'd been made a fool of. He ground a knuckle into the scar on the palm of his right hand and watched as the image of concentric circles never quite formed in front of his eyes.

He was tired. He'd walked a long way to get to the mining domes, and had as far to go again to get back to his hostel. He would have to hurry if he was going to get back before dark.

He'd asked the day clerk about taxis, but the woman had just laughed. "What idiot," she'd said, "would want to take a chance with a job like that on a world like this?" He'd then asked her about renting a car, but that would have cost as much as buying one, and cars were very expensive here. So he'd walked.

Still, his day's effort hadn't been completely wasted. Bedik's change of manner from amused politeness to cold, hard distance could only mean that the name Arin Braeth had meant something to him, in spite of his denial. His father must have made a big impression to produce that strong a reaction even after eleven years. So other people should remember him too.

If Arin Braeth had died eleven years ago, Bedik would have just said so and not have shut up as if he were concealing something, however he felt about Rikard or his father. And what could he conceal but the fact that Arin Braeth was still alive?

The idea excited Rikard so much that he walked half a dozen blocks before he realized that he hadn't been keeping

track of where he was going. He stopped at the next intersection and pulled out his map.

As he was trying to locate himself on it, two men came
up beside him, took his arms, and walked him quickly toward
an alley. For just a few startled moments Rikard could do no
more than let the two men carry him along. Then something
clicked in his mind. His father would never have put up with
this.

He stopped so suddenly that the two men were swung
around in front of him, their holds on his arms momentarily
loosened. He jerked free and while his assailants were still
off balance, hit one in the face with a right jab and backhanded
the other across the side of the head with his left. Then he
turned and sprinted away without waiting to see whether the
men fell or not.

He stopped when he was safely out of reach. The would-
be muggers picked themselves up off the street. Their faces
were angry and confused, but they said nothing. They turned
and quickly walked away.

Rikard's heart was pounding; his hands felt numb. He'd
nearly been taken again, but once more he had reacted in just
the right way. There was a lot more of his father in him than
he'd given himself credit for. His experiences on Gorshom
had misled him, compounded by his desire to deny his father's
influence. For some reason, that made him feel good.

He was, after all, his father's son, in more than just a
biological sense. He had absorbed a lot from his father during
his first thirteen years, if only from stories and by emulation
of his manner. And except for Gorshom, when he'd been too
young, he'd just never had an opportunity to put his father's
teaching to use. Until now.

Except for the fact that he was tired of running from trouble, the experience exhilarated him. This was what people
felt when they went searching for thrills. If he had been back
home, he would have been horrified at himself for finding
that he enjoyed it. As it was, here on Kohltri, it might make
the difference between living and dying. Predators always
culled the weakest of their prey, and if he enjoyed danger, it
would make him seem stronger to his enemies, and less vulnerable.

Feeling more confident than perhaps he had a right to, he

went back to the intersection. He seemed to be in one of those parts of the city that didn't correspond to his map. The only thing he could do was to head in the general direction of the port as quickly as his tired legs would take him and keep to the more heavily traveled streets. After all, it was one thing to enjoy an occasional thrill; it was another to stupidly put himself in danger, as he had done too many times already.

By midafternoon he came to a street name that corresponded with one on his map. He was right on course but still several hours walk from the hostel. He put his map back in his pocket, looked up, and saw Emeth Zakroyan. She was standing right in front of him, hip cocked, arms crossed. She was dressed in leathers, and the 5mm fifty-shot machine pistol was still on her hip.

"You just won't learn, will you?" she said.

"I don't know what you're talking about."

"Nonsense. You've been talking to Boss Bedik."

"Yes, I have. The night clerk at my hostel thought he might have known my father."

"Nobody knows your father. And nobody cares. But Solvay *does* care that you're still prying into his private business."

"You go ask Bedik what I talked with him about." Rikard kept his anger under control.

Now that he knew what that "private business" was, he understood Solvay's desire to keep it secret. If anybody in the rest of the Federation found out that Solvay was taking a big rake-off on the export of balktapline, he would be arrested at once. Fleeing to the surface of Kohltri wouldn't do Solvay any good. Kohltri was a refuge by convention only. If the Federal government really wanted him, they would just come down and get him.

"I'm not going to waste my time with Bedik," Zakroyan was saying. "I'm not going to waste any more time at all. You were warned on the station, and you chose to ignore it. You were sent down here, and still you persist. Solvay has had enough of you, and it will be my pleasure to take you out."

"Now wait, wait just a minute." He held his hands up defensively and backed off a step. "You've been following me. You must have talked to the same people I've been talking to. Doesn't what they say confirm my story?"

"It only confirms that you're covering yourself with a false trail. It doesn't prove anything. Now come on. Do you want it right here in public, or shall we go somewhere in private?"

"Why won't you listen to reason?"

"Reason has nothing to do with it." She straightened and uncrossed her arms. Her right hand rested easily on the butt of her gun.

Rikard sighed. The only thing he could do right now was to buy a little time. "Let's go."

She pointed, he went, she fell in step beside him.

They were still heading toward the port, but after a couple of blocks Zakroyan took Rikard's elbow and steered him into a courtyard. He had no plan of escape yet, but he wasn't going to let Zakroyan kill him without a fight, even if it was only a token.

From the courtyard they went into a dim lobby, with stairs going up one side. They went past these, down a hallway toward the back of the building. At the far end Zakroyan opened a door and shoved Rikard out into a narrow alley. She pushed him along ahead of her until they came to a wide place with two other doors opening off it.

If he was going to put up any resistance, now was probably the time. The only trouble was, Zakroyan was too alert and could drop him before he did more than take a step toward her. She shoved him roughly against a wall, drew her gun. Rikard tensed himself to spring, and one of the doors opened. Leonid Polski stepped out.

The tableau froze for a moment. Zakroyan was startled, but her gun never wavered. Rikard suddenly lost track of what he had been half planning to do. Polski looked at them both with mild surprise.

"A little backyard murder?" Polski asked blandly.

"Nothing to do with you," Zakroyan said, her voice flat.

"Of course not. How you doing, kid?"

"I was doing just fine until a couple of minutes ago."

"I guess she doesn't trust the city to do her work for her. Why don't you let it be, Zakroyan?"

"I told you, it's none of your business."

"It is now that I'm here. You want to shoot people, you do it while I'm not around."

"If you'd go about your business, I could do that."

Zakroyan's gun was aimed steadily at Rikard's chest. She'd have to turn ninety degrees to get a shot at Polski. He, on the other hand, dressed as an offworlder tourist, had no gun showing. If Zakroyan turned on him, he'd have to draw a weapon from somewhere.

Zakroyan considered the situation just a moment longer, then slowly lowered her pistol and carefully put it back in its holster. Only then did she turn to face the policeman.

"I've no quarrel with you," she said to him.

"And I've none with you—unless you hurt the kid."

"What's he to you?"

"I've made his acquaintance. Purely personal. I don't like my friends blown away from me."

"I'd advise you not to interfere."

"If you shoot him, you won't find Kohltri a refuge—not if I choose to come after you."

"You won't do that."

"Want to take the chance?"

"It might be interesting."

"I'm sure you'd enjoy every minute of it. Now let the kid go."

"You put me off this job, you'll have the Director on your neck."

"You interfere with *me*, you'll have the *Federation* on *your* neck. And on the Director's. And you know they'll come here, refuge or no, if a Federal cop is killed."

"Easy," Zakroyan said, holding her hands out from her sides. "Like I said, I've no quarrel with you."

"Then let me explain what's going to happen. Either you're going to let Rikard and me go without further hassle, or you're going to try and keep him, in which case one of us will die, and if it's me, you will too, in just a matter of days."

"They'll have to find you first."

"Don't be stupid. I'm wired. This whole scene is on crystal. As long as you don't mess with me, it will be erased in one hundred standard days. But if I go down, a Goon Squad comes in, and there's nowhere you can hide."

Zakroyan stared at him, her mouth hard. "All right, you

win this round. But remember one thing. I'm not the only one who's trying to kill your friend. At least two other tries have been made on him already today."

"Just don't let me see you do it."

Zakroyan turned and walked up the narrow alley. Polski looked at Rikard and visibly relaxed.

"You travel in rough company," he said.

"It wasn't my idea." Rikard could feel himself shaking with released tension. "Have you been following me too?" He drew a long, shuddering breath, then wiped the cold sweat off his forehead.

"Pure coincidence," Polski said. "Are you all right?" He took hold of Rikard's shoulder.

"I think so. Give me a minute so I can get used to the idea of living awhile longer."

"Take all the time you need. Where were you going when Old Iron Jaws found you?"

"Back to the hostel. I've just been to see Boss Bedik."

"Like I said, rough company. What'd he have to say?"

"Not much. It's what he didn't say that counts, though." Rikard told Polski what he thought Bedik's reaction to the mention of his father's name had meant.

"I think you may be right," Polski said, "but it won't do you any good if you get yourself killed. Let's get you home. You've had enough excitement for one day."

Rikard resented the patronizing attitude, but it didn't make any sense to protest. He let Polski lead him out of the alley by the other door. They went up a narrow hall to a shop, the nature of which he could not determine.

"You've got a lot of courage," Polski said as they passed through the shop, "or else you don't know what kind of place this is."

"I'm beginning to get a pretty good idea."

"Then why'd you try to talk to Bedik?"

"Because I thought he could tell me something. And he did."

"You're lucky you got out of there alive."

"Not at all. I'm lucky I got out of there with a loss of only twenty bills."

Polski just shook his head. Rikard decided not to press the point.

A block and a half from the shop they stopped at a parked floater. Polski opened a door for Rikard, then went around to the other side and climbed in behind the wheel.

"Expense account," he explained as the car lifted up five centimeters from the pavement. He drove through the maze of streets as if he knew them.

"You've been here before?" Rikard asked.

"Several times. Got awfully lost the first time."

"You're not down here for fun, I take it."

"Just wrapping up the tail end of a long investigation."

"Right, the thing I'm not supposed to ask about."

They pulled into a courtyard two blocks from Rikard's hostel, where there were several other vehicles in parking slots. To make room the plant shelves started high up on the walls.

"Thanks for the lift," Rikard said as they walked from the lot out onto the street. "I wasn't sure I could have made it back before dark."

"Assuming you could have gotten away from Zakroyan, you had plenty of time. If you had known the best way to go."

"I've got it marked on my map now."

"You're expecting to go back, are you?"

"I hope not. I'm pretty sure it would be a waste of time. But you never know about these things."

"Are you still determined to try to find your father?"

"Absolutely, especially now that I have some reason to believe he might still be alive."

"Look, Rikard, it's been eleven years, according to you, since he dropped out of sight. Maybe he is still alive. But even if he is, he didn't disappear without a reason. Maybe he doesn't want to be found. Take my advice. Find someone who'll sell you a ticket off Kohltri and go home."

"Are you afraid I'll get myself killed?"

"Exactly. You're not your father. You don't know the first thing about survival down here. Maybe Bedik won't come after you, but Zakroyan certainly will. And half the rest of the people of this city, if they thought they'd make a bill or two."

"I've survived so far."

"You've had good luck so far."

"That's true, I have. Look, I've got one more place to try. If that doesn't pan out, all my leads will have run dry, and there will be nothing left for me to do except go home. But I'm not leaving while I'm alive and have any chance at all."

"What is this lead of yours?"

"The Troishla."

"You're crazy."

"That's as may be."

"Don't you know what kind of a place that is?"

"I've heard stories."

"Well, they're all true, whatever they were. You walk in there, all that will happen is you'll provide those characters with some sport for an hour or two, and then they'll have your head on a stake."

"So I should just give up?"

"Yes."

"Would you?"

"I'm not you."

"You never learn anything by not trying."

"Learning does you no good if it kills you."

"I'm going to die anyway, so I may as well do it doing what I want."

Suddenly people began running from something behind them. They turned to see the golden, shining, serpentine transparency of a dragon descending to the street just half a block away.

"Let's move, kid," Polski said, grabbing his arm and rushing him along toward the hostel. They reached the door to the courtyard at a run. Polski shoved the door open and Rikard, beside him, looked over his shoulder to see the creature just meters behind them, its eyes looking directly at him. What appeared to be a forelimb was reaching for him.

With a yell he lurched against Polski and knocked them both sprawling through the door and into the courtyard.

Polski twisted over on his back and started an angry protest. He cut it short when he saw how close the dragon was. He grabbed Rikard's arm, dragged them both to their feet, and jerked Rikard across the court toward the hostel lobby. Rikard caught a glimpse of the dragon coming over the wall into the courtyard just as the door slammed shut with them safely inside.

# PART FOUR

## 1.

Rikard started out for the Troishla early the next morning.

Leonid Polski had stayed at the hostel until the dragon left and had tried to talk Rikard out of visiting the notorious tavern, but Rikard had been stubborn. Polski had refused to show him the route until Rikard told him he'd find his own way. Then the policeman had sketched in the streets on Rikard's false map.

He remained alert as he walked toward the west edge of the city. His experiences the day before had taught him that it could be fatal to let one's attention wander while strolling these streets. This time he saw the first set of muggers when they were still a block away. He detoured to avoid them.

A little while later he thought he noticed a woman following him. Without being obvious about it, he kept track of her, and after three blocks he was sure.

He checked his map while walking. Polski's route was plain, but the printed portion was totally unreliable here, and he didn't dare make another detour for fear of getting lost.

He kept on walking. After another block the woman had closed the gap to only a hundred meters or so. After another block she was walking beside him.

She was almost as tall as he was, and quite striking in appearance. She wore leathers, a gun on her hip, and her face had the same hardness Rikard had seen on all the other citizens of the city.

"Kind of far from home, aren't you?" the woman asked after she'd walked beside him for half a block.

"Everybody I meet says something like that."

"My, aren't we sharp this morning."

"State your business or leave me alone."

The woman grabbed Rikard's arm and jerked him around, and he, with the same motion, hit her on the side of the jaw. Her head snapped to the side and she staggered to her knees,

77

clutching for her gun. He kicked her hand away; the weapon went spinning into the street. The other pedestrians paid no attention.

"Lesson one," Rikard said. "Never talk to strangers." Then he turned and went on his way. She did not pursue him.

Once again he felt exhilarated. Maybe he would be able to survive in this city after all.

The only other trouble he had was when he passed through a neighborhood where children were playing, the first he'd seen so far. Several of the older ones, ten or twelve years of age, formed a jeering ring around him. They danced and yelled along with him until he'd gone three more blocks.

The buildings began to thin as he neared the western edge of the city. Between them were empty lots, not overgrown but carefully planted with trees, shrubs, and flowers. Rikard's theory was that the citizens' emphasis on horticulture was their way of compensating for an otherwise harsh psycho-social existence.

The street angled to the right. Beyond the bend he could see, three blocks away, the bulk of a huge building, right at the end of the street. It was the Troishla.

He stopped where he was, suddenly afraid. He had no doubts about his ability to get into the Troishla. His real problem would be in coming out again.

Everything he'd heard about this place had been bad, conjuring up images of brutality, perversion, and violence. He didn't know how much was exaggeration and how much the truth, and doubted that it mattered. He slowly walked a block closer, hating his fear and struggling to master it, and stopped again.

Whether the stories were true or not, he had decided that he was going to go in there and commit this world's two prime sins: talk to strangers and pry into their business.

He tried to think what his father would have done. He certainly wouldn't have just walked in cold. He'd have had some kind of plan, not so much of action but of attitude. He'd have decided ahead of time, based on his knowledge of the situation, whether to be humble or arrogant, silent or loquacious.

And he would have found all the exits. That was the first

thing Rikard could do. It would give him time to come up with some kind of plan for the rest of it.

He didn't want to be seen obviously casing the place. He walked a block to the north, losing sight of the building momentarily behind the other structures, then went back west to the street on which the Troishla stood, on his left now, five stories tall, isolated from the other buildings north and south of it by lawns.

The Troishla was an old building, older than anything else Rikard had seen in the city so far. There were even a few anomalous windows in the north-end wall, behind narrow railed balconies. The east front of the building was a blank, with only a single, large door at the end of the street one block to the south. There was no other door on the northern side as far as Rikard could see. There were only trees and woods at the back. It was right on the edge of the city.

He crossed the street that ran in front of the Troishla, to a double-sized empty lot between it and the next building north of it. This lot, like all the others he'd passed, was well tended, not left to weeds and junk. At the back of the lot, however, was wilderness, a forest. The Troishla extended twice as far back as the building now on Rikard's right. The trees came right up to its back wall and around its near corner.

Rikard stayed close to the wall of the neighboring building sixty meters north of the Troishla, and moved along it halfway to the forest at the back. From here he could easily be seen by anybody looking out the tavern's windows, if they were in fact transparent. Anybody who saw him would know he was a tourist, and any further caution on his part would be superfluous.

But if he hadn't been seen yet . . .

He walked quickly straight back into the woods. The forest beyond the lot was not dense, more like a wooded park. Fallen limbs littered the ground under the trees, the occasional shrubs were leggy, natural, untrimmed. Leaf mold lay thick on the ground.

He did not pause until the Troishla was all but obscured by intervening foliage. If he had made it undetected this far, he should be safe.

He wanted to see the back side of the Troishla, but the foliage obscured all details. He walked through the woods, parallel to the back wall, until he had come to its middle. Then, choosing his way carefully, so as to remain concealed as much as possible, he approached the tavern again.

He got to within fifteen meters before he decided he was close enough. He found a place where he could crouch down and peer under low, bushy branches. He was in shadow, and unless he disturbed the foliage too much, he should be invisible to anyone inside looking out.

There were two more doors in the back wall, one near each corner. There were more windows back here, especially at the top two floors. Each had a minuscule balcony barely deep enough for one person to stand on. There were no outbuildings, power blocks, or external stairs. There was no obvious correlation between the arrangement of windows here and those on the north end of the building. After a moment he carefully backed away.

He retreated a hundred meters or so, until the tavern was almost out of sight, then continued around to the south. He moved cautiously, as quietly as he could, keeping one eye on the Troishla, to make sure he couldn't be seen and to keep from wandering too far away and losing sight of it altogether. His toe came up hard against something, and he fell.

He lay still for a moment, waiting to hear if anyone had taken notice. The woods were silent. He picked himself up cautiously and looked down to see what had tripped him.

He kicked whatever it was free from the ground. The end that had been exposed looked just like broken stone, though of an unusual amber color, but the part that had been buried had a different texture and sheen.

It was about as big as his head. He bent down to pick it up. It weighed a lot less than he expected. The undersurface was broken off and looked as if it had been made of some kind of porcelain or plastic, he couldn't tell which. The part that had been exposed to the elements was not in fact weathered, but artificially made to look that way.

He saw that there were other, similar fragments all around his feet, protruding slightly from the ground, their earth colors not that different from the leaf mold. It looked like the site of a ruin. Rikard could not tell from their arrangement on the ground what the shape of the original building might have been.

He kicked up another chunk buried even more deeply than the piece that had tripped him. The "stone," almost russet, showed no weathering or signs of organic attack. He knocked the two stones together. They did not chip or crack.

Judging from the way the stones had been embedded in the soil, the way the roots of the trees grew around them, and the locations of the trees themselves, growing among the detritus, they had to be very old.

Kohltri had been colonized less than a thousand years ago. That might have been enough time to bury these stones as deep as they were, but it was not long enough to have caused the destruction of what they had originally been a part of, unless whatever had once stood here had been deliberately torn down.

The material of which they were made looked like nothing he had seen elsewhere in the city, or on any other world, though there was a vague resemblance to weathered quartz. These fragments would have to be very old indeed to have crumbled naturally, as they appeared to have done.

That indicated that these pieces of plastic or porcelain were the remains of a previous civilization. The bartender across from Boss Bedik's dome had mentioned a people called the Belshpaer, and had said that the materials that the mines extracted were the remains of an even earlier civilization. . . .

He heard something moving farther back in the woods. He crouched down closer to the ground, though there were no bushes here to hide him. He held his breath. His hearing became super sharp. After a moment, the sound came again, like someone walking through the woods.

He stayed frozen in his crouch, trying to think of some plausible explanation for his being here. He could not see who was making the noises; they were too far back in the woods. But he thought he could detect a strange quality to the sound which he couldn't put his finger on.

The footsteps, if that was what they were, were moving away from him. Once he thought he heard somebody speak, or rather, three or four people speaking in unison, in strange, thin voices. But the distance was too great, and the intervening foliage muffled the words, if they were words.

The sounds died away. He waited, then straightened to his feet. He remembered the Troishla and glanced nervously over his shoulder. There was nobody there; he could barely see the building through the bushes and trees. The only thing he heard now was a bird calling somewhere.

Whoever or whatever had been walking through the woods had distracted him for too long. He dropped the pieces of "stone" and, keeping one eye on the Troishla, the other on the ground at his feet, hurried south through the trees.

He went past the end of the tavern and angled back toward the city so that he would come out of the woods behind the next building south. This was a commercial building, and conventional for Kohltri. It had no exterior windows at all. He pressed himself against its wall and moved back toward the Troishla until he could see the whole of the tavern's southern face. Like the north end, it had a few balconied windows but no doors.

He backed away and went around the south end of the building, away from the Troishla. He came back to the street half a block from the tavern. There were only a few cars on the street and no pedestrians. Although he felt terribly conspicuous in his offworlder clothes, nobody paid him any attention.

He wasn't sure that his reconnoitering had accomplished anything. But now there was nothing more he could do but go in. He hoped he would be able to come out again.

## 2.

He opened the front door of the Troishla and stepped into a high, vaulted room with exposed rafters ten meters overhead. There were two tiers of galleries against the far wall reached by stairs at either end. There was a long bar under the galleries, and thirty or more round tables, with five or six chairs each, filling up most of the rest of the room. Only the area in front of the door was clear.

The tables were over half filled, and there were about twenty people at the bar. A door on the first gallery overhead opened, a man came out, went to the next door, and went in. Chandeliers hung on chains from the high rafters. The air was thick with tobacco and other smoke, the smell of alcohol in various forms, and the not-well-muted rumble of the patrons.

Most of these people were dressed in leathers, but a few had fancier attire—not tourist clothes, but something else. Everyone wore a gun of some kind. There were at least three card games in progress. Somebody in a far corner laughed too loudly.

Rikard could allow himself only a moment to size things up. He was too obviously a stranger and could not walk in as if he belonged here, but if he hesitated too long, it would look as if he were uncertain about being here at all.

He tried to think how he would act if he were someone on the run, come to Kohltri to avoid arrest and trial. But assuming the role of a refugee would be dangerous; he didn't have the right attitude to pull it off. Someone would be sure to find him out. His best bet was to play it straight for the moment.

He walked up to the bar, moving toward an empty place near the end at the right. He felt eyes on him as he crossed the room. Nobody said anything; he did not falter. He dared not show the fear he felt. If he did, they would be on him in an instant.

He reached the bar and took a stool. There was no one else near him. He tried to figure out the best strategy for this situation while he waited for the tender to serve the other customers.

The only thing he was sure of was that he would have to behave as if he were not afraid. The scar on his right palm was itching fiercely. He forced his mind to relax, his shoulders to unhunch, his hands to unclasp. He looked around the room again. The tender had seen him and was working his way down the bar toward him.

Rikard looked at the faces of the men and women. They were hard, grim, and frequently sad. Some were old, some young, most middle-aged. Some were laughing, but there was pain and anger behind their eyes. Rikard's father, too, had had that hard, mean look, but there had always been laughter behind his eyes. His father was not like these people at all.

Somehow that realization eliminated his fear. He still understood the danger he was in. He was still aware of the hostility in the room. If anything, he was more perceptive than before. But he was no longer afraid. His scar stopped itching.

The tender got to him at last, his eyes hard and nasty.

"Croich on the rocks," Rikard said softly. His voice was calm and perfectly under control.

"What are you, some kind of a wise guy?"

"You don't have croich?"

"Now, how the hell am I supposed to get croich on a godforsaken planet like this? You want croich, you go back where you came from."

"Got anything like it?"

"Mertha, frolem, nelsh whiskey."

"Nelsh then, on the rocks. Do you serve lunch?"

"Sandwiches."

"The biggest one you make." He put a couple of bills on the bar and stared the tender in the eyes as the other took the money and moved off.

The people who'd been watching him returned to their own interests. Nobody bothered him while he waited. He was tempted to think that maybe this place wasn't quite as dangerous as everybody had made it out to be.

A moment later the tender returned with a glass of amber whiskey, a plate on which lay a huge sandwich cut in quarters, and change. Rikard had won round one. He thanked the man and left the change lying on the counter. The nelsh wasn't much like croich after all, but the sandwich was very good.

He ate slowly, as if he had all the time in the world. When he finished eating, he downed the rest of his drink and signaled the tender that he wanted another. The tender brought it, took his money, and came back with the change.

"Maybe you could tell me something," Rikard said. "I'm trying to find somebody, and I understand that this might be a good place to ask. Is that right?"

Even as he spoke, all conversation within earshot stopped.

The tender mopped the bar in front of Rikard without looking at him. His face was set in an expression that reflected the tension in the rest of the room. Rikard didn't have to look around to hear the silent attentiveness.

Up till now the patrons had not deemed him worthy of more than the barest notice, but they had not forgotten him or truly accepted him. And though they had gone on about their own interests, they had heard his conversation. His last words had been spoken in silence. Now there was only the occasional sound of a chair leg scraping on the floor as somebody with his or her back to the scene turned to get a better view.

Rikard waited a moment longer, but the tender didn't answer his question.

"He came here about twelve years ago," Rikard went on at last. "I can trace him for two-thirds of a year, and then he disappeared." The smell of danger was thick in the air.

"Didn't anybody tell you it was a good idea to mind your own business?" the tender asked.

"This is my business."

"I don't see it that way. It's the business of the man you're hunting where he is, not yours."

"But it's my business to want to find him."

"That's too bad."

"Would money make things better?"

"Look, kid, nobody tells a stranger where somebody is. You haven't got the kind of money that buys information like that."

"How do you know?"

"I don't see your assistants carrying it in wheelbarrows."

Rikard couldn't help but chuckle, which possibly saved his life. His good humor broke the tension of the moment, but the contest was still on. It was just going to go into another round. His life was still in danger, but at least the tender didn't despise him.

"You're right," Rikard said, "that kind of money I don't have. Look, I can understand not passing out a guy's address to every tourist that comes along. But not everybody who's looking for somebody is an enemy. Sometimes one friend tries to find another. What happens then?"

"Same thing. A friend knows where his friends are. He doesn't need to ask directions."

"Even after eleven years?"

"If your friend didn't tell you where he is, he didn't want you to find him."

"Unless he's dead."

"You think he's dead?"

"No. Somebody else I talked to reacted in a strange way, which I don't think he'd do for a corpse."

"Then there's not much I can do," the tender said. "This guy may be a friend of yours, or he may not, but *I* don't know you. And I don't talk to strangers."

It was the end of round three. Rikard took a sip of his drink. If he wanted to leave now, he'd be allowed to depart in one piece. But he had nowhere else to search after the Troishla. And he hadn't lost this contest yet.

He drew a wet circle on the bar and looked back up at the tender, who was still watching him. "Everybody starts out as a stranger."

"Almost everybody," the tender agreed.

"Granted. But for those who don't already have a connection, there's got to be some way to become known."

"Sure, hang around for a year or so."

"It doesn't take that long."

"Not always."

"So maybe there's some way I can establish my credentials a little more quickly."

"Credentials!" the tender repeated, and started to laugh. There were other appreciative chuckles from around the room, and an occasional comment. Rikard had lost again, but he was providing a good show. As long as he did so, he was probably safe.

He glanced casually around at his audience. They were enjoying this contest. But most of them would be perfectly happy to teach him a lesson if he made any kind of mistake.

Some faces were angry. Those people would jump on him now if there weren't so many other patrons present. One or two people looked bored. One or two others, including a very attractive young woman, seemed to have no hatred at all in their eyes. Rikard nodded and smiled at one of these last, then turned back to the tender. The man was waiting expectantly.

"The man I'm looking for is my father," Rikard said.

The tender raised an eyebrow. "And he disappeared eleven years ago?"

"He left home almost fourteen years ago."

"Then I'd suggest you leave well enough alone."

The contest was over. Somebody at one of the tables muttered, "We don't want any Fed spies around here," but there were few assenting replies. As far as most of the patrons were concerned, Rikard had lost fairly.

The tender went off to serve other customers. The noise level in the room returned to normal. The man three stools to Rikard's left suggested that he finish his drink and get out, but almost everybody else had returned to their business. Only a few people were still watching from their tables.

Rikard took a long pull from his drink and thought that maybe the man's advice was pretty good. Then two people, a man and a woman, came up to the bar on either side of him. They stood too close to be friendly.

"I think maybe you've been here too long," the woman, standing on his right, said. Rikard had watched her face just moments before. It still expressed hatred. And now he didn't dare leave, because it would look as if he was running from these two people.

"All I want to do," he said, "is find out if my father is alive or dead. If he's dead, I'll visit his grave, and that will be the end of it. If he's alive, I want to see him just once, and *that* will be the end of it."

The woman grabbed his arm. "Maybe you didn't hear—"

"Shut up, Lesh," her friend on Rikard's left snapped. She did. "Don't mind her," the man went on. He was not at all friendly. "She gets a little impatient. But you're cool. You've been amusing so far. Go on and tell us your story." There was no humor in his expression whatsoever.

Rikard wondered how much he should say, but now was not the time to be coy. "My father is Arin Braeth," he said. "He left my mother and me almost fourteen years ago, after his money ran out. He said then, and I believed him, that he was going to make his fortune and come back. But he never did come back.

"I started tracking him down two years ago, and I've traced him here. Records show he stayed in the city for over two hundred days, and then the records stop. He checked out.

There's no record of death, for whatever that's worth. I talked to Boss Bedik, and he won't tell me anything, but I think he knew my father back then. He acts as if my father is still alive. And now I'm here.

"And that's all there is to it." He finished his drink.

"I've heard of Arin Braeth," the man said.

"Hell, Arbo," Lesh whined, "you've heard of everybody."

"Shut up, Lesh.".Arbo's voice was icy. "But I don't believe you're Arin Braeth's son," he said to Rikard.

"Why not?"

"Arin Braeth was a Gesta, and one of the best. He ransacked Valerian. He sold guns to Tropos. He helped put down the Menn Thark uprising. He traded bhang of Asmarth. A guy like that has lots of children. But none of them bear his name."

"My mother was the one woman my father married," Rikard said. "It was his last adventure. And I can prove I'm his son. I have the identification."

"That proves nothing," Lesh said. "Do you know how easy it is to make identification tickets? Why do you think all these tourists come here? To buy and sell stuff they can't get at home. And one of those things is IDs. Any kind you want, made up in any name you wish."

Another man came up to the bar behind Arbo and leaned around him across the counter so he could see Rikard.

"What do you want your old man for anyway?" he asked.

"To find out what happened to him after he left my mother and me. My mother died because he didn't come back as he said he would. It took her three years to do it. My father should know what happened to her. And because I care about what happened to him."

"You're screwy," the man said.

"So what? That doesn't make me different from anybody else."

"What I want to know," Arbo said, "is what made you think you had any business coming here in the first place."

"To Kohltri? I—"

"To the Troishla."

"I was told that somebody here might know what happened to my father."

"And didn't anybody tell you that coming here for any reason might be a bad idea?"

"Yes, several people."

"And you came here anyway."

"It was my last lead. I—"

"You're nothing but a tourist," Lesh said. "Who are you running from, hah? Nobody. You've got no business here."

"Finding my father is my business."

"So what if your father's dead?" the man behind Arbo asked.

"Then I can go home."

"Okay, he's dead."

"Show me the grave."

"This has gone on long enough," Arbo said. "I don't like people nosing around, asking personal questions."

"Tell me another way to find my father," Rikard said, "and I'll be happy to take your advice."

Arbo stepped back from the bar and put a heavy hand on Rikard's shoulder. Rikard had been waiting for this moment, but still didn't know how he was going to defend himself. But before Arbo could start anything, a drunken face pushed in between them and glared at Rikard.

"I don't like you," its owner said, his breath heavy with stale alcohol. Arbo's hand fell from Rikard's shoulder, and the drunk pressed in closer.

"I'm going to smash you," the drunk went on, eyes blurry, face half slack.

"May I defend myself?" Rikard asked quietly.

"Sure," Lesh said from behind him. "However you like."

But Rikard was spared the trouble. The drunk was suddenly jerked away. A rather small man of middle age had him by the arm, and when the drunk saw who it was, he lost all fight.

"Just going to smash him," the drunk said.

"Not today," the little man told him. Arbo watched with approval.

"But, Gareth, this tourist's been in here asking personal questions."

"So it's not up to you to stop him," Gareth said. Several other patrons who had been closing in shuffled and backed off a pace or two.

"But if I don't, who will?"

"Maybe nobody. And in any event, Arbo was here first. Just back off, Dorong."

"And if I don't?"

"You must be even drunker than you look."

"Come on, Gareth, what if I don't back off?"

Gareth calmly took Dorong by the throat with one hand and squeezed until the drunk went to his knees, gasping and choking. Then Gareth hit him in the face with his other hand until the blood flowed from Dorong's mouth and nose.

"Don't try to find out," Gareth said. He let go of Dorong, who staggered to his feet, clutching his battered face. There was a soft murmur from the other patrons. Arbo just grinned.

Then the little man turned his attention to Rikard. "Okay, kid, you can ask your questions." He shot a silencing glance at Arbo, who was about to protest. "Just be very careful."

"Thank you," Rikard said. He didn't trust Gareth's motives, but he couldn't back down now. "Did you know my father, when he was here eleven, twelve years ago?"

"No, I didn't. Knew the name, of course, but I never met him."

"He was very public for about two-thirds of a year. Boss Bedik knew him, and I'm sure other people would have too. Could you suggest somebody who might have known him, or direct me to someone else who could help?"

"I'm afraid not." Gareth's face was bland.

Rikard turned to Arbo. "Would *you* know anything to help me?" he asked.

"Only been here seven years," Arbo said, and leaned against the bar.

Rikard turned to Lesh, but she just stared away. He turned back to Gareth.

"Who else can I ask, then?"

"I don't know," Gareth said. Somebody at a table snickered. Rikard was being given the runaround. He was disappointed, but not surprised.

"I guess," he said, "having your permission to ask questions doesn't necessarily mean anybody has to give me answers."

"That's right," Gareth said, and went away.

A lot of people were laughing at him now. He turned back

to the bar, carefully suppressing his anger and humiliation. It was one thing to be tested, but another to be deliberately made a fool of.

There was nothing more he could learn here. His value as entertainment was wearing off, and if he tried to push any farther, these patrons might find more fun in killing him. He touched the scar on the palm of his right hand and watched the image of concentric circles appear and disappear. For just a moment he wished he could meet Gareth outside somewhere.

# 3.

Arbo and Lesh went away. Rikard stood at the bar, trying to decide what to do next. He knew he was lucky to still be in one piece, but that didn't assuage his frustration.

He felt someone move up to him, intruding on his meditations. He turned to see the attractive young woman he'd noticed earlier. She put an empty mug on the bar, and the tender came to fill it.

She looked up at Rikard. She was shorter than he by about thirty-five centimeters. "You're doing okay for a greenhorn." Her face was as hard and smooth as it was attractive, but there was no hatred in her eyes. She wore leathers and a gun, but she was not the same kind of person as the rest of the patrons.

"I figure I'm lucky I'm still standing on my own feet," Rikard said, keeping his voice steadier than he felt.

"There were a couple of close moments there," she agreed. The tender came back with her beer, then moved on. "But I've got to give you credit. You handled yourself very well. That they let you stay here is proof of that. How long have you been on Kohltri?"

"This is my fourth day. Think they'll let me out of here alive?"

"Sure. Gareth is on your side for some reason." She sipped

her beer. "You don't belong here. You did all right, but you're not one of these people."

"Neither are you. I can see it in your eyes."

She laughed. "Was that story you told true?"

"Yes, it was. There's a lot more to it, of course."

"And you've followed him all the way here from wherever?"

"Pelgrane. Yes. It's been a long two years."

"You must either love him a lot or hate him a lot."

"That's obvious, isn't it? Otherwise I wouldn't be here. When I was a kid, I thought he was the greatest guy in the world. Then he went away and didn't come back. My mother did die because of that. As to how I feel about him now, I don't know. But I'm going to find him, if I live long enough."

"And what happens when you do?"

"That depends on whether he's alive or dead. But aside from that, there are some other things I've been thinking about doing."

"So, finding your father is not the end-all of your career."

"Now, that would be kind of silly, wouldn't it? Though it's been my driving force for a long time. It's something I've got to do, a kind of a threshold I have to cross."

"Why did he come here?" She took another pull at her beer.

"He was after money. Why else? We'd always been well off. He had a fortune left over from all his exploits before he met Mother, as I learned later. It was all invested on Pelgrane. But he wasn't a very good investor, whatever else he might have been. When I was twelve we went broke.

"That was when he began to talk about the treasure. I don't know what it was, but he said he knew where he could lay his hands on a lot of cash, more than he'd ever had before. It seems he'd always had clues as to where it was but hadn't bothered to think about it until the money ran out. Then all the pieces came together, as it were.

"He said he was going to go out one more time, that he might be gone for a year. But he never came back."

"Do you think he would have if he'd found what he was looking for?"

"For a while I was sure of it. He and Mother were a real love story ever since they first met. He gave up adventuring for her. She gave up her titles for him. They moved to Pelgrane, where neither was very well known. I can't remember there ever being a moment's unhappiness between them.

"And then I decided he'd changed his mind, found the money and run out. That's when I gave up on him, since he'd given up on us. But now I don't know. He said he was going to be gone for a year, but it took him two years just to get here. Apparently he didn't know where the treasure was as well as he thought he did. And the way he disappeared, after being here for two-thirds of a year—well, I just don't know."

"Who was your mother?"

"The Lady Sigra Malvrone."

"Ah! Of course. I remember hearing stories about that. She was kidnapped, wasn't she?"

"Yes. They wanted a ransom, but her family had no money, only titles. And even with their connections, they couldn't raise the amount the kidnappers wanted.

"But Mother's brother, my uncle Gawin, had friends who knew my father. They asked him to help. And he did, and got her back, and destroyed the kidnappers in the process. He fell in love with my mother, she fell in love with him, and that was that. Uncle Gawin never forgave my father— nor himself, for that matter, though he was the only member of my mother's family who ever came to visit us."

"How romantic."

"Well, it was, the way my father told it. And my mother told it the same way. And though Uncle Gawin had a different opinion of the whole affair, his version was more or less the same. And as long as Mother was happy, he was satisfied. I never saw him again after Father went off."

"And so your father left your mother one last time, to make just one more fortune."

"Yes. It would have been something he could cash in quickly. My father was incapable of holding a job."

"And you don't know what this 'treasure' was, but you've traced him here."

"And I think he's still alive." He told her about his meeting with Boss Bedik.

"If your interpretation is correct," she said, "then he might be. Well, how are you doing so far? Do you have any more leads?"

"Nothing. You saw what happened here. I know he's on Kohltri somewhere, but nobody will admit to having seen him."

"I'm not surprised. You're probably asking your questions in all the wrong places." She finished her beer and signaled the tender to bring her another.

"So what are the right places?"

"You wouldn't know them."

"That's obvious. I'm a tourist, I don't know anything about Kohltri. Give me some names."

"These places don't have names."

"You're playing with me, just like Gareth."

"I'm sorry. I shouldn't have said anything. Even if I told you where to go, it wouldn't do you any good. You wouldn't know how to ask the questions, and you'd get hurt or worse before you got any answers."

"That's what they said about this place."

"It's different. The Troishla is dangerous, like a den of hyenas. The places I mean don't play games with you like they did here."

"That's as may be, but I've come this far, and while I appreciate your concern, I have no intention of giving up now. I've spent too much time and too much money coming here. I'm not going to waste that now that I'm so close. I wouldn't be able to live with myself. I've got to see this out. So if you have any ideas at all, please tell me. Where can I go next?"

"You really want to put your life on the line? You've done so well it would be a shame to get yourself killed now."

"So what do I do, just stand here until they throw me out?"

"If you weren't such an obvious tourist, you might be able to get away with it. You've got talent."

"Okay, so how do I stop being a tourist? Everybody who wasn't born here started out as one."

"Not really. They were already citizens of Kohltri before they ever got here. They just shed their tourist disguises after a few days and melded right in—if they lived that long."

"Like you?"

"I don't live here, I'm just a visitor. But I'm not a tourist, not the way they mean it here."

"Okay, sorry. I know, mind my own business. But you know these things; I don't. How do I stop being a tourist?"

"It's not easy."

"I never expected it would be."

"Do you really want to do this?"

"Hell, no. I'm only here for the fun of it. Squandered three lifetimes' income to get here just so I could play games."

"Sorry." She stood silent for a moment, sipping her fresh beer.

Rikard regretted his outburst, his lack of control. Especially since this was the first person since he'd come to Kohltri with whom he felt comfortable talking—if he didn't count Leonid Polski, now that he thought about it. And she could help him, if she only would. He signaled the tender for another drink.

He turned his back to the bar and leaned his elbows on the polished wood behind him. There were more people in the big room now. Only occasionally did anyone glance his way. If he didn't start anything, there would be no trouble. He saw Gareth over at the other end of the room, near the stairs going up to the galleries. Dorong the drunk was nowhere in sight.

"Hey," the woman said, "look, I'm sorry I got you all upset."

Rikard looked down at her. She was younger than he by a couple of years. How had she gotten so hard so soon?

"No problem. I shouldn't let it get to me. If I'd been talking to Arbo, he would probably have just blown me away."

"Not in here, but he sure would have rearranged your face. But only because you're a tourist. You've got the makings of a first-class Gesta."

"Thanks, I guess. I tried exploitation once. Worked at it for a whole year. Lots of excitement if you don't mind being hated by most of the locals you have to deal with. Of course, I was pretty young then. Maybe I could do a better job of it now."

"A Gesta isn't the same thing as an exploiter. Exploitation is a business. Being a Gesta is a way of life. You go adventuring for the fun of it. No, really. There aren't too many of us, but your father was one. If you find him, ask him why he did what he did."

"Is that why you're here, for the fun of it?"

"Sure. And to lie low for a while. And just for the fun of it, I'm going to take you on. If you want to find your father, you have to ask in the right places, and even to get into the right places, you have to look like you belong there. On your own authority, if nothing else. Give me a week with you, and I bet I could teach you enough so you'd be able to go anywhere. Coming back again would be your own problem, of course."

"You mean that?"

"Sure. If somebody doesn't do something about you, you won't get home tonight. Dorong's got a grudge, but he doesn't dare take it out on Gareth. So you'll be the target. If not tonight, tomorrow or the next day. You see, just by coming in here, you signed your death warrant."

"I've been set up before, but—okay, I'll take the chance. If you're willing to teach me, I'm willing to learn. What will it cost me?"

"Nothing, I'm flush at the moment. Just pay attention, and I'll do what I can. Okay?"

"Fine. How do we start?"

She stuck out her hand. "I'm Darcy Glemtide." Her grip was firm and strong. "And you're the son of Arin Braeth."

"My name's Rikard."

"Okay, Rik, we start now. Pay up."

He did, then they left the Troishla. He couldn't help but wonder what the "tough" parts of the tavern were like.

"You're staying at some hostel downtown," Darcy said as they walked away from the building. "The first thing we do is find you a new place to live. You're spotted, and they'll come for you—whoever they are. I know just the place. It's out of the tourist section, off an alley, has two other exits, and is probably more comfortable than the place you're in now. And since I know the owner, you'll have no trouble getting in. Just let me handle everything."

"I'll be more than happy to."

# 4.

Although the walk back to Rikard's hostel took a few hours, they had no trouble on the way. There he packed his one suitcase in a matter of moments. Then, with Darcy carrying his recorder, he checked out just as night was beginning to fall.

As they walked through the city, Darcy kept her free hand on the butt of her laser pistol. Rikard's suitcase was an invitation to a mugging, but nobody bothered them.

They came to a very narrow alley and waited for some moments to make sure they hadn't been followed. Then they entered the alley, which had several back doors opening onto it. Darcy led him through the third door on the right, into a small courtyard, little more than a patio, with the leaves of the ever-present plants almost meeting overhead. Beyond an archway opposite them was a hallway running right and left.

They turned right up the hall and went through the second door on the left, into a room furnished with a couch and a couple of chairs. Darcy handed Rikard his recorder as another door on the right opened and a man came out, a heavy shotgun pistol in his hand.

"It's you, Darcy," he said. "Come to pay me a visit?" He watched Rikard closely.

"I need that room you have." Darcy took a wallet from an inside pocket and handed the man a couple of large bills.

"For him?" The man nodded his head at Rikard as he took the money. Darcy nodded back.

"Have fun." The man went out the way he had come in.

"Come on," Darcy said to Rikard. She led him through a third door in the far wall, into another corridor. They passed three more doors, the hallway elled to the left, and they went on to the end.

She opened the last door on the left and ushered Rikard into a comfortable sitting room. It was clean, brightly lit, and well furnished, but there were no windows, and the phone was a nonvideo type.

"Let me show you the other two exits," she said. Rikard put down his suitcase and recorder and followed her into a well-appointed kitchen, already stocked with food. A section of the cabinets swung out, revealing a narrow, unlit passage, which led to the street.

"You can't get in this way," she explained, showing how the door at the other end worked. "Always check before you go out to make sure you aren't being seen." She indicated a globe eye next to the door. Rikard looked through and could see the whole street beyond.

"There isn't usually much traffic there," Darcy went on. "Use this exit only if you have to."

She led him back to the kitchen, then to the third room, which served as a bedroom and sanitary. There she showed him another secret door behind the bookcase. Beyond was another dark passage, which ended in a hallway.

"You *can* come in through here," she said, "but again, don't let anyone see you." She stepped out into the hallway, and Rikard followed, looking back to see how the door worked.

They went left a few meters to where the hall elled to the right, then on past two doors on either side to the end, where another door opened onto a more conventional courtyard with all the usual plants in containers on the ground and on brackets on the walls. There was another door at each end of the courtyard. The street entrance was across from them. They went out so Rikard could see the place and recognize it from the outside. Then they went back to his rooms the way they had come in the first time.

"Always use the front entrance," Darcy said, sitting in one of the big chairs in the living room, "unless you have no other choice. Mendel won't come out unless you bring somebody with you. When you first enter that little court off the alley, an alarm rings and he checks on you then. He did it just now when we came back."

"Are there lots of places like this?" Rikard took a seat on the couch. He was suddenly very tired.

"Lots, but none as good as this one. Or at least, if there are, which is a good bet, I don't know about them."

"What if somebody manages to find me here?"

"If he or she comes through Mendel's little parlor, they'll have to talk to his shotgun first. If you hear it going off, don't bother asking whether it's for you or somebody else. Just get out."

"Good enough. What's the charge on this place?"

"A hundred a week. Can you cover it?"

"Sure. For a while, anyway. I'd like to keep enough in reserve to buy a ticket off if I need to. How much did you pay him?"

"Two hundred."

"Let me pay you back." She took the proffered money. "Just how much danger am I in?"

"A lot. Not from Mendel. But from everybody else. You're off your turf. You've been lucky so far. I guess you know how to handle yourself well enough to get along most places other than Kohltri, but never forget that Kohltri is different. If you keep your head down, you may live long enough to know how to survive on purpose instead of by accident."

"Why are you going to all this trouble?"

"For the fun of it, like I said."

"Sure. Want some supper?"

"Thought you'd never ask."

Rikard pushed himself to his feet, went to the kitchen, made a selection, pressed the buttons, and set the meal out on the table. Darcy stood in the doorway, watching him.

"You don't believe me, do you?" she said. "That I'm doing this for fun."

"Oh, sure, but fun isn't enough. It's too pat. But that's your business." He sat down, and she joined him.

"It's true," she said, digging into the roast. "I've got absolutely nothing to do right now, and you're a challenge. Not too much of one; you've got lots of potential. But enough to make it interesting."

"Okay, I'll accept that, I guess."

They ate in silence for a few moments.

"I don't mean to pry," Rikard said after a while, "just making conversation, you understand. But how did you get into this business?"

"You really want to know?"

"Sure, but like I said, I'm not prying. You've heard my

life story. Or part of it. What made you become an adventurer, a Gesta as you call it? The fun of it?"

"Sort of. It's not always fun, you know."

"My father used to love to tell stories. I thought he was just making them up. After I left Pelgrane, I found they were all true. He didn't always have fun either."

"Most of it is fun, though. Or, not really that, but exciting. That's the real reason, I guess. Life was dull."

"As what?"

"An archaeologist, can you believe it? At least, that's what I got my degree in. It's paid off too a couple of times. But the idea of spending my life in some university, going on sabbatical digs whenever funds could be found . . . well, I didn't like that. My family thought it was great.

"So anyway, I got my B.S., and my father gave me a big graduation check. The next day I hopped a lighter to some place I'd never heard of, and I've been going ever since."

"Ever get tired of it?"

"Nope. I've been more places and known more exciting people than any dozen normal people ever will. I've been rich more often than I've been poor. I'm not tired of excitement. The farther I go, the farther I want to go, and someday I'll make my mark. But there's plenty of time for that."

"Seems like it would be kind of a hard life." They'd finished eating, so Rikard cleared off the table.

"Oh, it is sometimes. Especially at first. All I wanted then was to get out and away. I wouldn't have lasted half a day here then. But that first year I wasn't up against this kind of stuff. Just a kid out alone with my money. My father's rich. That check was a big one, and it took me almost a year of traveling to spend it all."

Rikard got them each a beer, and they went to sit in the living room.

"I'd learned a lot by then, of course," she went on. "So when the money ran out I found somebody who could use my knowledge of archaeological techniques. We went to Aakan, and excavated the great pyramid there. And then the people who owned the pyramid found out, and we had to leave in a hurry. That was my first time outside the law. And I liked it."

"So you just kept going."

"Sure. I don't know about most people, but I found the adventure addictive."

"I think I know what you mean." He told her about the muggers he'd fought off and the exhilaration he'd felt afterward.

"That's it exactly," Darcy agreed, "though getting mugged's not the way I'd look for thrills."

"Me neither. Okay, so now I know about you, a little bit. What's next on the program for my education?"

"Nothing more for today. Get yourself rested up, and tomorrow we'll go out and get you some new clothes."

After she left, Rikard stood for a long moment, looking at the closed door.

# 5.

He woke the next morning to find Darcy Glemtide standing by his bed.

"Do you always come in unannounced?" he asked.

"Just part of your education. I've been here about five minutes. Long enough to have killed you a dozen times in any number of ways. Or drugged you. Or whatever. You're going to have to learn to be more alert, even when you're asleep. Tomorrow when I come in here I'm going to dunk you with ice water. So be on your guard."

"It seems a rather drastic way to make a point."

"A bullet in the head is even more drastic, but I'm not trying to make a point. I'm trying to condition you so that you'll wake at the first sound of intrusion. It takes a long time to learn that without help, and a lot of people never do learn it, because they get killed first."

"I guess I'm pretty used to civilized society. Is that kind of sleeping vigilance really necessary?"

"Absolutely. What if I'd been Dorong?"

"Somehow it never occurred to me that they'd come and get me in my sleep."

"You're naive."

"Yes, I guess I am. Okay, I'll bet you a bill you never get to douse me with that ice water."

"It's a bet. Now get up. We've got some shopping to do."

"I sleep nude."

"So?"

"So I wasn't aware that our relationship had progressed to that degree of intimacy."

She smiled slowly. "It hasn't." Then she went back out to the living room.

He joined her a few moments later and offered to fix breakfast. She accepted readily.

"So we're going to buy me clothes today." He pushed the buttons on the kitchen console. She sat at the table.

"That's right," she said. "You won't get anywhere dressed as you are, even if you stay away from anybody who already knows you."

"I thought about getting some leathers, but a very considerate clerk told me I shouldn't."

"And she was right. You don't dare buy new leathers. You don't know how to wear them. Now if Arbo, for example, went out and bought new leathers, anybody who saw him would still know he was Arbo, and if they didn't know him before, they could soon tell, just by watching him, that he belonged here and knew what he was doing and would leave him alone. If they didn't have some other reason for messing with him."

"But they don't know me." Rikard took the plates from the range and set them on the table.

"That's it exactly." She started eating as if she were hungry. "You'd look just like some tourist who was trying to pass by wearing leathers. And that would be the end of you, because the first person who saw you would want to test you and teach you a lesson for your audacity."

"So what good will it do me to buy these leathers, then?"

"You buy old ones secondhand. Lots of strangers come here, people who fit right in. If you're dressed in old leathers, you'll look like one of those. Of course, the first time you open your mouth you'll give the whole show away. The disguise is thin, but it will pass casual observation. You'll be able to walk the streets—most of the time."

"Do even old-timers get mugged?"

"They sure do. But that's another problem. What we're concerned with now is enabling you to move around the city without having to worry about the casual person on the street.

"And there's another thing. Almost everybody here wears some sort of light body armor under their clothes." She leaned back from the table and opened the top few buttons of her shirt. She pulled the collars back to show a close-fitting garment of softly shimmering gray.

"You'll need a set of that too." She buttoned her shirt back up and returned to her breakfast. "It's proof against plastic pistols, needlers, freezers, daggers, light jolters, and helps a lot against everything else. It's not easy to buy a good set. You can't buy it new, and the secondhand sets on the market are there usually because the last owner didn't need it any more."

"Like dead, you mean?"

"Exactly. And that usually means the armor has been damaged. The set I'm wearing, for example, has no left sleeve. I can't tell for sure, but I think it was taken off by a shotgun. But sometimes you can find a whole set. The only problem with those is that they aren't always of standard quality, and some are outright fakes, but I think I can tell the difference."

"Is this going to cost a lot?" Rikard finished his eggs and toast.

"A bit. About three fifty altogether, maybe more." She gathered up the plates and put them away. "I know a place, though, where you can get your money's worth. Ready to go?"

They left his rooms by the main entrance. Keeping to the less frequented streets and alleys, they went west and south.

"You should be seen as little as possible," Darcy explained. "We don't want somebody to recognize you later and remember you were a tourist today."

"If we had a car, that would be easy to do."

"It would, but who's going to lay out thirty to seventy thousand unless they're planning to stay awhile?"

"That's more than I'd care to spend. Those prices are ridiculous. Is it because so few are imported?"

"You've got it. And the ones that are, are secondhand, at that, and parts are scarce. Occasionally a local will take the

chance, and if she's got the fare, go out to some other world,
buy up cars and parts, and if she isn't caught before she gets
back, she can make a killing."

"A lot of smuggling goes on then?"

"It's Kohltri's second largest industry, after the mines.
Working in the mines doesn't pay well, but they're safe, and
you don't need any skills. Smuggling stuff, either in or out,
can make your fortune, but your chances of survival are
ve-e-ry low. Even if you get past the station, some people
here make a living knocking off smugglers."

It took them about an hour to get to the secondhand shop.
This turned out to be a rather large establishment, one of only
three sharing that particular plant-filled courtyard. There were
no other customers present and only three clerks.

"That's why I wanted to get here early," Darcy said.

"I know. The fewer people who see me the better."

"First thing is underclothes. The armor will chafe without
it. You don't have to worry; it's all clean, at least in this
place."

They found the right stacks and quickly picked out six sets
soft silky shirts and pants.

Rikard was appalled at the prices. "This is going to come
to more than three fifty."

"You could get by with less, if you don't mind smelling."

"No, go ahead. I won't have to dig into my reserve just
yet."

They had more trouble with the leathers. Rikard was too
slender for most of what they saw, or too tall for the rest.
But at last they located an old outfit on a rack near the back
of the shop.

"Looks a little odd," Darcy said critically, examining the
material of the jacket. "That's why it's marked down. See?
The jacket is just a little long below the belt. And this fancy
stitching across the shoulders. And the color is off." It was
a tan a few shades lighter than anything else in the store.

"If it fits, do I have a choice?"

"Not really, I guess. Oh, well, you see a lot of strange
clothes around here. It's just that I wanted you to be as
inconspicuous as possible."

"Do these boots and gloves come with the suit?"

"Sure looks like it, but they cost extra."

"I'd need boots anyway, wouldn't I?"

"Yes, and the gloves too. Okay, now for light armor."

"Do they ever sell medium or heavy?"

"Medium sometimes, if you don't mind looking like a cyborg, but nobody wears it unless they have good reason. Heavy armor you can only find if you know the person who's selling it. And once in a great while somebody will have a set of smashed-up battle armor. But none of that stuff would do you any good. Go on the streets in it, and you'd meet an ambush before you'd gone three blocks."

"Okay, so light armor it is."

This was kept in another part of the shop, and there wasn't much of it. Most of it was of the shimmery gray that Darcy wore, some a dirty white, a couple were bluish, and one was copper colored. All but three sets were damaged in some way or other. And of those that were whole, one was much too large, and the other was cut strangely so that Rikard couldn't get into it when he tried it on. That left the copper-colored suit, which fit remarkably well and was marked down.

"I don't know," Darcy said. "It feels a little soft."

"Maybe another shop."

"Possibly, if we want to wait until tomorrow. Too many people up and around now."

"Would we have a better chance at better armor?"

"About the same as here. And time is important. I think this will do you okay. If you get into real trouble, even the best light armor won't help all that much, and anyplace else it would cost more."

"Okay, so let's take it."

Their purchases took all his remaining cash. "I have a credit account," he said, "but I don't know how to get to it. At the hostel they took credit."

"Mendel will take care of it. Just knock on his door. He'll make the transaction for you."

"Very handy."

"He's a good man."

"You seem to know an awful lot for someone who's just here on a visit."

"I've been here before. And besides, if you move in my circles, you meet people who know things. Word gets around."

They left the shop, carrying his purchases. They weren't

too bulky so Rikard was able to handle most of them, leaving Darcy with one free hand in case she needed to draw her gun.

"We're running a risk now," Darcy said. "Someone might be interested in trying to take all these packages from us. But if we have the stuff delivered, there'll be somebody who knows where you are, at least approximately, and I count that as the greater risk. Now one more stop, then we'll go back to your place. Fortunately, it's on the way."

"Where is that?"

"We're going to get you a gun. If you go around in leathers without one, people will take you for a fool or a fake and take you out just for the fun of it."

"I have a gun if I need it."

"You do? Where'd you get it?"

"It's my father's."

"You mean you brought it with you? How'd you get past inspection?"

"How does everybody else bring stuff past inspection?"

"If you're bringing it here and know the people and have the fee, it's no problem. But most other worlds aren't as easy to run as Kohltri. How'd you do it?—don't tell me if you don't want to."

"No problem. It's that suitcase I have. That was my father's too. It's got a probe-proof compartment."

"Well, how about that. I've heard of that kind of thing, but I've never seen one. Does it really work?"

"It has so far. I'll show you when we get back."

They had no trouble on their way to Rikard's hideout, though more than one person eyed them and their packages covetously. When they were safely inside, they dumped their bundles on a chair in the bedroom, and Rikard got his suitcase from the closet. He laid it on the bed and opened it. It still held most of his clothes, all of which he took out.

"See if you can find it," he challenged.

Darcy looked the suitcase over very carefully as Rikard put his things away. She touched it everywhere, turned it upside down, tried the latch, twisted the handle, probed the lining.

"I give up," she said at last.

"It's in the bottom, of course, but the latch is on the hinge outside, and it will only work when the suitcase is held open like this." He held the top at a right angle to the bottom, then reached behind to touch one of the hinges. A small square outline appeared in the bottom lining.

He let the top fall all the way open, stuck his finger at the back corner of the outline, and the whole square opened up. Below was a compartment, much deeper than the thickness of the material of the suitcase. Inside was a bundle wrapped in a cloth.

"A real four-D box," Darcy said with amazement.

"It is. Not a big one. But probes can't detect it. I think there's something else about it too, a warp when it's closed, so that even a polydimensional probe couldn't tell what was there, even if it detected the compartment." He took out the bundle, closed the compartment, and it disappeared completely.

"I sure could have used that suitcase a little while back," Darcy said.

Rikard unwrapped the bundle. It contained a gun in a holster, with a belt to be worn on the hip.

"My God!" Darcy exclaimed when she saw it. "That's a megatron." It was a big gun, heavy, carrying six rounds of 20mm ammunition.

"My father gave it to me before he left. He had about a dozen guns, but this one was special, he said. It's pretty old, I think, but it's in perfect condition, and it works beautifully." He held it out to her. She took it from its holster. "It's loaded," he said.

"It's a beauty. It can stop almost everything. Have you fired it?"

"A few times."

"Good." She handed the gun back to him. "So, now why don't you get dressed, and we'll see what you look like. I'll wait in the living room." She went out and closed the door behind her.

Rikard quickly took off his tourist clothes and dressed in his new silks, armor, and leathers. He pulled on the calf-high boots and gauntleted gloves. Then he strapped on the holster belt and set the gun into it. Feeling a little self-conscious, he went into the living room. He stood and let Darcy look him up and down.

"By damn but you look good," she said.

# 6.

Rikard felt inordinately pleased at the compliment He wasn't sure why her opinion of his appearance should be so important to him, but he had suspicions, which he carefully suppressed as being inappropriate to the circumstances.

"That's good," he said, "because unless I want to stop eating, I don't have enough money for a ticket out of here — at least not at the prices I've been quoted."

"I didn't know you were that close to the end of your cash."

"One bill short of the price of a fare is short enough."

"Now look, didn't you say your father came here thinking he could make a lot of money fast?"

"That's right, but the 'fast' part turned out to be wrong. Maybe the 'lot' part was wrong too."

"Arin Braeth was no fool, not according to the stories I've heard. What do you think?"

"I think he found whatever he was looking for. The longest he stayed on any other world before he got here was twenty days. He was on Kohltri Station for nine days, then was down here on the surface for over half a year before he disappeared."

"Okay, what I'm saying is this. I'm willing to stake you against ten percent of your share of whatever your father found."

"In spite of what I said, he may not have found anything. To have gone so far for so long with the last of the money and to come up with nothing in the end would make a lot of people ashamed to come back."

"Was your father like that?"

"No, I don't think so."

"Well, then?"

"He may be dead."

"So? Look, I never knew your father, but I've known people like him. Hell, *I'm* like him in my own way. Nowhere near his caliber, of course. But from what you told me, and what I've heard elsewhere, if he was after treasure, it would be a big one.

"Gestae are aware of their reputations As long as your father stayed at home, he didn't have to worry about that. He'd capped his career with a daring and romantic rescue. Follows then retirement to glorious obscurity. A fitting way out, something that I'd like to do someday.

"So though I don't know your father, I know the type, being one myself. I'd be willing to bet that whatever it was he was after, it could be told about as a suitable sequel to the rest of his life, something really big, like an Aradka artifact or a lode of dialithite or the secret of the Taarshome or something like that. Don't you agree?"

"That's fantastic, like looking for a mountain of gold."

"Three Aradka artifacts have been found; the Book, the Scepter, and the Eye. Several thousand dialithite crystals are in museums. And I know for a fact, because I was in on the excavation, that the Taarshome were finally proved to have really existed. That was just three years ago."

"Yes, I know, but—"

"Okay, so maybe it was only a good blackmail prospect he was after. You want to take up my offer or not?"

"Absolutely. I just don't want you to throw your money away on a harebrained scheme."

"You're not harebrained. If there's no money, tough on all of us. I've made millions. Most of it's gone. It won't hurt me to lose a few hundred or a few thousand more. I'll make it all back somewhere else."

"Darcy, I'm sorry, I was thinking about the money, not you. You've been more than generous so far, and I'm grateful. I'm willing to accept your generosity for as long as you care to give it." He reached out and squeezed her shoulder.

"Well, hey, come on, let's not get mushy. I'm just offering a loan, making an investment."

"Okay. I accept."

"Good. Now let's go out for lunch. I want to see how well you pass."

They left his rooms and went back on the streets. They moved among the people as if they belonged there. Nobody gave Rikard a second glance, but they kept away from the parts of the city where Rikard had been before.

"If somebody who knows you sees you," Darcy explained, "they'll want to find out which is the real you, and that could mean trouble."

They found a little restaurant where Rikard wouldn't meet anybody he knew, nor any of Kohltri's more dangerous citizens.

"Not everybody here is a murderer," Darcy said as they sat at a booth.

"I'd begun to figure they were." A waiter came over and took their order.

"No," Darcy said. "Many people become killers once they get here. It's a matter of survival. But killing someone on Kohltri isn't always murder, like it is out in the rest of the Federation. It takes a special kind of mind to kill someone in cold blood."

"Have you ever killed anyone?"

"I have. In self-defense. After the pyramid affair on Aakan, there were just four of us, and two weren't in any condition to do anything but go along for the ride. We had the ship and got off just ahead of the local patrol.

"And then Oremf decided he was lonely and tried to rape me. It was very easy to kill him, though it took me a long time to get over it emotionally. That was when I learned to fly a lighter. Oremf was our pilot, and with him dead and Lars and Sfrenbow too hurt to help, I had to figure it out by myself or we would have just zipped on forever. It took my mind off what I'd just done, and what had almost been done to me. I remember the whole business very clearly; it was the real turning point in my life."

They stopped talking while the waiter brought their meal.

"Have you ever killed anyone?" Darcy asked when the waiter left.

"No, I never have. I find the idea appalling. But if I'm going to stay here, I guess I might have to."

"Most worlds in the Federation are a lot rougher than Pelgrane."

"So I've learned in the last two years. But how many worlds like Kohltri are there?"

"In the Federation, only this one. I've heard of other refuges elsewhere, and some of them are supposed to be even meaner than Kohltri. But I've never been to any of them, and I don't expect to go. Kohltri is enough for me, and I only come here when I have to. I'd much rather be on worlds like Saber, Erls Palace, Krishna, places where something besides survival is the main goal of life."

"Have you ever been to Terra?"

"Twice. It's a pretty civilized place. One of the best universities in the Federation is there."

"I'd like to go someday, just to see what it's like."

"It's an archaeologist's paradise, just like any of the species home worlds are."

"Is that why you went?"

"Of course. And to sell artifacts. That's mostly how I make my money. But time enough for my life later. Right now we've got your education to worry about. You're going to have to learn how to use that gun."

"I've shot it before."

"That's not enough, unless you just want to wander around seeing the sights. But you're going to be talking to strangers, prying into other people's business. People around here take exception to that. The chances are that at least once you'll be in a situation where your skill with that megatron could mean the difference between life or death.

"But more than that, if you know how to use the gun, if you have any ability at all, it will show in your manner, in your confidence, and people here can read things like that. If somebody confronts you and you don't *know* you can defend yourself, they'll know that and try to take you out. But if you feel confident that you can put them away first, they'll know that too and they'll leave you alone. The better you are with a gun, the less often you'll have to prove it. And that's important."

"Okay, I believe that. So when do we start?"

"This afternoon. I called up a friend of mine last night, and he'll meet us here."

"Aren't *you* going to teach me how to shoot?"

"I could, but my friend will be better than I am. I'm a better shot, but he's a better teacher."

"Is he safe?"

"You're learning fast. Yes, he is. I've trusted him with my

life a couple of times. He's not easy to get to know, but he's one of the best people in the Federation."

Rikard had been watching the other patrons as he and Darcy ate their lunch and talked. The people in the restaurant represented a complete mix of ages and types, though all wore leathers and guns. Nobody paid any attention to him, so he assumed that he did in fact look as if he belonged here.

Just as they were finishing he saw Leonid Polski come in.

"There he is," Darcy said, and waved to the policeman. Polski saw her and came over to their table. He, too, was wearing leathers, but the gun on his hip was a police blaster.

"Hello, Darcy," Polski said, sitting beside her. "How are you doing, kid?" he asked Rikard.

"You know each other?" Darcy asked.

"We met up on the station, and I happened along once when he was in a tight place. You're looking pretty good," he said to Rikard. "Is he your pupil?" he asked Darcy.

"He is. You know his story?"

"A bit of it. So you want to learn to shoot?"

"Darcy says I have to."

"She's right. Well, this is neat. If you've got Darcy Glemtide for a guide, you may live to see your father after all, if he's still alive. How'd you two get together?"

Rikard told him briefly about his visit to the Troishla.

"I'm impressed," Polski said. "I didn't think you could do it. But so much the better." He turned to Darcy. "So how are you doing?"

"Okay, under the circumstances."

"Get caught opening tombs again?"

"Not caught, or I'd not be here."

The policeman laughed. "Darcy's got quite a reputation. She's 'contributed' more archaeological artifacts to private collections than anyone else alive."

"I take it you two go back a long way." Rikard felt oddly ill at ease.

"Quite a few years," Darcy said with a smile. "And not always as friends."

"We first met on Total Foam," Polski said. "She and a couple of others had just opened a prize archaeological site and made off with about six million in jewelry and artworks. I was supposed to bring her in."

"Nobody else even got close to me," Darcy said, laughing. "Dozens of clucks all over the place—*after* the fact, mind you—and we still had all the stuff in our hot little hands, and not one of them could even touch us. But Leo knows a thing or two, and I completed the sale half an hour before he came in. Tightest squeak I've ever had. But at least all those pretty things are where people can see them now, not locked away in dusty storage bins, where the local authorities wanted them."

"That's her soft spot," Polski said. "She can't stand to see those treasures hidden away. She wants them out where everybody can enjoy them."

"Well, hell, if you're going to violate the past in the first place, why keep what you've found out of sight?"

"She's good," Polski went on. "She's a suspect in about a dozen cases, but nobody can pin anything on her."

"Look who's talking. It's Leonid Polski here, the youngest colonel on the Force, who broke up the smuggling ring on Zendar. That had been going on for twelve years, and even Captain Eleyo couldn't touch it. I'm just glad I wasn't involved in *that* one."

"It wasn't your style, Darcy. They were taking out contemporary artworks and robbing the artisans blind in the process. Darcy, on the other hand," he said to Rikard, "was the first person to enter the Tower at Vel Daren, and I mean the first since it had been sealed some forty-two thousand years ago."

"How'd you hear about that?" Darcy asked, surprised.

"I know Meylin. He's the one who bought the Throne."

"Wasn't he involved in the Lea Rashkovan kidnapping?"

"He was indeed. That's how I know him. I'm the one who put him away."

"Now *there* was a kidnapping," Darcy said.

"I know," Rikard said. "I've heard of it." He was beginning to feel very much the "kid" indeed. He'd heard of all those exploits. "It seems that I've made the acquaintance of some rather impressive people."

"More than you know," Darcy said. "I was on Fartax when Leo and a suicide crew of Goons took out the Warmonger."

"While Darcy made off with her private collection of bronzes."

"Well, she wouldn't need them any more, and after *you* got through with the place, it was easy."

"Find any buyers?"

"Not yet. They're still too hot."

"I'm wired."

"I know. So you can be sure none of them will show up for at least half a standard year." They both laughed.

"Maybe you could tell me one thing," Rikard said. "What's the difference between a Gesta and a police officer?"

"Her 'salary,'" Polski said, "is erratic and large. Mine is regular and small." He and Darcy laughed again.

Rikard felt very young indeed.

# 7.

An hour later the three of them stood at one end of a deserted warehouse. At the other end was a target, leaning against several rows of sandbags. Pockmarks on the wall around the target testified to this place's frequent use, as well as to the inaccuracies of some of its users. Rikard was sure he'd add his share to the total.

Polski had locked the door after them when they'd entered to avoid any interruptions.

"If somebody comes in while we're practicing," he explained, "they may want to have a little duel. It's happened more than once."

They moved up to the target until they were only ten meters from it.

"No sense shooting any further," Polski explained, "until we see how both you and the gun work. That's a big old clunker, and I want you to get used to just shooting it before we try any real target practice. I take it you've fired it before."

"A couple of times, at a range on Pelgrane. Their setup was a lot better than this."

"Sure, a regulation field-stop, never any strays or ricochets, self-masking targets. But we're in the backwoods now; we have to make do with what's available. How much ammunition do you have?"

"Four boxes."

"Ninety-six rounds. Great. You can buy more later, Darcy will show you where. Let me see your gun for a minute."

Rikard handed him the weapon, then took off his gloves and tucked them into his belt. Polski took the pistol and turned it over and over.

"It's a good gun," he said at last. "Old, but well made. I'm not familiar with the manufacturer, but then you hardly ever see a megatron these days." He aimed it at the target and squeezed off three rounds in rapid succession. The noise was loud. Three large holes appeared in the target, clustered in the middle of the bull's-eye.

"Very smooth." Polski handed the pistol back to Rikard. "You've got yourself a good weapon there. Can you strip it?"

"My father taught me."

"Good enough. Now you've got three live rounds yet. The target's almost healed. Take your time and shoot. Don't try to hit the bull's-eye. Just shoot and get the feel of it."

Rikard raised the gun and aimed. He squeezed the trigger gently. The gun roared and jumped in his hand, and a large hole appeared at the edge of the center spot.

He glanced at Polski and Darcy. Their faces were blank. He aimed and fired again. Another hole appeared, a bit farther off, on the other side of the spot. He relaxed for an instant, then fired the third round. It hit almost dead center.

"Are you sure you need practice?" Polski asked dryly.

"Well, maybe I was just lucky."

"Could be. Or you've shot a lot more than you admit. Or you have a natural talent."

"I've shot this gun three times, six rounds each time. My father also let me try out some of his other guns once."

"Okay, you're a talent. Let's back off to twenty meters and see how you do."

They went to the next mark back and Rikard reloaded. This time he didn't hit the center spot at all. Polski's relief amused him. For a while the policeman had thought he was being put on.

"Okay," Polski said, "you are human after all. But you're

still good. Six months' practice and you'll be able to hit anything. Let's back up again."

At thirty meters Rikard felt he was lucky to hit the target at all.

"At least you're not flinching," Polski said. "You'll do all right. Now watch." He drew his own gun. "Hold it like this." His left hand supported and steadied the right. "You're squeezing properly, that's good." He didn't fire—a bolt from the blaster would have taken out the whole target and put a hole in the back end of the warehouse.

Rikard held the gun as he'd been shown, steadied his breathing, and for a moment was distracted by the sense of concentric circles as the butt of the gun pressed against the scar on the palm of his right hand. That was supposed to have helped him shoot. All it did was distract him. He relaxed. The sensation faded. He took careful aim, and this time he got all six rounds within the third circle.

He fired another six rounds, and then they went back to forty meters.

"You learn fast," Polski said. "It will take more than one afternoon, of course, but when we finish today, you'll at least know what you can do and what you can't. Now here's another thing." He proceeded to give Rikard more advice on how to stand, how to hold the gun, how to aim.

Rikard reloaded and fired all six rounds. He hit the target every time, even at this range. With every shot he felt himself relaxing more, growing more confident, growing more aware of just what he was doing.

When they'd emptied the second box, Polski called for a break. They went all the way back to the far end of the warehouse, a hundred meters from the target, and sat on the benches there.

"Think I'll ever be any good?" Rikard asked.

"You're already better than half the people on Kohltri," Darcy answered. "Just because they all wear guns doesn't mean they all know how to use them. Of course, at the point-blank range of your average mugging or gunfight, that hardly makes any difference."

"Where the hell did you find those leathers?" Polski asked, non sequitur.

"At Tandy's," Darcy said. "They're a little odd, but they're what fit him."

"Odd's not the word for it. Sorry, Rik, I'm not picking on you, but when I first saw that outfit of yours some kind of bell began tinkling in the back of my head, and it's driving me buggy."

"They don't make me too conspicuous, do they?" Rikard asked.

"A little, but not badly. There's quite a variation in the style of leathers, and nobody should pay any attention—unless they'd seen that cut somewhere before."

"They weren't made on Kohltri, now that you mention it," Darcy said. "*Have* you seen anything like that elsewhere?"

"Yes, I remember now, on a man who was a representative of the Anarchy of Raas. His were specially made, and the equivalent of light armor in protection. I think it had other qualities too, but I was in no position to ask, and the body didn't offer the information. I really didn't pay much attention at the time, but that particular shade is what reminded me. So it looks like you got yourself a better set of leathers than you thought, Rik."

"That's good to know. How about this armor?" He unbuttoned his shirt. "Darcy says it's odd too."

Polski's eyebrows went up when he saw the copper-colored light armor Rikard was wearing. "Ah, Darcy, any more of those where that came from?"

"No, Leo, sorry."

"Too bad. You don't recognize it?"

"Can't say I do."

"That stuff's made in Abogarn for their secret police. You can't buy it anywhere in the Federation, and even civilians of the Abogarn Hegemony can't obtain it. I wonder how it got here."

"Is it special?" Rikard asked.

"Let's put it this way. What you've got on now, leathers and light armor as a combination, is as good as heavy armor. Only a magnum machine pistol, a megatron like yours, or a blaster could penetrate it. Unless they aim for your head, of course. A shotgun blast wouldn't feel good, but you could walk away from it. And you got this stuff at a discount?"

"That's right," Darcy said with a grin. "Quite a bargain, eh?"

"I'd say so. The leathers might bring a thousand from someone who knew what they were, the armor two thousand easily."

"And I laid out five eighty-five total," Rikard said, "including the underwear."

"You'll never find a bargain like that again," Polski said. "Did those boots come with the leathers?"

"They did. And the gloves. Want to see them?" He took the gloves from his belt and handed them to the policeman.

Polski took them, examined them, then held out the right one, palm up, for the others to see.

"Look here." He pointed with his finger. "That fine mesh by the thumb. That's a bionic switch. Whenever this guy drew his gun, it completed a circuit between the gun and a surgically implanted sighting device connected to his eyes."

"That's really weird," Rikard said. "How did it work?" That was what the operation his father had had done on his hand was supposed to have accomplished.

"I'm not sure," Polski said. "I mean, I've never examined a setup like that firsthand. All I know about it are fourthhand reports in journals and so on. But as I understand it, the gun produces an image in the user's eye, showing exactly where a bullet fired at that instant would hit, while another system in the user's eyes spots the target and adjusts for range and movement, showing him where to point the gun. How it all *looked* to the user, I have no idea."

"The guy must have looked awful weird with all that stuff wired to his body."

"Not at all. I'm wired, for example, but only to a transmitter. Everything I see and hear, whether I'm awake or asleep, is recorded. If I want to be private, I just give the word and the monitor switches off. But the recording goes on. If I want witnesses, I just give another signal, which you'll never see, and the monitor comes back on. I can call for help, receive orders, and so on. I'm always in contact. And none of it shows on me.

"Same for whoever was wired to wear this glove. All you'd ever notice would be a small scar on the palm of his right hand, where the bionic switch made the connection through this glove, between the gun and his own surgically implanted system."

"A scar like this one?" Rikard said. He suddenly felt short of breath. He showed Polski the palm of the right hand.

"How did you get that?" Polski asked quietly.

"When I was ten my father took me to a hospsital on Dasopreen. It was supposed to make me a better shot, but it didn't work. When I get tense or upset, the scar itches, and I have a habit of rubbing it. When I do that, I sometimes get a sensation of concentric rings floating in front of my eyes."

"Let me see your gun," Polski asked. Rikard handed it to him. "Your father wouldn't have had a range finder planted in you if there was nothing you could use it with. Right there, see, on the butt, that plate. Did you get any sensation of rings while you were shooting?"

"Once or twice. They distracted me. Like I said, the system didn't work."

"And did your father leave you any gloves like these when he left?"

"I don't think so. Mother sold a lot of his stuff after the second year. We were running awfully short of money. She even sold his guns, but I kept this one, since he'd given it to me before he left."

"I want to see you shoot this gun with that glove on."

Rikard felt his chest contract. It was too much to hope that this was the missing connection, which even his father hadn't known about. He put on both gloves. Then he stood, took the gun back from Polski, and at a hundred meters from the target, raised the gun to shoot.

Time seemed to slow down. Without a moving target it was hard to gauge the effect, but from his own movements he guessed the slowdown to be about ten to one.

The concentric circles formed in front of his eyes. He could see them clearly for the first time. There were three fine rings centered on the center of his vision. Off to one side and down a bit was a small red spot. It moved when he moved the gun. The red spot moved toward the circles as he brought the gun up. He didn't have to sight along the barrel. Everything was being done for him.

The circles in his eyes haloed the target. The red spot,

adjusting for range and movement, showed him where the bullet would hit.

When the red spot centered on the target, he squeezed the trigger. He could almost see the huge slug arcing out to strike the target exactly where he had aimed. Just to be sure, he put five more rounds in the same hole.

He lowered the gun. The circles disappeared. His time sense returned to normal.

"He didn't even aim!" he heard Darcy cry.

"Like hell," Polski muttered. "The guy's a wired-on killing machine."

# PART FIVE

## 1.

During the next three days Polski continued to work with Rikard until he was comfortable with how his built-in range-finding targeting system worked. Moving targets proved more difficult to hit, but Rikard's native talent was real, and he learned quickly.

Meanwhile, Darcy continued to coach him on the way of life on Kohltri. They spent a lot of time out in public, observing the people, absorbing the feel of the city.

At last she decided he was ready to start asking his questions in the right places. They had breakfast in Rikard's rooms, then went out into the city. "We'll be going into some strange places," she said. "Kohltri has a secret, and we're going to see part of it."

"I thought Kohltri had lots of secrets," Rikard said.

"Perhaps it does, but this one is special. Humans aren't the only people who live here."

"I haven't seen anybody but humans."

"You won't see the Atreef very often, but there are almost as many of them in the city as there are human people. Their city interpenetrates the human city at many places, and there is some communication between the two species, but not much."

"Atreef. I've heard of them, I think."

"It's possible. They're not a major species, in numbers, culture, technology, or history, but they're interesting. They have their own ways, which are different from ours, of course, but they're not incompatible with human psychology."

"Come to think of it, I think I may have seen one once." He told her about the time he'd glimpsed what he'd thought was two people in one set of clothes.

"Yes, that was an Atreef. They don't often cross the human streets."

"But where do they live?"

"These big blocks of buildings are only a shell. The Atreef live in the areas inside. They have their own buildings, their own community superimposed over ours, but as separate from it as white squares are from black on a chessboard.

"And that's not a bad analogy. If the human parts of the city are the black squares, we're like bishops who can't ever travel on the white. But we're going to change colors today."

"It sounds fascinating, but why?"

"Because while no Atreef live in the human part of the city, a number of humans live in the Atreef part, people who have fled the human society of Kohltri in fear of their lives."

"Why aren't they just followed?"

"As I said, it's a secret—of sorts. Not many people remember the Atreef are here. The few times they are seen, they are wondered about, then forgotten again.

"You see, when Kohltri was founded, it was intended to be an experiment in bispecies coexistence. But it didn't work. No matter how hard the managers tried to get the two peoples to live together and so on, they just drifted apart. At last the experiment was abandoned, and only the mines kept anybody interested in coming here.

"Then, about five hundred standard years ago, the first Boss came. Kohltri was a backwoods, out-of-the-way planet, and he holed up until the heat died down. Only he liked the place and stayed on. His successor made the first arrangement with the station director of that time. And in short order the criminal refuge we find here now had evolved. And because the criminals here are not out messing around in the rest of the Federation, it's tacitly allowed to continue."

"What did you do, a study of this place?"

"Nothing less. I first came here because of the Belshpaer ruins out in the wilderness. But what I found here in the city fascinated me as much, if not more. And besides, most of the ruins have been picked over already, and those that haven't been are awfully hard to get to."

"So you gave that up and researched the present population instead. Didn't Solvay give you a hard time?"

"He did, so I went elsewhere. I found the planet where the experiment was designed and did my work there. And prowled around down here, when I knew better how the system worked. The records are pretty good up to about four hundred years ago, even if they're hard to find."

"Well, as a Local Historian to an archaeologist, may I congratulate you on your research. And we're going to visit this alternate society, the one left over after the bispecies experiment failed?"

"That's right. If your father is alive and hiding among the Atreef, nobody out in the human part of the city would know it, but certain of the Atreef would. Now remember, they know about us and don't completely approve. They're generally nonviolent, but can be big trouble if you mess up."

"Okay, I'll just follow your lead."

"Real good. Now up this alley, and keep calm."

They passed between close-set buildings, turned a corner, and emerged at one end of a narrow street. It was, in many ways, similar to the one they'd just left. The walls fronting it were blank faced, possibly enclosing courtyards. But the buildings weren't as tall, and they were made of plastic instead of glass and steel and porcelain. The corners were all rounded. Everything was white and bright and smooth and clean. And Atreef—built like four-armed centaurs with a squashed-in horse's body and looking very much like two people in one set of brightly colored clothes—walked everywhere.

The street was closed off at the other end too and was intersected at the middle by a cross street. As they walked to the corner, Rikard allowed himself to gape at the Atreef pedestrians.

The Atreef were much the same height as humans, but a lot bulkier to accommodate four arms, two front and two back. Their four legs were close set on a short lower body. They walked on their toes, like dogs or rashteks, and wore shoes.

It was easy to tell the males from the females, though they both wore pants and shirts. The Atreef women were well endowed with four breasts.

Like humans, they were hairless except on the head, but the males were beardless. Their skin colors were generally warm, from pale yellow-cream through oranges and terracottas to deep Tuscan reds. But skin color did not seem to be the mark of separate races, as it tended to be in humans.

Neither was their hair color a racial characteristic. It was much like human hair, except that occasionally it had a bluish tone.

Their faces were round, bluntly prognathous, yet remarkably humanlike. They had no tails. Rikard had half expected that they would. Their eyes, when they looked at him, and they frequently did, were blues, violets, black, very wide and attractive. They smiled a lot and showed lots of carnivore teeth. They had five fingers and a thumb on each hand.

Their clothes were brilliant, many-colored, and covered a range of styles broader than Rikard had seen anywhere. They stood out brightly against the stark white of the buildings.

"Is there a party going on?" Rikard asked.

"No, it just seems that way. They take things a lot less seriously than we do."

They reached the intersection. The ends of the cross street ended in cul-de-sacs just like the one they were on. Each end had only a narrow, crooked alley continuing. Darcy turned them to the right and across the street.

"There are little exes like this inside almost every block of human buildings," she said. "Fascinating, isn't it?"

"It is, very. They don't seem to fear us."

"They don't. Nobody's ever killed an Atreef and lived to tell about it."

They entered a courtyard, as bright and white as the street. Unlike human courtyards, there were no plants here. But when they went on through a side door into an anteroom, they entered a different environment altogether.

It took a moment for their eyes to adjust to the dimness. The air was delicately perfumed, and the scent changed moment by moment. When he could see again, Rikard saw that color was everywhere, in the deep carpets, the rich hangings, the pictures, in the enameled woodwork which was all hand carved in ornate realistic and geometric patterns.

"We are going to meet," Darcy said softly, "one of the few Atreef who has adopted human ways. He is very touchy about it, so be careful. The Troishla is a child's playground compared with this place. But you won't see a hint of it."

# 2.

They waited in the dimness. After a few moments a male Atreef came through an inner door and greeted them. His voice was soft and melodious.

"We'd like to speak with Dzhergriem," Darcy said.

"Dzhergriem no longer lives here."

"I hadn't heard. I apologize for the intrusion, but perhaps you could give us his new address?"

"I'm sorry but I cannot. If you know Dzhergriem, then you know he likes privacy. Most unfortunate, but true. And as I have no connection with his 'business,' I wouldn't know where to direct you. He left these premises a year ago."

"I see. Thank you very much for your time."

The Atreef inclined his head and watched them go. Rikard did not know how to read his expression, but he got the distinct impression that the Atreef had been relieved by their quick departure.

"He doesn't approve of us," Rikard said when they were back on the bright white street.

"Not at all. None of these people do. But they'll tolerate us. The Atreef who have become like Kohltri's human citizens, however, will not tolerate anything."

"Okay, so what do we do now?"

"Try to find Dzhergriem. He smuggles drugs, for sale in the human part of the city mostly, and is a particularly nasty character, but he keeps in touch with everything in the human city, as well as the Atreef parts. If we can find him, we should be able to talk to him, and he'll know something, that's for sure."

"Do we go knocking on doors?"

"More or less, but not around here. These are all law-abiding citizens, and want to have less to do with Dzhergriem than with us."

"What if that guy back there was just giving us the brush-off?"

"Then we'll come back when we find out, and he won't do it again." It wasn't a threat, just a statement of fact.

They walked to the end of the short street, through a narrow, crooked alley, and back out into the human city.

"Are all the Atreef enclaves accessed in the same way?" Rikard asked.

"More or less. But they don't like sightseers."

"It's too bad the bispecies experiment didn't work."

"I agree. But I guess we're none of us really ready for that kind of thing yet."

They spent two hours going from one place to another. Rikard let Darcy do the talking. At each place her approach was different. Sometimes she asked about Dzhergriem outright. Sometimes she just asked if she could get some Pyrodoxine or some other drug. But the answers were all the same, in effect. Nobody knew.

At noon they took a break for lunch in a little restaurant halfway to the edge of the city. As they were finishing, two large men came up and sat down at their booth, effectively blocking them in against the wall.

"You've been asking for Dzhergriem," the one next to Darcy said.

"That's right," she answered. Her gun was between her and the man next to her, so she couldn't have drawn it if she had wanted to. "Can you tell us how to reach him?"

"We could," the man next to Rikard said, "but we'd rather you didn't do business with him."

"I'd rather we did, but maybe you could serve us just as well."

"Of course we can. You want Pyrodoxine? We got it, good stuff too. Put you out like a light, no hangover. You want Malixa? We got it. Prettiest pictures you ever saw, and you can still walk around in public. And we got good prices too."

"The only thing that bothers me," Darcy said calmy, "is why Dzhergriem lets you deal."

"Hey, listen," the man next to Rikard said, "he's a busy man. What he doesn't know won't hurt him."

"So I figured. Okay, here's what I want. Arin Braeth."

"What's that?"

"It's a him, not a what. If you don't know, you can't help us. That's all. Good-bye."

"Now hold on," the man next to Darcy said, "you want some dope or not?"

"Not. I want Arin Braeth. Dzhergriem might know where he is. You don't. Good-bye."

"I don't like games," the man next to Rikard said.

Without even thinking about it, Rikard reached down between the man's legs and grabbed hard. He drew his megatron with his left hand and pointed it at the other man, the end of the barrel just centimeters from his forehead. The man who's genitals he was squeezing went white and gasped, his hands fluttering on the tabletop. The other man went red and didn't move a muscle.

"And I," Rikard said softly, "I don't like games either. So who's first? Balls or brains, it makes no difference to me." He squeezed a little harder and touched the other man on the bridge of the nose with the gun barrel. He felt absolutely calm, his mind perfectly clear.

Darcy pulled her own gun and pointed the laser at the face of the man across from her. Rikard let go but kept his gun steady.

"Okay," he said, "since it comes down to this, let's get our trouble's worth. You know how to get to Dzhergriem?"

"Yeah," the man across from him said. The one beside him was still trying to catch his breath. "He's in the Blue Rose, between Varo and Nelsh, north side."

"Nice of you to keep such close tabs," Rikard said. "Now, here's what's going to happen. You two are going to get up and walk out the door. You will not turn around or you will die and I don't care what kind of armor you're wearing. Understand?"

They both nodded, then got up from the booth and walked out. There was some soft jeering as they left. One of the patrons shouted, "Good work, kid."

"Very good indeed," Darcy said, putting her gun away. "I'd almost think you didn't need my help any more."

"Nonsense." Rikard holstered his own gun and let his hands shake a moment on top of the table. "I just acted on impulse." He was surprised at how easy it had been and at how quickly he had acted "And I guess that kind of thing wouldn't work with Dzhergriem, would it?"

"Not at all " She put one hand on his two clenched hands and felt him shake. "No, I guess you still need me after all." She smiled warmly. "Shall we go see if the old boy is at home?"

"Might as well. I'm not going to calm down if I sit here and think about what just happened." And yet, he felt deeply satisfied. In spite of his reaction now, he had enjoyed his dominance of the situation.

They left the booth. Rikard paid for the meal, and they went back out on the street.

On Blue Rose Street, in the middle of the block between Varo and Nelsh, on the north side, was a narrow passage between buildings. They entered cautiously, ready for an ambush, but the crooked alley just opened onto the end of a short Atreef street, as usual.

Darcy stopped the first four-legged pedestrian and spoke one word, "Dzhergriem."

The Atreef woman looked them up and down with large violet eyes and made a face which Rikard interpreted as distaste. "Last court on your right, at the corner," she said, and hurriedly moved away.

"She didn't like us one little bit," Rikard said as they walked toward the court entrance.

"Not at all, and I don't blame her. People who do business with Dzhergriem aren't nice people."

There were three doors off the court. One was a clothing store, another was a shop for some kind of merchandise Rikard couldn't identify. The third had curtained windows. They went in there. Beyond was a dim anteroom, as richly furnished as the other one they had tried.

"Is this typical?" Rikard asked as they waited for their eyes to adjust.

"Very. They care little for outward appearance—except their clothes, of course—but put great value on the luxury of their dwelling places inside."

"Do they work the mines too?"

"No, they don't. They are an isolated society on this planet, and don't have any offworld trade that I know of. I couldn't guess what their economic basis is."

After a moment or two, an inner door opened and an Atreef woman came out to meet them  She said nothing, but waited for them to speak first

"We'd like to talk with Dzhergriem," Darcy said

"If you'll tell me your business," the Atreef responded, "perhaps I could help you "

"We're looking for information, not drugs "

"Please continue "

"A man came to Kohltri about twelve years ago, and after something over half a year disappeared. I think Dzhergriem might have known him, or known of him. I'm hoping he'll be able to tell us whether this man is still living, and if so where he might be now."

"I see. It is possible. Would you care to entrust me with this man's name?"

"I'd rather not, if it is possible to speak with Dzhergriem personally."

"Would you be willing to pay a fee?"

"Yes, within certain limits."

"One moment, please." The Atreef woman went back to the other room and closed the door behind her.

"Very polite," Rikard commented.

"All the more reason to be on your guard. Remember what I told you about his being sensitive about adopting human ways."

They had to wait only a moment, and then the inner door opened again and the Atreef woman beckoned them to enter. This inner room was as pleasant and luxurious as the outer one, and furnished with stools with strange backs and seats made to accommodate the Atreef's four-leggedness. There were also a couple of comfortable-looking human-type chairs.

"You will not be required to leave your weapons," she said, "but I must caution you, if you are not already aware, that to draw them will bring an automatic response." She wore no gun herself; none of the Atreef Rikard had seen had. He could only assume there were weapons concealed in the walls.

The Atreef woman opened another door. "Follow me, please," she told them.

They went through into a corridor, at the end of which

was a stairway leading down. It turned twice before ending in another hallway.

"This is Belshpaer work," Darcy said, examining the odd plastic of the walls. It was the same material as the "stone" Rikard had stumbled over behind the Troishla, vaguely translucent, pale ocher and yellow.

"It is," their guide said. "Their ruins underlie much of the city."

After about ten meters, the corridor turned a sixty-degree angle to the left. A few steps more took them through a tall, wide doorway, also on the left, into a hexagonal room.

"The Belshpaer were trilaterally symmetric," Darcy commented. "I believe all their rooms were hexagonal."

"That is correct," the Atrèef woman said. "You know something of the Belshpaer?"

"A little. I'm an archaeologist."

"And this man you seek, he is a part of your archaeological business?"

"I'm afraid not. It's another matter altogether."

They passed through two more hexagonal rooms of different sizes and into an irregular tunnel. It was roughly circular in section, and had been cut into the rock around them.

"Did you build this?" Rikard asked.

"No, we did not. We don't know who did. It was excavated after the Belshpaer, and there are other tunnels like it, but we don't know their origin."

At last they came to a modern door set into the side of the tunnel, which went on into darkness. Beyond this door was a lush, perfumed, carpeted room, furnished exclusively in velvet-covered Atreef furniture in deep, rich reds, bright yellows, dark greens.

"Dzhergriem will see you here," the Atreef woman said. "Forgive the lack of appropriate chairs, but I think you will find the couch quite comfortable. When you have finished, you may find your own way back upstairs. I strongly suggest you do not stray from the route we have taken."

Then she left. Another door opened at once, and a tall, old Atreef gentleman entered.

"I am Dzhergriem," he said, gesturing toward the couch with two of his four arms. "Please be seated."

They all three sat. Rikard was trembling with tension—and excitement.

"The man you seek," Dzhergriem went on, "why did he come to Kohltri?"

"He thought he had found a source of fast wealth," Darcy said. "He traced it here from Pelgrane."

"That could be many things. Please do not be reticent."

"We don't know what it was," Darcy explained, "only that he thought it was here and could be taken away quickly."

"Something not perhaps common here," Dzhergriem mused. "But again, that could be many things. People come here seeking fast wealth all the time. A few find it. Most don't. I see no light in this direction. Very well, who was this man?"

"My father," Rikard said, "Arin Braeth." He told Dzhergriem precisely when his father had come, where he had stayed, and when he had disappeared.

As he spoke, Dzhergriem drew back, his hands clenching his knees. "You were wise not to reveal the name upstairs," he said. "You would have been gently expelled."

"You know him, then?" Rikard felt the tension mount, and strove to keep it out of his voice.

"I know of him rather, yes," Dzhergriem said, his voice very low. If he had been human, Rikard would have thought that he was suddenly afraid.

"You don't know where he is, then? Or what happened when he dropped out of sight?"

"I do not. You know more than I. I'm sorry, I cannot help you."

Rikard glanced at Darcy. He was sure Dzhergriem was lying, and Darcy's expression indicated that she felt the same way. Rikard started to speak again, to pursue the point further, but he hesitated, aware that the Atreef was even more tense than he. He remembered Darcy's words of caution and changed his mind.

"That's too bad," he said instead. "Is there anyone else I might ask?"

"I know of no one," Dzhergriem murmured. There was something about his tone and posture that made Rikard think he was on the thin edge of violence.

"I see," he said. "Thank you very much for your time. The lady mentioned a fee."

"As I have been of no service to you, there will be no charge."

"Thank you again," Rikard said. He got to his feet, and Darcy followed suit. Dzhergriem remained seated as they left.

"He does know something," Rikard said tightly as they walked up the tunnel toward the Belshpaer chambers.

"Of course he does, but you were right to let it go. We would have died without knowing it if you'd questioned him further."

"That's what I felt. But I can't understand it. Was he afraid? And of what?"

"He was afraid of you." They went through the hexagonal rooms to the corridor beyond.

"But why would he be afraid of me?"

"I don't know. I'm familiar enough with the Atreef to be able to identify his reaction, but I don't understand it at all." They climbed the stairs to the hallway at the top and walked along it to the inner room. The Atreef woman was not there. They let themselves out into the bright white courtyard and to the street.

"He knows something," Rikard said again, "but he won't say. And why in the world would he be afraid of me, with all the defenses he must have in that hidey-hole of his?"

"I'm sorry, I don't know."

"Maybe he had something to do with my father's disappearance. Or maybe he's trying to protect him."

"It could be either one, but I don't think we'll ever find out. Now don't give up. There are other people to ask. It's just that I thought Dzhergriem was our best bet. Come on, let's get out of here."

# 3.

They did no more searching that day, but went out early the next morning.

"We're going to try to find a 'sponsor,'" Darcy explained. "That's someone who specializes in protection."

"You mean he'll keep his people from demolishing your business if you pay him money?"

"No, not that. There are plenty of those in the city. What I mean is a person who, for a fee, will help a newcomer adapt to Kohltri."

"Like you're doing with me?"

"Well, not exactly. This is a one-shot for me. Sponsors are professional. They teach newcomers things the way I'm teaching you, and they protect the newcomer until she is well adjusted. There aren't many sponsors, and their rates are high. They specialize in embezzlers, swindlers, and others who come to Kohltri with lots of money and not much street savvy. By the time the sponsor is through with them, they have plenty of the latter and not much left of the former."

"If you hadn't offered to help me, how would I have gotten in touch with one of these sponsors?"

"The night clerk at your hostel might have told you, but it wouldn't have done you much good. You don't have enough money. And even if you had, you're not the right type. You're not a criminal. But an embezzler, they would have seen her coming, and somebody would have steered her to a sponsor right away. After a couple of days trying to survive on their own, they would have agreed to the deal without too much grumbling. The usual arrangement is the chance to learn how to live in exchange for half her stake, more or less."

"You think my father might have gone to one of these? But he didn't have any more money than I have, less even."

"What I think is that a sponsor's agent would have approached your father, not the other way around. Being who he is, they would have thought he was well off, even if he wasn't. If your father turned the sponsor down, they would have kept a close eye on him, if only to see if they couldn't get him to agree to the service after all. Not that he'd need it."

During the morning they located three such sponsors. They were not hard to find. But none of them had been in business when Rikard's father had come to Kohltri.

Darcy bought them lunch, and afterward a tender told them that a certain Mareth Davinis had been working as a sponsor for almost twenty years. They got the address and went to her place just outside the port district.

The courtyard there was exceptionally well planted. Most of the plants were the same as those Rikard had seen elsewhere, but there was a wider variety than usual and some species that he had not seen in any of the other courtyards.

Davinis's office was one of six openings onto the courtyard. It was quite modern and luxurious. They were met by a receptionist who asked them their business, which Darcy stated in her usual oblique way. After a moment's wait, they were ushered into a larger inner office.

It was tastefully if expensively decorated. There were a large desk, several chairs, a couch, cases full of book cartridges, pictures on the wall. The carpet on the floor was of unmistakable Atreef manufacture. Rikard could see its true beauty in the brighter light of this office. If the Atreef ever decided to begin interplanetary trade, their carpets would bring a good price.

Mareth Davinis, seated behind her desk, was a handsome woman of 150 or so. Her face was strong, her hair not yet grayed, and her handshake firm.

"Let me say at the beginning," she said as they seated themselves, "that my business is usually to keep people hidden, not tell where they are. But tell me what you want, and I'll see what I can do."

"We appreciate your position," Rikard said before Darcy could speak, "but I don't think you'll have any ethical conflicts. In any event, my name is Rikard Braeth, and I'm looking for my father."

"Braeth. I've heard the name, I think. Wasn't there a Gesta some thirty years ago with that name?"

"That was Arin Braeth, my father. He left home about thirteen years ago, came here, lived in the city for two-thirds of a year, then disappeared. You may have known him then."

"I see." Davinis's cordiality visibly cooled. "Yes. Arin Braeth. Yes, I do know the name. But don't you see, if he disappeared, either he died or went underground of his own accord. If he died, I can't help you. If he chose to drop out of sight, I wouldn't help you if I could."

"What if he disappeared against his will?"

"I don't know that."

"Look, Msr. Davinis, my father came here to recover a fortune of some kind, specifically so he could come back home with it. I have reason to believe he thought he'd found it.

"Now, I don't want to take his fortune away from him, if he did, or force him to return home, or even to get unpleasant about his leaving in the first place. I just want to find him and find out what happened to him. If he's dead, I'd like to know that, see his grave if it can be found. If he's alive, I just want to see him, hear his story, tell him mine, and let him make his own decision as to what he does next."

Davinis leaned back in her chair. "It seems to me that he's already made his decision."

"I don't believe that. If you knew him, even if only by reputation, you know what kind of a man he was. He was not the kind to quit, or give up, or avoid trouble. I knew him quite well, even though I was only a kid when he left. If he didn't come back, with or without the money he hoped to find, it could only be because he's dead or is being kept somewhere against his will."

"I can see that you believe that. Nevertheless, it's not necessarily true."

"I know. But think about it. You heard of him when he was out making a name for himself. He came here openly. He lived in the city openly for over half a year. In your business you know the comings and goings of people. You would certainly have heard of his arrival, even if you never offered to do business with him. You would have heard about it when he disappeared. If he's dead, if you know that, what harm to tell me?"

"None at all, I guess."

"Exactly. Then, since you won't tell me, I can only assume that he's still alive and that you know that he is "

"That doesn't mean I know *where* he is."

"Of course not. But I think you do, or at least have an idea  Must you protect him even from me?"

"Yes. I don't know you. You say you are Arin Braeth's son. But you can't prove that, I don't think. Show me your ID, and I'll show you another one proving I'm Arin Braeth's mother—which I'm not. So you see, there *is* an ethical conflict. I'm afraid I cannot help you."

"Oh, but you already have." Rikard got to his feet. "Thank you for your time." He extended his hand. Davinis shook it uncertainly. Then Rikard and Darcy left quickly.

"You did that beautifully," Darcy said as they got to the street.

"You've been a pretty good teacher." He was covered with goose bumps of excitement. "And it's the way my father would have done it. And now I know he's still alive—unless Davinis is a lot better liar than she seems to be."

"I don't think so. And I think you're right. And if that's true, then we still have a chance. If he can be hidden somewhere, he can be found."

"What I don't understand is why? Why he'd either hide voluntarily or let himself be hidden against his will. Something happened here eleven years ago. Maybe he found his treasure, and he's being held by somebody until he tells them where it is."

"For eleven years? I don't think that's it."

"Okay, let's examine the two most obvious possibilities. First, he didn't find the treasure, or more likely found it and it was worthless. Now, I can understand some people would be so let down that they couldn't face up to having been suckered in on a wild-goose chase for two and a half years, and would just hide away out of shame.

"But not my father. He would have yelled a lot, kicked a few walls down, cursed himself for his stupidity, then calmed down and come on home. I've seen that reaction, though for lesser cause. He wouldn't crawl in a hole. He'd want Mother to comfort him. He cared more for her, and for me too, I guess, than for money or his pride. So that's not the explanation.

"The second possibility, then, is that he did find what he was looking for, and it was what he thought it was, or close enough. Now, I can understand that some people, suddenly confronted with enormous wealth, might not want to share it, and would just go off alone to spend or hoard their loot in private.

"But when my father married my mother, he had a fortune, a big one. He shared it then. He lost it because he didn't understand how to invest it properly. He was no businessman.

"But money for him was just a tool, a means of achieving another, more desirable end. And that end was to live a comfortable life with his family. So just finding the treasure wouldn't drive him into hiding.

"And hide where? Here? If he were going to go off somewhere, it would be out in the Federation, or maybe in the Crescent, or the Abogarn Hegemony, or somewhere else where his money would do him some good. If anything, he'd become a Gesta again, not a hermit."

"Maybe he did go off."

"No, he never left Kohltri."

"Look, Rikard, ships go out of here all the time that aren't on the record. There's an awful lot of smuggling. I bet three out of five ships leave Kohltri with no record at all, and the rest have their records falsified."

"Don't kid yourself. If I dared go back up to the station, I could show you. Every ship arriving or departing is logged. Every ship. Some of the codes confused me until I learned down here about all the supposedly secret transport going on. But it's not secret, at least not to the people who run the station. Anton Solvay knows what comes in and goes out. He keeps it quiet because it's part of his control over this whole racket."

"Are you sure?"

"Absolutely. Look, you weren't far off. Thirty-seven percent of all ships are on one register. Their manifests are in plain language. They dock in, dock out, all according to accepted procedure.

"But there's another register, fully sixty-three percent of all traffic, and half of it's in code. Including ships that never touch the station but orbit farther down and send their own shuttles.

"And there's a code for passengers and the like—very simple, I broke it in an hour. More people arrive here than leave, and all those who do leave, especially on the second register, are very carefully identified. I guess Solvay wants to keep track. And none of the people who left Kohltri between when my father arrived and ten days ago was my father. I know that for a fact."

"My God, you're not kidding."

"I'm not."

"But if you're right, then your father really could be here."

"He *is* here. Maybe he's dead, but I don't think so. If he were, none of the people we've talked to would have been so protective of him, or afraid of him. He's in hiding somewhere. Maybe it is his choice, I don't know. But he's here, he's alive—and Davinis is protecting him."

"I think you're right, and she is. But in that case, there's absolutely nothing more we can get from her, or from any other sponsors. They form a very tightly knit guild. If one were to talk, she'd be dead within an hour and the pieces spread out all along the streets. So that's closed, and too bad."

"But we're not finished yet, are we?"

"Not at all. If either Dzhergriem or Davinis had been willing to talk, it would have been the fastest way to find out where your father is. But if they won't tell us, somebody else will. There are plenty of finks on Kohltri. It will just take more time."

"So what's next?"

"We just noise it about that we're looking for Arin Braeth and that we're willing to pay for the information. Quietly, of course. Word will spread, and sooner or later somebody will offer to tell us—for a price. But it will take a while."

"Then the sooner we get started the better."

"I agree. We'll just make the rounds of the bars and—"

And everybody was running.

"It's a dragon," Darcy said, clutching Rikard's arm.

"Where?"

"Over there, at the corner."

He could see the golden orange glow of the creature as it came onto the street. They ducked into an alleyway, following several other people. A moment later the dragon appeared at the alley mouth, its head, if that was what it was, stretching forward on the end of its transparent serpentine neck.

The alley was a dead end, and there were no other doors. There were six or seven other people trapped with Rikard and Darcy. All they could do was cower and wait.

Everybody stood very still. The two eyes of the dragon wandered back and forth, as if it couldn't see very well. Then they seemed to focus on Rikard for a moment.

And then the dragon just went away.

# 4.

Rikard and Darcy spent the next three days visiting as many bars, taverns, and pawnshops as they could. Everywhere they went, they asked for Arin Braeth, but no one was able to help them, and the word of their search had not yet brought anyone forward with information.

They finished up the third day at the Rathrayn Restaurant, a place that was as different from the Troishla as it was possible to be. One had to go through one of the worst parts of the city to get to the narrow alley off which the Rathrayn was located, so one wasn't likely to stumble across it by accident. On the other hand, while it was hard to find, it was safe for practically anybody to be there, even tourists.

It wasn't an exceptionally large establishment. Twenty tables seated eighty customers downstairs, while two rooms upstairs could accommodate forty more. Rikard and Darcy were seated in the main room.

"We don't seem to be having an awful lot of luck finding informants," Rikard said after their steaks came.

"We've only just started," Darcy said. "Something like this takes time to percolate through to the right people."

"I suppose if it's been eleven years and more a few more days won't matter. But I'm impatient."

"Be impatient all you want. Just don't hold your breath."

"That's what I find myself doing. I guess it's knowing that he's here and alive—"

"So far as we know. Our deductions may be wrong."

"I know. I remind myself of that whenever I start feeling too antsy."

"Look," Darcy said around a mouthful of steak, "I know it's none of my business, but what are you going to do when you find your father, assuming he's alive?"

"I'm not really sure. If he's in trouble, try to help him get out of it, for a start."

"And then what? There's the money, of course. But even as I'm looking at you I can see that that's not your only motive any more. Right now you tell me you want to rescue him. At other times I think you're more interested in revenge. Look, Rik, it doesn't really matter to me, but if you're not sure of yourself, you could blow the whole deal right at the last minute."

"I see your point. There was a time when I wanted to forget him altogether. And then, it's true, I did want revenge. After all, my mother died because he didn't come back. I hated him for that. I guess I still do, to some extent, but the time I spent tracking him down—hell, if he had come back the day after he dropped out of sight here, it still would have been too late for Mother. And he was trying, I know that now. He really was looking for treasure. And now, the way things are looking, the only conclusion I can come to is that he wasn't able to come back to us, even if he wanted to.

"It's a funny thing, you know. My father and I were always close, in a strange kind of way. Not the same way fathers and sons usually are, I guess. That first year he was gone I missed him an awful lot. By the end of the second year I was starting to put him out of my mind. It hurt too much.

"And during the last few days I've begun to realize that I've always envied him for his past, for what he was before he settled down. I've told you about my one try at exploiting. And now, ironically, I find myself becoming like him at last. Is that what he wanted me to be? He gave me that operation, after all, so that I could shoot like an expert.

"And lots of other things. If I stop to think about it, it gets very complicated."

"I can imagine," Darcy said. "You know, I don't think I've thought of my parents much since I left home."

"How long ago was that?"

"About six years. Every now and then, when I think of it, I send them a gram telling them I'm still alive. Sense of duty, I guess. I don't miss them at all."

"It must be easier that way. If I just plain hated my father, just wanted my share of his money, whatever he found, it would be easier. Right now I don't know."

"Have you ever thought about what you would have done if you hadn't decided to come looking for your father?"

"At odd moments. I never come up with any good answers."

"No ideas at all?"

"Sure, lots of ideas. I wanted to be an actor, a mathematician, a novelist, run a model shop. I've wanted to be all kinds of things. The one thing I never did want to be was a Historian. Which, of course, is what I turned out to be."

"And after you've found your father and settled all that, then what?"

"Darcy, I just don't know. If he's found his treasure and I get my share, who knows, travel around for a bit. Otherwise I'll have to work as a Historian somewhere for a while. That's all I'm trained to do. It will give me time to make up my mind."

"Sounds awfully dull."

"Yes, it does."

"You know, Rik, I've been watching you. Every day you're getting better and better, and I think you're enjoying this search for its own sake. You've made a good start at being a Gesta, like your father was. Why not continue?"

"Believe me, Darcy, the thought has crossed my mind. But I'm not sure it's really the kind of life I want."

"It can be whatever kind of life you make it. Gestae are not all the same. Some survive by their wits, some by force, some by money, some by political connections. Take your pick, or choose something else. The only thing we have in common with each other, as Gestae that is, is the desire to travel as far as we can to as many places as we can to see and do as many things as possible. How you do it is up to you."

"How about you? How long will you go on being a Gesta?"

"Until I get tired, or unable to survive other than by re-
tiring, probably. I—"

"Excuse me," a man said, suddenly appearing by their
table. "Is either of you Rik Darcy?"

"Rikard Braeth and Darcy Glemtide," Rikard said, suddenly wary. "You've kind of bundled us together."

"I'm sorry. I guess I got the message garbled. But you're
the people I want. You're looking for Arin Braeth, right?
Hey, are you related?"

"He's my father."

"No kidding. Well, now it makes sense. Anyway, my boss,
Avam Nikols, sent me to tell you she may have some information to sell. Are you interested?"

"We might be," Darcy said. "Can you give us any partic-
ulars?"

"Sorry, I'm only the messenger boy. If you want to talk
to Nikols, come to shop 4, court 1143, Toad Street. She'll
be there all afternoon, okay?"

"Okay. Thanks a lot."

The man smiled and left.

"Well, what do you make of that?" Darcy asked.

"I thought it would take longer."

"You never can tell, but that wasn't what I was referring
to."

"You mean the 'Rik Darcy' bit?"

"Exactly. Didn't he strike you as just a little too friendly?"

"I had my hand on my gun the whole time."

"It could be a setup."

"It could, but can we afford not to check it out?"

"No. But let's not rush." She went back to work on her
steak. "Take your time and enjoy your lunch."

# 5.

Shop 4 sold new leathers. Rikard and Darcy asked the clerk for Avam Nikols and were directed through a back hall into a large room where about a dozen people waited.

"Which of you is Rik Darcy?" a woman standing just inside the door asked. The other people, seated in chairs and at low tables, watched.

"I'm Rik, she's Darcy."

"Don't be funny."

"I'm not. You got the word wrong."

"Okay, okay, so there's two of you instead of one. Makes no difference. I'm Avam Nikols."

"I understand you have information to sell."

"I have information, but it's not for sale."

"I don't presume you're giving it away?"

"My, you're a smart one."

"Come on, Nikols," Darcy said, "what's the game?"

"I just wanted to see who was looking for Arin Braeth."

"Idly curious?" Rikard asked. "My name is Rikard Braeth. Arin's my father."

Nikols laughed as if Rikard had told a joke. She was standing close enough to Rikard that he could smell the whiskey on her breath.

"And what do you think I am, stupid?" she asked, still laughing. "You're not Arin Braeth's son. You're an impostor." Her face got nasty. "We don't like impostors."

"But he is, you know," Darcy said quietly. She put a hand on Rikard's arm as if to restrain him. "Why should he lie?"

"To make it easier to snoop in other people's business. We don't like snoops."

"You don't like much of anything, do you? Do you have something for sale or not?"

"Not."

"Then we'll be about our business and leave you to yours."

"God, I hate you big-mouth smart-asses. You're not going anywhere. We don't like our friends to be messed with, and we're going to make an example of you."

"Arin Braeth is no friend of yours," Darcy said. They were not going to be able to get out of this room with just talk. They would have to fight.

"What's it matter?" Nikols asked. Four of her friends got to their feet. "You're a snoop and a spy, and you're prying into business that doesn't concern you. That's enough for me." She reached out to take Rikard by the arm. He moved without thinking, eluding her grasp. He slashed once with a stiffened hand at the side of her neck, and she fell.

He felt split in two. Part of him was intensely aware of everything in the room and was thrilling with excitement. Another part was aloof and observant, and appalled at what he'd done. He looked down at Nikols. Her head lay twisted too far around. He'd broken her neck.

Everybody else in the room seemed frozen. Then one of the four people who had stood up jumped forward, fists flailing.

The two parts of Rikard's mind merged. He stepped to one side at the last instant and brought a closed fist backhanded into the back of the man's head, sending him stumbling past to crash into the wall.

One of the women at a low table started to draw a gun. A tight red laser beam from behind Rikard speared her through the chest. The woman screamed, her gun fired noisily but harmlessly into the ceiling. The beam from Darcy's gun flashed again but missed another man who was also drawing a pistol.

Rikard found his own gun in his hand. Time seemed to slow by a factor of ten. The concentric circles were centered on this man's face. Rikard watched as the man finished his draw, ever so slowly it seemed. The red spot, off to the side, moved toward the center of the target. When the spot and circles merged, he pulled the trigger and was picking a new target even as the head of the first man exploded.

He shot three more times, then all movement ceased. Darcy had downed another woman with her laser. There were seven dead, one unconscious against the wall behind them, and six more standing or sitting as still as they could.

Rikard relaxed his hold on the gun just a bit. His time sense returned to normal.

"Let me make one thing clear," he said. "I am who I said I was. Arin Braeth is my father. If I find out that any one of you has hurt him in any way, I'll come back. Now, does anybody have anything to say to me?"

There was only silence.

He backed toward the door, felt rather than saw Darcy turn to precede him, to make sure the way was clear. He passed through into the hall, closed the door, then they turned and ran down back to the shop at the other end, guns still drawn. The clerk was already over against the far wall, his hands up. Rikard and Darcy left the shop and courtyard, and put their guns away when they got to the street.

They didn't run from the neighborhood; that would have drawn attention. They didn't delay either. They went back to the Rathrayn and quickly downed two beers apiece before either said anything. Then Darcy started giggling. Rikard just felt cold and hard. He didn't feel excited any more.

Darcy's giggling bothered him, but when he looked at her he saw she was nearly hysterical, not amused. The other patrons were staring at them.

Darcy gasped and gulped and stopped giggling. "My God." Her voice was squeaky and uneven. "My God but you're a holy terror."

"So it would seem." His voice sounded to him thin and far away. "Thanks to my father. I've just killed five people, Darcy. I'm trying very hard not to scream or get sick to my stomach."

"What the hell, throw up all over the place if you want to. We nearly *died* back there."

"They didn't have a chance."

"They didn't give *us* a chance! If you hadn't been wired, we'd be hash all over their floor. You got those four shots off in *less than one second*!"

He opened his mouth to say something, but nothing came out.

The other patrons were talking among themselves as some kind of message spread from table to table. All eyes were on him.

"They just got the word about what happened," Darcy

said. "I don't think you're going to run into any more casual trouble, but you might have to keep on the lookout for ambushes and snipers."

"A wired-on killing machine," Rikard murmured. "That's what Polski called me. And it's true. But my *father* did this to me. Why?"

"Maybe he knew you'd come after him someday if he didn't come back, and wanted to make sure you would be able to get to him."

"Not unless he was planning this three years before he left." He ordered another beer and forced his stomach to keep it down.

# 6.

Rikard woke late the next morning. His head pounded with the effects of the drinking spree he and Darcy had gone on the night before. He remembered Darcy's threat to douse him with ice water if she ever found him asleep, but she was not here. She had gotten as drunk as he last night, and was probably at home, feeling just as bad.

He pulled himself out of bed, took a long, hot shower, and a Kerotone pill which eased his hangover. He dressed, then called over to Darcy's place on the nonvideo phone to see how she was. He got no answer, but someone was knocking at his door. He hung up and let her in.

"Thought I'd give you a little rest this morning," she said. "You feeling better?"

"Kind of raw around the edges, but I'll heal. How about you?"

"I'm fine. Look, Rik, I know it's not easy the first time you have to kill someone. I went through it too. But it wasn't like they gave you any choice."

"I know that. I'm glad to be alive."

"If you want to take a couple of days off, come to terms with it, that's fine with me."

"That would just leave me more time to think about it. Let's get on with it and maybe I'll feel better. Have you had breakfast?"

"On the way over."

"I just got up myself. Let me fix something before we go." He went into the kitchen and pushed buttons. She followed and sat at the table.

"You've established a reputation, you know," she said as he brought his plates to the table.

"The way some of those jokers were talking last night, you'd think I was a hero or something."

"You remember that? Well, they're just jokers, like you said. They don't matter. But they were right, in a way. Most people don't walk into an ambush like we did and live to hear themselves talked about later.

"And now you've got a reputation. You'll be spotted wherever you go. In a way that's good. Most people will leave you alone. And you'll get answers from a lot of people who wouldn't even talk to you before. But others will want to test you, see if what you did is a true reflection of your abilities or just luck."

"That makes me feel real good." Rikard ate his eggs as if he were hungry.

"It isn't as bad as all that," Darcy said. "After a while, people will learn that you don't shoot up places just for the fun of it. Give it a while. They still don't know you. When they do, things will get smoother."

"You talk as if I were a public figure."

"You are. The only way to have avoided that would have been to kill everybody else in Nikols's office. And if my judgment is correct, you'll become more of a figure as time goes on. You just don't have it in you to be anonymous."

"That's what I've been until now. I think I prefer it."

"The hell you do. And besides, it's all over now. Like virginity, once gone, it can never be recaptured."

"Nonsense. What about all those people who retire and fade into obscurity?"

"They're not forgotten, not really. Your father was not forgotten. But don't be upset. You're traveling in good company, as well as bad."

"Like who?"

"Like Leonid Polski, for one. You finished? Let's go."

In the third tavern they visited, they saw one of the women who'd been at the shoot-out in Nikols's office. She was sitting over in a corner, talking with two friends, and didn't see them come in. Rikard and Darcy ignored her. They went up to the bar and asked their usual question.

Before the tender could answer, they heard a commotion coming from the woman's table. They turned and saw her staring at them, white faced. Her two companions were staring too and edging away as if to get out of the line of fire. The woman looked around, seeking a way out, and saw none. She was trapped.

"Let's go talk to her," Darcy suggested.

"She's scared out of her mind. Leave her alone."

"She was perfectly willing to watch you be dismembered yesterday. She lives with fear every day. Talk to her and let her go."

"I don't like to terrorize people. And besides, will it do any good?"

"One way to find out."

They went over to her table and sat down. Her two friends had evaporated.

"Listen, man," the woman said, trying to back through the slats of her chair. "I had nothing to do with it. I was just there watching."

Darcy started to speak, but Rikard stopped her.

"It makes little differerence." He kept his voice soft and not unfriendly. "You were there, and not on my side. Right?"

The woman gulped and nodded.

"So I owe you nothing, and you owe me a straight answer. Do you know where Arin Braeth is?"

"No, no, I don't, really, but Aben Arshaud does. He always used to say how he was a friend of Braeth's before Kohltri. Go ask him. He'll tell you."

"I appreciate the information," Rikard said. "Where can I find Aben Arshaud?"

The woman told him.

"Thank you," Rikard said. He and Darcy stood up from the table. "Now let me say one thing," he went on. "If you've sent me into another ambush, you'll do better to be offplanet because I'll come for you. Do you understand?"

"There's no ambush, honest to God!"

"All right." He turned away, and Darcy followed.

"I thought you didn't like to terrorize people," she said.

"I don't."

"Well, you sure do a good job of doing it. Even I was frightened, and I'm on your side."

The compliment pleased him, and he flashed a smile at her. "We can't always avoid unpleasant tasks." But in the privacy of his own mind, he wondered. He thought he should be upset about what he had done, but he wasn't.

"We'd better check out this guy Arshaud before we go see him," Darcy suggested when they were back on the street.

"I agree. It's too pat."

They asked around in the neighborhood of the address the woman had given them. Everywhere they got the same answer. Aben Arshaud was an old hijacker who'd come to Kohltri about twenty years ago. He'd opened a hardware store and had stayed out of trouble ever since. He was somewhere in his fourth half century, a little bit crazy, and the devil to mess with, but easy to talk to if you didn't mind long conversations. He kept an eye on everything that went on in the city, though he kept to himself most of the time. He ran an honest store.

Not everybody they asked knew him. Darcy had never heard of him before. But those who did know him all agreed. Whatever he might have been in the old days—and hijackers were not the nicest of people, even by Kohltri's standards— Aben Arshaud was a pleasant enough character now. Except that if anybody gave him trouble, they got burned; nobody had ever robbed his store and survived.

They had lunch, then went to see the man himself. His shop was easy enough to find, and well stocked. There were three clerks and a constant stream of customers. On Kohltri, more than on most worlds, a hardware store was an important business.

None of the three clerks was old enough to be Arshaud, so they asked one of them where the boss was. The clerk directed them to a back room. There was a set of heavy shelves loaded with tools against the inside wall and just beyond it an ancient desk where they found an old man going over stacks of invoices. He looked up as they entered, a bland smile on his face.

"Aben Arshaud?" Darcy asked.

"I am," the old man answered. Some animation came into his expression as he looked at her.

"We've been told," Darcy went on, "that you once knew a man named Arin Braeth."

"Arin Braeth? Sure, I knew him. I knew him way back when. We went out a couple of times together. He was one hotshot kid, he was. Why, he was just an infant when we first met, and he was already my match in just about everything except cold-bloodedness. Couldn't say we were friends, exactly. He didn't approve of me. No, indeed. Said I hurt too many people. But what the hell, he was no innocent himself. Just had a different style, that's all. Why, I'd been out dashing around for a hundred years before he'd had his first adventure. If he'd kept on, he'd have gotten hardened too, but no, he pulls a goody and marries a Lady and drops out. Doggone, I envied him. *I* never met anybody I liked enough to drop out for."

"Did you know him here on Kohltri?" Darcy asked, seizing a gap in the flow of words.

"Hell, yes, I sure did. Why, he wasn't surfaced three days before he came knocking on my door. Glad to see a familiar face, he said, even mine. Goddamn but it was good to see him again. Always did like him, even if he was a bit prissy. He had that way about him, you know. If you lived through the encounter, you liked him. Yes, sure I knew him here. But that was a long time ago."

"We know he was public for half a year or better," Darcy said, "and then he disappeared. We have reason to believe he's still alive."

"Oh, yes, he is, yes, definitely, no doubt about it, though I haven't seen him since then. Nobody has, as far as I know. Become a hermit he has. Some trouble back then, I don't know exactly what. He was looking for something, and I think he found it, or almost found it, but something happened, I don't know what, and I don't think he ever got his hands on what he came for, but I couldn't say for sure. No, haven't seen him in eleven years or more. Get a note from him now and then, though. He's changed. Whatever went wrong did something to him. But he's still alive. Oh, my, yes, absolutely."

"You know where he is, then?"

"Oh, well, now, I wouldn't want to betray an old friend. Not that he's that old, not yet eighty I'd wager, just a kid yet really. No, I couldn't say anything about that."

"We don't mean—"

Rikard put his hand on Darcy's arm and stopped her. "We appreciate your position," he said, "and we thank you for your confidence."

"Well, now, don't rush off."

"I'm sorry, we have lots of other business. Thank you again." And with Darcy in tow, he left the shop.

"Rikard," Darcy said when they were back on the street, "where are you going? You could have leaned on him a little bit and he'd have talked."

"I don't think so. He's not as senile as he seems to be. Let it sit a couple of days, then we'll visit him again."

"Whatever you say," she muttered. But she smiled as if she approved of his taking command.

# 7.

They went back two days later. Aben Arshaud was out in his shop, tending a counter. He raised his eyebrows when he saw them come in. He finished with his customer and turned to them.

"I thought you'd come back," he said. "Especially after I found out who you were. Msr. Glemtide, I've heard of you. You're making quite a reputation for yourself. And Msr. Braeth, let me look at you. Arin told me he had a family, but I never thought I'd meet any of them. Yep, you're his son all right. Same eyes. Same set to the mouth. Can't mistake it. It's a habit of his, couldn't be picked up by an impostor. You'd have to live with him from birth."

"I was hoping," Rikard said, "that once you found out who I was, you'd be a little more willing to talk to me."

"But why didn't you tell me who you were two days ago?"

"Would you have believed me then? Nobody else has "

"No, I guess not, and I would have been angry at the supposed trick and I wouldn't have taken the time to look at you closely and I would have kicked you out or worse. He and I were never really friends, but we knew each other, and I wasn't about to give away any secrets."

"Why did my father disappear?"

"I don't really know. He never told me what he was looking for, but one day he said he'd found it, and he was going out with a couple of people to get it. He never came back. But I got a letter. He said only that something had gone desperately wrong, and he didn't dare show his face. Well, whatever happened, it had to be bad for him to react like that. Your father's no coward, not any way."

"Thank you, that's good to know. And you say you hear from him every now and then?"

"I do. But he's changed, I can't quite put my finger on it. There are some bad things out there beyond the city. Whatever he ran into could have been pretty awful. But he's not the same man he used to be. Be ready for that."

"All right, I will. Then you'll tell me where he is?"

"Yes, I will. I don't think you mean him any harm. If you did, you'd not get a hint. But you're like your father in many ways. I can tell even from these two short visits. We weren't what you'd call friends. He never approved of my running guns and explosives. I used to be a pretty nasty character, you know, but your father never was. Hard, yes, and cruel sometimes, and certainly ruthless, but never mean or nasty. He just wasn't that kind. So when you went off without leaning on me and came back figuring I'd have heard who you were, well, that's just like him."

"Where is he?" Rikard asked softly. He felt Darcy's hand squeezing his shoulder reassuringly.

"Now, I've never been to his place. He asked me not to come. So I can't give you precise directions, but if you can't find it the first time, come back and I'll try again."

"Where is he?" Rikard asked again.

"Sorry," the old man said. "I ramble on." And he told them.

# PART SIX

## 1.

The next morning, with Darcy's help and advice, Rikard found somebody who would rent him a car. Darcy had suggested a floater rather than a wheeled vehicle, since he would be going out of town quite a way and there might not be roads that far out.

The daily rental was steep, and before he could take the car he had to put down a deposit equal to the floater's replacement value, which on Kohltri was almost as much as a standard fare to the next world. The rental charges would be deducted from that and the rest returned, if and when he brought the car back.

The deposit had taken over half of Rikard's reserve money, but Darcy had a scheme which she thought would make them a few bills. Because of that, and because she didn't want to intrude on Rikard's reunion with his father, she had decided not to accompany him. So he drove through town alone.

The floater was an old one, and the controls were unfamiliar to him. He drove carefully and had almost reached the southern edge of the city before he felt comfortable with the vehicle.

Aben Arshaud had given quite explicit directions, despite his protestation of never having been to Arin's hideout himself. And he had left Rikard with the feeling that while everything he had said about his father had been true, it hadn't been the whole story.

Rikard had to let it go at that. He would find out everything firsthand from his father when he got to him.

The south side of the city did not end as abruptly as it did on the north and west. There was a transition area of warehouses, then he passed through an extended region of farms and processing plants.

Agriculture was as backward on Kohltri as everything else. The crops were actually grown on the ground, protected only by hothouse shields covering an area almost as big as the rest of the city. Rikard didn't know much about farming, but he felt sure they could be getting no more than four crops a year.

The smooth crystal roof of the farms was interrupted only occasionally by the square shape of a processing plant. Less frequent were the mining domes, with their concrete aprons and lawns. Rikard saw no human workers in the fields, but the equipment he did see was archaic.

The road ran south, fairly straight and level, past the farms and into the prairie-veld beyond. There were only a few scattered trees here, unlike the forests on the north where Boss Bedik had his offices, or on the west where the Troishla was located. There were even occasional isolated houses, all well fortified. Life in the country was no easier than in the city.

After driving for about an hour, he saw what looked like a village up ahead. He slowed when he came to it. Unlike in the city, the buildings here were well separated. There was no other street parallel to the road he was on, and only three short cross streets. He drove through at a moderate pace.

When he came to the other side, four people, all carrying drawn guns, stepped out from behind the last building and waved at him to stop. Arshaud hadn't warned him of this.

Rikard stopped the floater but didn't turn off the engine or get out. One of the four people, a man, came up to the window on his side. A woman went up to the other window. The other two, another man and woman, stayed in front of the car.

"Toll," the man said.

"I don't understand," Rikard answered.

"You came through Logarth. You've gotta pay toll."

"How much?"

"Four hundred."

"What if I can't pay that much?"

"We take the car," the man said matter-of-factly.

"I don't have cash. Will you take merchandise?"

"If it's worth four hundred. Whatcha got?"

"Body armor."

"Way out here? What for?"

"I have no idea. I was just told to take it out to the first road going east after here, and somebody would meet me."

"Dumb idea. Okay, let's see what you got."

"It's in the trunk. I can't open it from inside."

"Well, get out and show us."

Rikard got out of the car and went around to the back. He grabbed his gun, and time slowed down.

Through the concentric circles in his eyes he could see the "toll takers'" guns come up ever so slowly. He fired at the near man first and, as his target jerked backward with a huge hole in his chest, he fired at the woman on the other side. He saw her head explode as he aimed and fired at the remaining man in front of the car, felt a bullet crack past his own head, and fired at the other woman, whose left shoulder came away. Then the first body hit the ground.

He jumped over the near man, got in the floater, dropped the gun onto the seat beside him, and hit the accelerator. When the village was out of sight behind him, he pulled over to the side of the road, stopped the car, and sat, shaking, for a while.

His reaction, he realized, was more because of the narrowness of his escape than from the fact that he had killed four more people. He knew they would have killed him for his car once they had found he couldn't actually pay the "toll."

It was a neat setup. And it had been too close a thing. One bullet had nearly hit him. When he got back to the city, he would mention this little incident to Arshaud. He hoped that the old pirate had a good explanation for failing to warn him of the trap.

When his hands were steady again, he reloaded his gun and put it back in its holster. He had almost taken the holster off when he'd gotten in the car back at the rental place, in order to sit more comfortably. If he had, he would be dead now. Never take it off, he told himself over and over, never take it off. The technology of the gun had gotten him through this trap, but he'd had more than a little luck. He started the car again and drove on.

A few kilometers farther on the road entered some low hills. He came to a dirt track leading east, as Arshaud had said he would, and took it.

A thin forest rose up around him as he drove on: widely spaced trees, tall and slender, with few leaves. The ground was hilly and the track uneven, but the floater, riding thirty centimeters above the surface, had no difficulty negotiating it. After a while the ground became rocky, and the floater began lurching. Rikard elevated it to seventy centimeters and drove on.

A flash off to his right attracted his attention. Half a kilometer away, through the trees, he saw the coiling, glowing, yellow and orange transparency of a dragon. Rikard tensed as he drove on, but the creature did not seem to notice him.

A little later the road dipped down into a broad river valley. Near the water he came upon the first of the ruins, mostly tans and light browns in color, though a few were ocher. There weren't many, and most were badly broken, but by the hexagonal outlines of their foundations he knew they were of Belshpaer origin. He made a mental note to ask Darcy more about these long-vanished people when he got back.

He passed slowly among the jumbled and weathered plasticlike material of the ruins, some of them still with fragments of upper floors, until he came to the riverbank, where he turned south again. Some of the buildings here were more complete, and one of them was where his father was supposed to be living.

The thought made his heart hammer. His emotions were mixed about this meeting, and after the frustrations of the last two years, he had difficulty believing he would really find him. He wondered what he would look like, whether his father would remember him. Would his father even care?

He came to a building, of which only the bottom story was still standing. It had obviously been patched up. He stopped the floater and got out.

It was quiet. Nobody came to greet him. Nobody shot at him. The crude repairs to the building indicated that somebody lived here. Whether his father or somebody else, the resident was either away, asleep, or hiding.

"Is anybody home?" Rikard called. There was no answer. He went to the makeshift door of the ruin and knocked. There was no response. He pulled it open.

There was a room with a rough bed in one corner, a stove in another, and another door on one of the inside walls. Odds and ends of junk lay everywhere, including an unusual pistol. It had a burned grip, a bulbous frame, something like an automatic slide that projected over the back, and a flaring barrel with what looked like a spark coil in the middle Either the person who lived here had another gun or nobody ever came around

This wasn't like his father at all, especially leaving a weapon out in the open like that Whatever had happened eleven years ago must have been really bad.

The room had a strong lived-in smell. His father couldn't be far away. Rikard called out again, not too loudly, just in case he was near. There was still no answer. He opened the inner door and in the hexagonal room beyond saw stacks of dried animal skins.

He couldn't imagine what anybody would want with animal skins. Artificial leather and fur lasted longer, were better looking, and felt better to the touch. Maybe his father ate what he caught, but still, why save the skins?

Rikard went back outside to his car. It would be better to wait out here in plain view than inside where he might be assumed to be trespassing. He was getting a growing feeling that the person who lived here might not be his father after all. Everything about this place felt too different, even accounting for thirteen years.

He didn't have to wait long. The sound of uncertain footsteps came from behind a pile of rubble near the river. Then a face showed itself over a low wall.

"Got nothing worth stealing," the man said. He was more than a century old, dirty, hairy, and twitchy. It wasn't his father.

"I know that," Rikard said. He kept his hand lightly on the butt of his gun. "I didn't come here to steal."

"Well, in that case," the hermit said, coming into full view, "welcome. Don't get many visitors."

"Thank you." Now Rikard knew what some of the skins were used for. The hermit was wearing them. "I'm looking for Arin Braeth."

The strange old man, grinning broadly, tottered toward him. "You've found him," he said. "I'm Arin Braeth."

# 2.

Rikard was surprised at the assertion and started to deny it. But the old hermit's behavior indicated an unsettled mind. Rikard didn't know what would happen if he called the old man a liar.

"I thought Arin Braeth was taller," he said instead.

"Taller, no, I'm not taller. Always been this height. You sure you want Arin Braeth?"

"I thought I did, but he was a taller man." He was intensely disappointed. If this was who Arshaud had been corresponding with for the last eleven years, then his father might be dead after all.

"No, no," the hermit said, "I'm not taller. Now, my partner, he was taller, tall as you are. Handsome devil too."

"I see. Ah, how did you come here, Arin Braeth?"

The hermit was far older than his years. He smiled, evidently pleased that Rikard had accepted his identity.

"Well, that's quite an interesting story," he said. "Old Sed Blakely and I were partners."

"I see. Who is Sed Blakely?"

"Like I told you, he was my partner. Tall fellow. Pretty clever too. He cheated me."

"I'm sorry to hear that. Where did it happen?"

"Beyond the tathas place." His expression became grim and morose. "And now I'm trapped. Trapped forever."

"I'm afraid I don't understand."

"You don't know Sed Blakely. He wanted it all. So he had me go in past the creepies, hand him out the stuff, and then, instead of helping me get out, he went off and left me."

"That was a terrible thing to do."

"Damn right. And it's true too."

"I believe it," Rikard said, though the hermit's story didn't make any sense.

"You'd better. Want to see my skins?"

"Sure." The hermit was insane. But whether he was pretending or actually believed himself to be Arin Braeth, there still might be something Rikard could learn from him.

The hermit led him into the patched-up hovel that was his home and into the room stacked with skins.

"There are places, you know," the hermit said, "where rich people will pay a lot of money for real skins and furs, just because they're real."

"You must have quite a treasure there." Rikard hadn't thought about black-market furs. Each of these skins, once properly treated, would be worth several hundred bills.

"No treasure," the hermit said, "just skins. How did you find me?"

"I know an old friend of yours, Aben Arshaud."

"Oh, yes, him. I send him letters every now and then."

"I didn't know there was mail service out this far."

The old hermit laughed and went on laughing so hard that Rikard thought he was going to have a fit.

"There's no mail service here." He almost choked in his paroxysm. "No power, no*body*." He suddenly became completely sober. "Nothing can get past the creepies."

"Then how can you send a letter?" Rikard was wary of the hermit's sudden change of mood.

"Sometimes a farmer comes by. He takes my letter if I give him some skins to sell in the city."

"I'll take a letter for you if you like."

"Would you do that? How many skins do you want?"

"None. I'll do it for you because you're Arin Braeth."

"That's very kind of you. Just a minute, I'll go get it."

The hermit went back to his main room, and Rikard looked over the dried and smelly skins. Now that he understood their worth, he was curious. They were of various sizes, some only a dozen centimeters long, some over a meter. They varied in their texture and in the pattern of their colors, from simple smooth brown to striped and spotted cream and tan and black and even maroon. There had to be a lot of wildlife down here by the river to provide the hermit with so many pelts.

It seemed to be taking the hermit an awfully long time to find the letter. Rikard went to the door and saw the old man sitting on his bed. He was holding a piece of paper but was staring at something else in the palm of his other hand.

"Arin?" Rikard said. There was no answer. Rikard stepped into the room. "Arin? Are you all right?"

The hermit didn't move. Rikard went up to him, afraid that he might have had a stroke, but before he touched the old man's shoulder, he saw what was in his other hand, what the hermit was staring at so intently.

It was three irregularly rounded stones, each about as big as the end of Rikard's thumb. They were transparent and had hearts of pale iridescent fire. Beside the hermit, on the bed between him and the wall, was a leather bag, bulging with hundreds more.

Rikard crouched down to look into the hermit's eyes. The old man's gaze was transfixed; spittle drooled from his slack mouth. There was only one thing Rikard knew of that could produce such an effect.

Afraid to break the old man's trance, Rikard straightened up, then reached around behind him and took one of the stones from the bag.

"If they were cut and polished," the hermit whispered, "then they'd really show their fire." His voice had lost most of its madness. It was now a soft purr with a new kind of fascination. But he was not talking to Rikard.

Rikard held the stone, as big as the end of his thumb, and looked into it. As it warmed in his hand, he began to feel a sense of exhilaration, joy, and peace slowly come over him.

It was dialithite, the hypnotic stone found only on a few old worlds. Everybody knew about dialithite, but few people ever had the opportunity to see it, let alone touch it. Rikard had seen one once, cut and polished and a little larger than this one, in a carefully guarded display in a big museum on Benarth. And there were hundreds of perfect stones, just like this one, in the handmade leather bag.

As Rikard held this one and stared into the fiery depths of colors beyond human vision, he felt the power and the peace the gems were reported to convey to those who did so. If he were to just look at it without touching it, or just hold it without looking at it, he would feel no effect. But when he held it and gazed at it at the same time . . .

He clenched his fist convulsively, breaking the spell he

was falling under. The hermit still sat, staring at the three stones he held. Even more carefully than before, Rikard put the stone back. Without it, he felt deprived.

"No wonder Arin Braeth was cheated," Rikard said softly.

"Yes, no wonder." Sadness was mingled with fear in the hermit's face as he began to arouse from his trance. Quietly, quickly, before the hermit could recover completely, Rikard returned to the skin room. A moment later the hermit joined him, holding only the piece of paper now.

"Here's the letter," he said. "It's already written. Will you take it to Aben?"

"I will." Rikard took the letter and glanced at it. The handwriting was large and clear.

"Are you sure you don't want any skins?"

"Meeting you is reward enough," Rikard said. The letter was very short. It took him just a second to read it.

> *Dear Aben. I am doing fine. Please don't look for me. I'm afraid of Sed Blakely. How are you? Sometimes I think he's looking for me. It was a terrible thing. Love, Arin.*

"Where is Blakely now?" Rikard asked as he put the letter in a pocket. The hermit's story was beginning to make sense. This prematurely aged old man was Sed Blakely, who had abandoned Arin Braeth after taking the dialithite. He had simply changed roles.

"I don't know," Blakely said. "He went away." His voice fell. His gaze grew distant. "He's lost. I don't know where he is."

"Do you suppose he felt bad about cheating his partner?"

"I should hope so. I hope it drove him crazy. It would drive me crazy. If I had cheated my partner like that. Sitting in some hole probably, fondling his treasure. Never do him any good. If I could just get my hands on him . . ." He choked off into silence, his eyes fixed on nothing.

"Poor Arin Braeth," Rikard whispered. He took the man by the shoulder and led him back to his front room and sat him on his bed.

"Poor Arin Braeth," the hermit whispered back.

"Where are you now, Arin Braeth?"

"Lost in the caverns. Dead by now, for sure. The tathas. They wouldn't let me leave."

"Could you tell me where the caverns are?"

"No. I don't know. I've forgotten. I knew once, but not any more. It's been so long, so long alone."

"Can I do anything for you?"

"Bury me. I'm so tired."

"I will. When the time comes. And thank you for talking to me."

"Why, it was my pleasure." The hermit's voice was sprightly again, as if nothing had happened. "Come by again."

"I will."

Rikard left the hermit sitting on his bed and went out to his car. He could find him again if he wanted to.

He felt a jumble of emotions as he drove away. He had held himself in control during the strange conversation, and now it came out all mixed together. The hermit was so pitiful. His father had been so badly wronged. And the dialithite stone had been so fascinating. That was a treasure worth his father's time and effort.

If Rikard wanted revenge for what Blakely had done to his father, he could find nothing better than the hermit's present torment. Rikard pitied him in spite of that, but he was not yet hard enough to end Blakely's misery by killing him.

At least he now knew why his father had disappeared so suddenly eleven years ago. It was some comfort that his father had not just gone into hiding, had found the treasure he had been looking for, even if he'd never had the chance to bring it back—except for the stones Blakely had, half of which Rikard could argue were his.

Now Rikard thought he understood the reactions of many of the people he had talked to in the city. They thought they were protecting Arin Braeth, and their concern for his father's safety was reassuring. They also didn't know about the dial-ithite, or somebody would have come for it long ago, dis-covered the truth, and have killed Blakely for it. And Blakely's progressing madness foretold that that would happen soon enough.

It was easy to explain everybody's mistake. After all, Sed Blakely had never come back to the city after he had abandoned his partner. His guilty conscience had driven him to hide out in these ruins. All anybody knew was what they learned from Arshaud, from the letters Sed had sent in Arin Braeth's name.

The other letters he had sent were probably much the same as the one Rikard now had. The earlier ones, perhaps, had been more convincing. No wonder Arshaud thought Rikard's father had changed. He just didn't know how much.

People must have liked his father a lot to keep on defending and protecting his ghost after all these years.

# 3.

Rikard drove back over the narrow old trail through the tall, thin woods. He slowed when he saw a group of people up ahead. He did not stop, but drove with one hand on the butt of his pistol, anticipating another ambush asking for "toll."

As he drew nearer, he saw that the six people had too many arms and legs. They were not human, but they didn't look like Atreef either. They were not animals; they were wearing clothes, but each had three legs and six arms.

He could have driven past, but wonder made him stop the car twenty meters from the cluster of trilaterally symmetric beings. It was an incredibly rare form for higher beings. The Belshpaer were supposed to have been trilateral, but they had died out millennia ago, or so he'd been told.

The six beings stood where they were, letting him look them over. They were dressed in soft, loose trousers and shirts, in pastel shades of blue, green, and violet. Even so, Rikard could see that their legs had three joints each. Their feet were encased in shoes. Their arms were triple jointed, ending in rosettes of fingers. Their bodies were columnar, their heads oval and tall, with three eyes radially placed. There were funnel ears between the eyes and an orifice of some kind below each eye. Their jaws seemed to be at the top of the head.

The skin of their faces and hands was a warm peach color. Under each subocular orifice was a patch of chocolate-brown hair. There seemed to be two each of three different sexes.

They stood and waited. Every now and then one of them rotated 120 degrees, presenting a new eye. They had no front or back. They carried no weapons.

Rikard could drive through them, drive around them, go back the way he had come. Instead curiosity got the better of him. He got out of the car and stood beside its open door.

One of the six came forward, walking by rotating on its three legs.

"Am I speaking your language?" the being asked. Its voice came from all three subocular orifices at the same time. It was a strange, triple-tenor voice, resonant and yet thin.

"Yes," Rikard said, surprised, "you are. Are you Belshpaer?" He tried to remember where he'd heard a voice like that before.

"We are. Are you the human known as Rikard Braeth?"

"Yes, I am. How do you know me?"

"We were waiting for you."

"Well, you found me. What can I do for you?"

"We wish to return to society."

"I'm sorry, I don't understand."

"We have not retreated too far, but we hesitate to show ourselves."

"You're very much in evidence now."

"That is because you are Rikard Braeth. We were not sure you would ever come."

"I seem to be missing a point somewhere. How do you know my name?"

"It has been spoken. You are the one."

"Which one? I'm sorry, I just don't understand what you mean."

"A moment, please." The Belshpaer returned to its companions. They stood together and seemed to be conferring with one another, though Rikard could hear only a low murmur at this distance. And then he remembered the voices he'd heard behind the Troishla. The Belshpaer voices were the same.

After a moment the one who had spoken came back to just within a meter of Rikard's car.

"We have been expecting you," it said, "but it would not have been *palshar* to have confronted you in the city. Are you indeed Rikard Braeth?"

"I am."

"Then you are the one to conduct us."

"Where do you wish to go?"

"To join the people. There are so many worlds."

"You want to leave Kohltri? I think it can be done."

"No, not leave, rejoin. We need a *verenth*. You are he."

"I—ah—don't think so. What's a *verenth*?"

"A *verenth*. To help us rejoin. Not a guide. A liaison. We have been down too long."

"I don't understand. I'm sorry, what do you want me to do?"

"Are you not he whose coming has been foretold?"

"I don't think so. I can't tell for sure, since I don't know what you want."

"We are not clear. I apologize."

"Look, I'm just here looking for my father. I think what you want is either a ticket agent or a social worker."

"I do not recognize the concepts. Perhaps we have come too soon."

"Perhaps. I'm sorry, I don't think I can help you."

"Perhaps you are right. We will have to try again." The Belshpaer stepped aside, and the others moved off the track.

Rikard got back in his car, confused and curious—and excited. Wait till he told Darcy about this! He drove slowly past them, then speeded up through the thin woods. At the same time he kept wondering, how had they gotten his name?

# 4.

The strange conversation with the Belshpaer occupied his mind all the way back to the paved road. He wanted very badly to talk to Darcy about it. Their very existence, not to mention the fact that they had known who he was, was a mystery he couldn't unravel alone.

He pulled onto the paved road and turned north. There was a pale golden light shining around the car. He looked behind him and saw a dragon settling down onto the pavement just meters away. The glowing points in its ambiguous body were as bright as its eyes.

He panicked and tried to gun the engine. He did something wrong, and it died instead and sank to the pavement. The dragon's head stretched out, yellow and orange and transparent on the end of its long neck, and butted against the door on his side of the car. Static electricity sparkled around the interior, and the smell of ozone filled the air.

With a lurch, Rikard threw himself out the door on the other side. He hit the dirt running and headed for some shrubs a few meters off. Still running, he pulled his gun and time slowed. He fired over his shoulder at the dragon, which was still nuzzling the car. The bullet seemed to have no effect. Then the ground gave way under his feet, and he fell through loose earth and tangled roots.

He struck bottom hard. The gun was knocked from his hand and the breath from his lungs. Dirt and gravel rained down on top of him, blinding and choking him.

He scrabbled frantically through the loose soil, found the gun, grabbed it by the barrel, and lurched to his feet. He backed away from where he had fallen. His face was covered with dirt. He wiped it away. When he could see again, he looked up. There was a patch of blue three meters over his head. He was lucky he hadn't broken any bones.

He could hear a muffled *thumf-thumf* coming from aboveground. The dragon was up there, moving around. Rikard had to get out of sight before it came down this hole after him.

He looked around the hole into which he had fallen. There was enough light so that he could see he was in a roughly circular tunnel like the one connecting Dzhergriem's hideaway office with the upper shop. It sloped down in both directions, narrowing as it did so. He couldn't see how far the tunnel went in either direction.

He backed down the left-hand passage, which wasn't as steep as the other, keeping his eyes on the hole overhead. The tunnel curved away behind him and abruptly ended in another old cave-in.

He could no longer see the hole through which he'd fallen. He let his eyes adjust to the dimness here and looked for side passages. The walls of the tunnel, dark and metallically iridescent, were unbroken, save for the blockage against which he stood. From overhead came the *thumf-thumf* of the dragon moving around.

He felt dizzy, as if the air in here were stale or noxious. It didn't smell bad. He glanced back up the passage the way he had come. The air up that way seemed to glow with light and brightness. He leaned against the tunnel wall, felt its cool, smooth surface, and slowly slid down to a sitting position. The dragon was up there, looking for him. He had to wait until it went away.

There was definitely something wrong with the air in the tunnel. He felt drunk. The light up ahead hurt his eyes, so he turned away from it. There was nothing to do but wait for just a little while. Waiting—that was all right. Waiting, just to be left alone. He could wait forever if he had to. All else was madness.

But this was madness. He had to get back to Darcy, had to find his father.

He looked around, but all he could see was the dark landscape superimposed on the dimly iridescent tunnel. He didn't know where he was. He didn't remember coming this way. He could see piled stones and wiry trees. But they were only images in his eyes. Really, he told himself, there was only the tunnel, wasn't there?

It seemed as if he had been dreaming a nightmare of

intolerable light, of exhausting activity. It seemed as though
he were just about to wake up to normal starlight and quiet
waiting. But he was in the wrong end of the tunnel. He had
to move, slowly of course, past the strangely familiar monoliths over there, past that oddly apertured pile of stones, that
tree of wires and plates, all of plastic, all darkly colored under
the black sky.

He moved slowly. Greater speed was possible, but not
desirable. He oozed along to the right end of the passage.
He had forgotten what made it right; it just was. But something was blocking his movements. He couldn't make it out
clearly. He reoriented himself and saw blue sky outlined by
a jagged hole. He was lying on his back under the caved-in
ceiling.

The return to near-normality shocked him. He still felt
lethargic, but he forced himself to his feet. He remembered
his gun and panicked until he realized he still had it in his
hand. If he had dropped it back in the tunnel, he wasn't sure
that he would have had the strength to go after it.

He holstered the gun and listened for sounds of the dragon
moving around aboveground. There were none.

His head was still fuzzy, but he knew where he was now.
He had to get out of this hole. Whatever dragons were, they
weren't insane like whatever had overcome him down here.
He'd rather have a quick, clean death than the slow moldering
end this place offered him.

The smooth wall of the tunnel had been broken here by
his fall through the roof. He climbed the sloping surface
laboriously, scrabbling for handholds, kicking toe holds in
the hard soil. As he climbed, just to keep his mind from
drifting back into the darkness, he wondered who had built
these tunnels. How far did they go, what made them shiny
and dark?

The intoxicating effects of the tunnel disappeared all at
once as his head came up to the surface. Now was not the
time to try to answer the questions he had asked himself.

He could not hear the dragon. He hauled himself up and
out of the hole. He could not see the dragon. He walked
slowly back toward his car. It had been nudged slightly off
the road but was not damaged. The dragon was nowhere in

sight, but the ground around the car was strangely marked. He got in, and the car started up with no problems.

Darcy had said, when she'd taken him to the streets of the Atreef, that Kohltri had a secret. There were more secrets here than she knew.

There were too many mysteries here, and all of them fascinated him, but he tried to put them out of his mind. The one mystery he was concerned with at the moment was the whereabouts of his father. He drove back to the city.

# 5.

He returned the car to the rental agency, collected the major portion of his deposit, and met Emeth Zakroyan in the courtyard as he was going out. She had her jolter drawn, its short knobbed antenna centimeters from his chest. He wouldn't be able to draw his gun before she zapped him.

"Took me a long time to find you," Zakroyan said. "That was a pretty neat trick, dropping out like that. You must have had some help."

"What do you want with me, Zakroyan?"

"Come, come, let's not play games."

"You're the one who's playing, not me. What are you, paranoid?"

"Not at all. You've been snooping around much too much, and you have to go."

"If you've been checking me out, you know exactly what I'm looking for. I've not been secret about it."

"Just cover, pure foam. I know and you know and Solvay knows what you're really after. There's no use denying it. We had you pegged from the start."

Her delusions were complete, her mind was made up, and she wouldn't care even if she were proved wrong. She was determined to kill him, but her paranoia made her play the game instead of just doing it outright. That, Rikard hoped, would give him a chance to get away.

"Let's move," Zakroyan said, gesturing him out the front gate.

"Where are we going?" Rikard wanted to stall her, distract her, anything to give him an opportunity to take advantage of her madness.

"Just move it. If I have to use this thing on you, I'll have to carry you, and if I do, I'll play with you before I kill you instead of doing it cleanly, and you won't like that."

He went. On the street she walked beside him, keeping the jolter right at his side.

"Just what do you think I'm trying to do here?" Rikard asked.

"Don't be funny."

"I'm not. I want to know."

"You know exactly what you're doing."

"I have my doubts sometimes, but what's your version?"

"You're bugging me."

"And you're bugging me." He had trouble keeping the impatience from his voice.

"So what?" Zakroyan snapped. "What are you, some punk cop, trying to take Kohltri apart? I can't let that happen, Rikard Braeth, or whatever your name really is."

"What's Kohltri to you? You don't profit off the mines, do you? You aren't hiding from the law. Why should you care?"

"You know, you're not as smart as you pretend to be. Kohltri is a good place, no matter what you think of it. And yes, I do get a cut of the take. And no, I'm not hiding from anybody. I *like* Kohltri, dummy, and I'm not going to let you mess it up."

"I really don't want to, you know."

"The hell you don't. The first thing you'd do, if you had the chance, would be to get Solvay kicked out of the directorship. And the new Director wouldn't be me, but some outsider. And he'd start an investigation, and right there all the mine profits would disappear. And half the population would get rousted out. No more refuge, no more money, no more good times."

"Do you come down here often?"

"Whenever I can. Turn here."

They went up a short street, through a courtyard, and into

a warehouse. They climbed the stairs set against the side wall
to the second-floor offices and walked in on Leonid Polski
going through the files.

"What the hell are you doing here?" Zakroyan cried. Her
frustration and anger stuck out all over.

"Looking for someone," Polski said calmly. "Put down
the jolter, Zakroyan."

"You're spying on me."

"How distasteful. No, I'm looking for the Man Who Killed
Banatree."

"Liar. Get out of here. You have no right to be here."

"You forget where we are. This is Kohltri. The only right
I need is the ability to enforce my actions."

"Will you shut up a minute?" Rikard snapped. The other
two started, as if they had forgotten him. "Now, if you'll
excuse me—"

"Don't try it," Zakroyan said, holding the jolter very close.

Rikard looked down at it, then remembered something
Polski had told him. "Everything but a megatron, a magnum
machine pistol, and a blaster, right?" Rikard asked him.

"Right," Polski answered.

Rikard moved a trifle. The tip of the jolter touched his
side; he felt a faint tingling but nothing else. Zakroyan's eyes
widened in surprise. Rikard took the jolter away from her.

"I should have thought of that when she first stopped me,"
he said.

"I could have been wrong," Polski answered dryly.

"What the hell is going on?" Zakroyan demanded.

"None of your business," Rikard said. "You through here,
Leonid?"

"Pretty much. Let's go."

Rikard tapped Zakroyan lightly with the business end of
the jolter. She collapsed in a heap. He dropped the device
beside her, then followed Polski out of the office.

"That's twice you've come on me now," Rikard said as
they crossed the warehouse to the front door. "Are you protecting me, or are you following Zakroyan after all?"

"Pure coincidence. And bad judgment on Zakroyan's part."

"She's psychotic." They let themselves out of the court
and onto the street.

"She never was very stable, as far as I know," Polski said.

"Which, of course, has only made her more dangerous. You want to press charges?"

"Against her?"

"Sure. Clear case of kidnapping. The whole scene was recorded. You were brought here against your will."

"But do those laws hold down here?"

"No, but you're still registered as a visitor, and as such, Federation laws protect you no matter where you are."

"Would the charges stick?"

"Possibly not, but they'd sure tie her up while it was all being investigated and tried."

"I'm surprised she doesn't fear you more than she does me. You can collect evidence anywhere. And Solvay needs to be investigated."

"I know, but there are regulations about what is admissible and all that. In your case, as an involuntary observer, everything I saw and heard is good. But if I went after Solvay, I'd have to have all the warrants and so forth or anything I got would be thrown out. Suspicion isn't enough. And I'm not after Solvay, though somebody probably should get on his tail."

"You're after the Man Who Killed Banatree?"

"That's right."

"But that happened seventeen years ago."

"It's taken us that long to trace his movements."

"And he's here?"

"We think so. Look, it's an interesting story, but too long to get started on now, and I've got things to do. I really was almost done up there."

"Sure enough. You know where I'm living?"

"No, but I know where Darcy stays. She'll tell me. When I get a chance, I'll come by and tell you the whole tale."

"Looking forward to it. Good luck."

"Same to you." Polski went off like a man with a lot of work to do.

# 6.

Rikard stayed off the streets for the next three days. Partly he wanted to avoid Zakroyan. Partly he wanted to think over what the hermit had told him and try to figure out what to do next. Darcy came by a couple of times to find out what he'd accomplished and to report on her own progress in raising some cash. And perhaps, he thought, because she wanted some company.

He had told Darcy about his meeting with the Belshpaer. She had been incredulous at first, but when he had described them in detail, she reluctantly believed him.

"I had heard rumors," she said, "that Belshpaer were occasionally seen far out of town near some of their ruins, but those reports were always made by loners and hermits whose word couldn't be trusted."

"They were probably telling the truth. But I thought the Belshpaer died out five or ten thousand years ago."

"As far as we can prove, they did, though there hasn't been as much archaeological study on Kohltri as the ruins deserve, of course. All we can prove is that the ruins that have been studied were occupied no more recently than five to ten thousand years ago, and that's really quite another thing."

"How come somebody doesn't come out here to study them?"

"Well, I did, and others have. But Kohltri is Kohltri. The academic types don't get along well here, in spite of the extensive ruins, and never come back for a second visit after they've had a taste of what it's like to live here. And there are lots of Belshpaer ruins elsewhere in the galaxy, and we know quite a lot about them from those."

"They had starflight then?"

"Oh, yes, and a technology at least as high as anything you can find these days, much higher than the Federation, in any event. They left ruins in all kinds of places. It's just that the most extensive ruins are here. They underlie almost everything."

"Seems like Kohltri would be an archaeological gold mine."

"It is, if the professors are prepared to deal with the citizens. Which, as you can imagine, they're not."

"How old are the Belshpaer?"

"I don't know when they started, but their peak as a galactic society came about the time humans made the first interstellar flight from Terra."

"That's old."

"It is indeed, at least in our terms. There are even older peoples, of course."

"Like the Aradka?"

"Exactly. And about them we know little more than that they existed."

"You really like this stuff, don't you?"

"I guess I do. I used to think I didn't, but it was the idea of academia I didn't like. The study of ancient races itself is fascinating."

She told him more about the Belshpaer but was unable to figure out how they had known his name or what they might have wanted him for. Neither could she explain what had happened to Rikard when he had fallen into the tunnel while escaping the dragon. Nor did she know anything about dragons, other than what was common knowledge.

She told him nothing about her own business except to say that things were maturing, and she would be showing a considerable profit in a couple of days, and without having to leave town as a consequence.

During those three days Rikard worked out a rough plan of his own, but he didn't want to rush into anything. He knew that he didn't yet know enough about life on Kohltri to be able to survive without a good bit of luck. And since luck, of course, could not be depended upon, he hoped to make up for any lack of it with caution and patience.

On the morning of the fourth day since his meeting with Sed Blakely, Rikard decided he'd waited long enough. He had reconciled himself to the idea that his father was dead, but he wanted to know for sure before leaving Kohltri. And besides, if there was more dialithite where Blakely's had come from, he wouldn't have to go back to the old hermit and try to take his share from him.

But one thing was clear. If he continued to ask for Arin Braeth, anybody who knew anything and was willing to talk would only be able to direct him back to Blakely. Everybody else would keep silent. It seemed, then, that the thing to do was to ask around about Sed Blakely, to see if that might lead him to his father instead.

He went back to Aben Arshaud's hardware store and found him in his office, going over invoices.

"Well, Rikard," the old pirate said, "how are you doing? Did you find him? You've been gone a long time. My God, boy, the day you left I kicked myself. I should have told you about the toll in Logarth, that village halfway there, but I guess you found out for yourself. What you *should* have done is gone off the road and circled around. A floater can do it easy. But I never go through there, so I clean forgot about it. What do you say, did you find your father?"

"Yes and no. I found the man who's been sending you letters all these years. Here's another one." He handed Arshaud the letter Blakely had given him. "But he's not my father."

"Sorry to hear that, boy. Must have hurt him real bad. I knew he'd changed, but not how much. You read this letter? Sure you did. So you know what it's been like. Pitiful, isn't it? What Blakely did to him must have been a real mind breaker."

"It was," Rikard said. He decided to be cautious and not correct the false impression he'd inadvertently given. "He told me all about it. Got left to the tathas, whatever they are."

"Tathas? Ugh, no wonder. That's a kind of fungus, Rikard. Grows down under the Belshpaer ruins. Didn't know I knew about that, did you? Well, I know lots of things. Those ruins are all that's left of a city that once covered the entire planet. You dig down deep enough *anywhere* and you'll find Belshpaer ruins. Can't live on this world for as long as I have and not learn that, not if you keep your eyes open and care to pay attention to what goes on around you.

"Anyway, under the ruins in lots of places there's this fungus. Don't know much about it except if you breathe the air around the stuff you start hallucinating, light hurts your eyes, you just want to sit down and wait for the end. And if you fight it, you go crazy. So if *that's* what happened to your father, no wonder he's not himself  Nothing you can do, boy Except maybe go gunning for Sed Blakely, if he's the one responsible."

"Do you know where Blakely is?" Rikard asked when there was a pause in the flow.

"Want revenge?"

"Not exactly. It all happened too long ago. I'm like my father—not cold-blooded enough."

"What about your father? *He* want revenge?"

"The man who calls himself Arin Braeth only wants to be buried when he dies."

"Poor old sucker. Maybe *I* want revenge. But if you don't, what do you want to see old Sed Blakely for?"

"To get the other side of the story. And to get back what was my father's. He found something, and Blakely took it from him. That's why he left him with the tathas."

"What was it?"

"I don't know. The old man was babbling."

"Old man? Hell, he's a century younger than me."

"Old man nevertheless. Older than you now. Old enough to die soon. And incoherent. Maybe they never did find what he was looking for. But if Blakely's alive, I'd like to see him just once and try to find out what really happened."

"Oh, well, no harm in that. It's just, don't you know that Blakely was a friend of mine too once. Don't want to hand him over to his killer."

"I won't kill him, I promise you, if my word is good for anything."

"If you're Arin Braeth's kid, and anything like him, your word is all I need. Now I don't know where Blakely is. He never came back. As I see it, your father escaped from the trap Blakely had set up and did him in out there, wherever they'd gone looking for the treasure."

"My, uh, father didn't kill him," Rikard said.

"I don't know, can't trust a crazy man. Sorry about that. Well, you can go out there if you want to. Maybe he's dead, maybe he isn't. I don't know where he is, but Pedar Gorshik does. He doesn't believe in any treasure, but he was the one who told your father where to go. Maybe he was in on the back-stabbing. No, I don't believe it. Gorshik's pretty dry, but he's not that way. You go ask Gorshik, he'll tell you where they went. After that I don't think I can help you. If Blakely is not there, nobody knows where he is. He didn't come back."

"Will Gorshik talk to me?"

"Sure he will. He doesn't care about Blakely. Never did like him much. Slip him a couple of bills and he'll tell you anything you want to know."

"Okay. Now where do I find Gorshik?"

"Not too sure about that. Haven't seen him in a couple of years. But go over to the spaceport and ask around there. They'll tell you."

# 7.

Rikard was tense as he reentered the tourist section near the port. He didn't know what would happen if he were seen by somebody who had known him earlier. He didn't want to have to defend himself. He stayed clear of the places he'd visited. It hadn't been that long since he'd left.

The locals paid him no attention, but the tourists looked at him as if he were some kind of killer. Which he was, he reminded himself. Still, it felt strange to be on the other side of the fence. He didn't enjoy the looks of apprehension cast his way.

He stopped at a tavern he'd never visited before and asked the tender where he could find Pedar Gorshik. At first the tender just stared blankly, obviously waiting for a bribe. Rikard let his face go soft and smooth, pulled his gun out, and laid it on the bar. The tender blanched and gave him an address across the street from Rikard's old hostel. Rikard put his gun away, gave the man a small bill, and left.

He was going to have to run the gauntlet after all. There was no sense in putting it off any longer. He went to the hostel and found the day clerk on duty.

"Do something for you?" the woman asked.

"I'm looking for Pedar Gorshik." Rikard waited for the clerk to recognize him.

"Right across the street, shop number one, last I knew. Got something to sell?"

"No. I'm looking to buy."

"Maybe I could help you. Gorshik charges high, and I haven't noticed that he's been doing much business lately."

"You know Sed Blakely?"

"Never heard of him."

"Thanks anyway." Rikard turned and left. She hadn't recognized him at all.

Shop number one, in the courtyard across from the hostel, was closed. Rikard went next door and asked about it.

"Oh, he moved out a month ago," the woman answered. "What's it to you?"

"Where'd he go?"

"Look, buddy, I don't know and I don't care."

He took out a few bills and offered them to her.

She looked at them and laughed. "You gotta be kidding. I don't sell nobody out for that little." She made a gesture, and two tough-looking men came out from a back room, carrying truncheons.

Rikard grabbed his gun, and time slowed. He did not shoot but used the gun as a club. He hit each man once across the face. They fell, and his gun was back in its holster before they stopped rolling.

"I'm offering you more than money," Rikard said quietly. He hoped she believed him.

"Yeah, sure, I get the picture. Listen, I don't know where he is, but you go to the Immigration office. They know there."

"Thanks a bundle," Rikard said. He dropped the money at her feet and left.

Returning to the Immigration office brought him full circle. The day clerk at his old hostel had not recognized him, but he wouldn't be able to fool the machines. He sat in one of the console chairs.

He felt very strange. The last time, he'd been an outsider looking in. Now he was an insider looking out. A couple of tourists came in, looked at him curiously, took chairs of their own, and pulled the hoods forward to ask their questions and state their business.

Rikard pulled his own hood forward. The screen lit up.

"Where is Pedar Gorshik?" he asked.

"Please state your identity," the screen answered.

"Rikard Braeth." He put his hand on the identification plate on the chair arm.

"Identity noted. You are in an anomalous position, Rikard Braeth, being not registered in any visitor facility nor listed as an immigrant to Kohltri."

"I'm staying with friends."

"Very well. What is your authorization for asking for Pedar Gorshik?"

"Personal authority. He knows where Sed Blakely was eleven years ago."

"As a visitor, Rikard Braeth, you are not authorized to request the location of unlisted persons without their prior consent."

"How about as a citizen of Kohltri?"

"In that case, you may ask."

"Make it that way then."

"Do you wish to become a citizen of Kohltri?"

"Is it reversible?"

"Only by your departure from Kohltri. A citizen of Kohltri is not liable to nor protected by Federation laws."

"Make me a citizen, effective the day I checked out of my hostel. Can that be done?"

"If that was when you acquired a private residence, it can be done."

"Do it. Will this be recorded?"

"Certainly."

"Is there any way I can erase the recording?"

"No, there is not."

"What would have been the notation had I not come in here?"

"Your last address would have been noted, that you had not acquired a new one. Implication that you were hiding out."

"How is the register compiled?"

"Anybody may record his present address."

"Is there an address for Pedar Gorshik?"

"There is," the screen said, and gave it to him.

# 8.

The building was old, the plants in the courtyard surprisingly ill tended. Door 3 opened onto a hallway, with more doors down one side and a stairway going to the upper floors on the other. It was a rooming house.

Rikard climbed to the third floor. It was dark here and smelled bad, of decay and waste and disease. For a man who "charged high," this was a remarkably poor place to live.

He found the right apartment and knocked. A weak voice told him to come in.

The room inside was dimly lit. It contained a dresser, a table, a chair, a bed, and nothing else. The bed contained a wasted form.

"Pedar Gorshik?" Rikard asked.

"That's me," the weak voice answered. "Sit down. You make me tired standing there."

Rikard picked up the chair and took it over by the bed.

"You're sick," he said, sitting down. "Can I get you anything?"

"Nope. I can still get to the john by myself, thank God."

"You ought to be in a hospital."

"You're new here. You ever been in a hospital on Kohltri? It's better to just die sometimes."

"They take your money?"

"If you've got any. If you don't, they experiment."

"Doesn't sound at all good."

"It's not. What do you want? I gave up the business a month ago."

"A number of people think you're still in it."

"Tough. I haven't fenced anything since I caught the crud."

"I'm looking for Sed Blakely."

"He's been gone eleven years or more."

"I know. I was told you know where he is."

"Who told you that?"

"Aben Arshaud."

"He had no business doing that."

"He trusted me."

"The more fool he."

"Arshaud's no fool. I'm not going to hurt Blakely."

"What else would you say? Look, friend, I'm not talking. You get rough, I'll just die on the spot. I don't care."

"Would money help?"

"Not at all."

"How about a ticket off Kohltri to a hospital you could trust?"

"*If* I survived the trip and *if* they could fix me up, *then* I'd have the law on me, and rehabilitation. No thanks."

"You know why he's hiding, don't you?"

"Sure, he finked on Arin Braeth some way."

"That he did. And that's why I want to find him."

"No dice. I didn't know Braeth, but he had a good rep, and whatever it was Blakely did to him, he probably deserves to be shot, but I'm not about to avenge one betrayal by committing another. Besides, for all I know, Blakely could be dead."

"He could be. If he is, I'd like to know that too."

"Sorry, kid, you'll have to go elsewhere."

"You're the one who told Braeth and Blakely where the treasure was, aren't you?"

"Hell, there's no treasure."

"I know that, but you told them anyway, right?"

"Sure. Braeth insisted. Damn fool. I thought he was brighter than that. And then his partner double-crosses him. He must have been getting old."

"Maybe. Look, I found Arin Braeth."

"Who squealed?"

"Arshaud. Like I said, he trusted me."

"And where is Arin Braeth now? Dead?"

"Not as far as I know. The man I found, the man everybody thought was Arin Braeth is still alive. He's a hermit living south of the city, crazy as a rorn. But it isn't Arin Braeth who's been hiding out for eleven years; it's Sed Blakely."

"You gotta be crazy yourself."

"No. Blakely double-crossed Braeth all right, but he's the

one, not Braeth, who's been sending Arshaud letters all these
years."

"Then where the hell's Braeth?"

"Where Blakely is supposed to be. Where's Blakely supposed to have been all these years, Gorshik?"

"God Almighty, you mean we've been protecting the wrong
man all this time?"

"Sure looks like it."

"But how do you know it's not Braeth? You're too young
to ever have run with him."

"I'm his son. I can't prove it, but it's true. That's why
Arshaud trusted me. He said I looked like my father."

"Hell's bells. Well, I don't know Braeth well enough to
see any resemblance. I only met him a few times, and that
was a long while ago. So you're really looking for your
father?"

"That's right. Where did you send them eleven years ago?"

"Ho, boy, if I wasn't going to tell you where Blakely is,
I'm sure not going to fink on Braeth, even if you hurt me."

"I don't want to do that. I'm not going to do that. I just
want to convince you that I have a right to know, that I just
want to see my father, not take advantage of him. Blakely
said he left my father with tathas. You know what that is?
Okay, so if my father is still alive, which I rather doubt, he
could sure use some help, don't you think?"

"If everything you've told me is true, he does. But I don't
know that. You sure look like any local hood to me."

"I didn't just a few days ago." Rikard told him briefly
what had happened since he'd gotten to Kohltri. The dying
man lay watching him, and when Rikard finished, Gorshik
sighed and smoothed the blankets over his body.

"Okay," he said, "okay. Maybe I'm wrong, but I don't
think so. I didn't get along in my business for as long as I
did by being a bad judge of character. And you don't sound
like a local. You're too innocent. So okay, I'll believe you.
You're just looking for your long-lost father. And after all,
he's probably dead by now, so what could it hurt?"

"Where's my father, Pedar?"

"If he's alive, and if he's still there, he's in a place called
the Tower of Fives, in a ruined Belshpaer city somewhere
east of here."

"How do I get there?"

"I don't know, honest to God I don't. All I know is that if there's any dialithite on Kohltri, it's in the Tower of Fives. Arin Braeth said dialithite came with dragons, and dragons are supposed to come from the Tower of Fives, and that's all I know."

# 9.

Rikard called Darcy as soon as he got back from visiting Pedar Groshik. She invited him over and, since he'd never been there before, told him how to get to her place. It was a comfortable three-room suite, not especially hidden away, though he was sure it had at least one secret exit.

She gave him a beer when he came in, and he told her everything that had happened to him since the last time he'd seen her.

"I'm really amazed," she said when he'd finished. She handed him another beer. "You came here with nothing, and now you've gone through half the city just as if you owned it. Anyone would think you were born to the trade."

"I suspect my father hoped I was. There were those stories he kept telling me. And there was that operation." He fingered the scar on the palm of his right hand. "It cost a fortune, I don't know how much, and I lost a year of school. Mother didn't approve, but she didn't object. I think toward the end there, just before she died, she finally accepted what it implied. Why do something like that to me if he didn't expect me to follow in his footsteps someday?"

"You were being primed for it during your whole childhood."

"I guess so. Anyway, now I know where my father is. Or where he was when he was betrayed. He's probably still there, or his bones at least."

"I still say it's amazing that you could have dug up so

much as quickly as you did. And followed such a convoluted trail. I don't know anybody else who could have done it."

"You could have," Rikard said, half pleased, half embarrassed at the compliment. "Or Leonid Polski."

She smiled. "Yes, I guess so. But we've been in the business for a long time. You just started." There was something odd in her expression. "I never did like klunkers, and nobody could ever accuse you of being that."

"Well, thank you. But, uh, I still haven't finished my search. I still have to find the Tower of Fives."

"Ah, yes. It's legendary. It's the center structure of a Belshpaer city supposed to be the largest and most complete set of ruins on the planet."

"What about the idea that dragons come from the Tower of Fives?"

"I don't know about that, but that doesn't mean anything. I'm not a student of dragons, though some people are fascinated by them. What fascinates me is the fact that you've actually seen living Belshpaer. I could almost give up all this other nonsense if I could actually work with real live Belshpaer."

"Really?"

"Well, almost."

"If I meet any more, I'll send them your way. What I want to know is how to get to this Belshpaer city and the Tower of Fives."

"I wish I could help you there, but I don't know where it is. I don't think it will be too hard to locate somebody who does. All we'll have to do is find one of the loners who prospects out of the city. New stories about the place come back all the time."

"Is it far from here?"

"Several days by car through some pretty rough country, or so I'm told. It will be a real expedition in any event. You'll need a jeep, supplies, a shelter, stuff like that."

"I'm running out of cash."

"No problem. My little scheme is almost worked through. It will take us a couple of days to find a guide anyway. By that time my deal will be finished and we'll have plenty of money."

"You're not going to get into trouble with this, are you?"

"My money deal? No, I don't think so. I know most of the people involved. Nothing really illegal. Oh, there's a little danger. There always is. But it will pay off, don't worry, and then we'll be able to afford any kind of expedition you want."

"Sounds good. So I guess I'll spend the time looking for a guide."

"Sure. But don't tell them what you're after. Let them think you've heard about artifacts or something you can sell. You go off on an altruistic rescue mission after a dead man, they'll laugh at you. Tell them you're in it for the money, they'll come right along for a cut."

"What should I offer?"

"A hundred a day plus 5 percent, or whatever they can carry, whichever is less."

"That's an odd way to do it."

"Maybe, but it's terms they'll understand. If you don't sound greedy, they won't trust you."

"Looks like I've got a lot to learn yet."

"We all do, Rik, but you're learning fast."

"I sure hope so. And I think I'm going to get on it right now."

"So late?"

"The evening's just begun. And I can't sit still."

The odd look came into Darcy's eyes again. Rikard felt as if he were missing something.

"Well, if you must, you must," she said.

Rikard got to his feet. "I'll talk to you tomorrow. Then maybe we could go up to the Troishla and you could introduce me to some of its charms."

"It's a deal. You've only seen the front room so far. It might be fun to run into Dorong or Arbo again, just to see their reactions."

"It might at that."

He took his leave and found his way out of the building.

As he crossed the courtyard to the street door, four people passed him going the other way. He went out to the street and stopped, suddenly indecisive.

Something tugged at the tail ends of his mind. The only thing he could think of was the four people who'd passed him, going into Darcy's building. There hadn't been anything special about them as far as he remembered.

He took another step and stopped again. He didn't know why, but he was alarmed. He tried to go on, but his feet wouldn't work. All his hair was standing on end. He had to go back to Darcy's apartment. He turned and hurried back through the courtyard.

The building was quiet when he reentered. He climbed to the second floor and stepped into the hall, at the end of which was Darcy's apartment. The silence was broken by the sounds of breaking furniture. There were no shots.

With an unnatural calmness, he walked to her door. Loud noises came through it, the sounds of fists hitting flesh. He put his hand to the latch. It was locked. He took an extra clip of shells from his pocket, drew his gun, and time slowed.

He kicked at the door latch. The panel splintered and broke in. Two of the four people he'd seen in the courtyard were holding Darcy down in a chair. The third, a woman, was hitting her in the chest and stomach with a truncheon. The fourth, a man, was directing the affair.

He fired first at the man on Darcy's left and then at the one on her right. They both slammed back, but the other two were between him and Darcy. A shot at them would go through and hit her.

In that instant's hesitation the man who was directing the beating turned and raised a heavy, thick-barreled shotgun pistol.

Rikard dropped to the floor, the shotgun went off over his head, and he fired upward, taking the man under the rib cage. But the woman's truncheon came through the air and smashed into Rikard's face. For a moment he was blinded by pain.

Before he could recover, he felt a foot crash into his gun hand. The megatron went flying. Time returned to normal, and he barely ducked another kick that was aimed at his neck. It glanced off his shoulder.

He grabbed the swinging foot the next time it came, and wrenched it around until the woman fell heavily beside him. He heard shouts and running feet in the hall.

The woman lashed out with her feet even as she tried to rise. Rikard rolled away, lurched halfway upright, and caught the woman on the chin with an uppercut, starting around his ankles, mainly because he couldn't stand any straighter.

Another woman with a drawn gun of some kind appeared

in the doorway. Rikard slammed the shattered panel in her face. Her gun went off half a dozen times into the floor. He dived for his own gun, the door bounced open, he grabbed the megatron, the machine pistol came up in the woman's hand. He aimed at the pistol and fired. The wreckage of her gun and her arm tore her chest away as it slammed her backward into her companion behind her in the hall. He fired twice more, blindly, into the darkened hallway. His gun was empty. He fumbled another clip into it.

There was a pause. He could hear voices at the end of the hall, out of his line of sight. He spared a glance at Darcy. She was slumped in her chair, watching him with glazed eyes. There was blood on her shirt.

"Rik Braeth, is that you?" somebody called.

"Yeah, it's me."

"We've got no argument with you," the anonymous voice told him.

"You do now." He sent a bullet through the wall near where the voices were coming from. There was a loud scream, then the sound of several people cursing and scuffling.

"Okay, Braeth," another voice yelled. "You've had it. We're going to take you out."

"Hold 'em," he heard Darcy whisper. "I called Leo when you left."

For some reason that bothered him, but he brushed it aside. "You just keep breathing," he said. He flattened himself against the wall next to the door.

A hail of bullets came in the doorway. Darcy groaned and rolled out of her chair before the arc of bullets reached her. As the angle of fire increased away from him, Rikard stepped out and sent five heavy slugs smashing into the two men against the far wall who were firing two machine pistols apiece. He jumped back, tripped on the clip he'd dropped when the truncheon had hit him, and went down.

The hall exploded. There was a roar and another explosion. A cloud of stinking smoke billowed into the room, bringing screams with it. There was a third explosion, then silence.

Then Leonid Polski stood in the doorway, his police blaster drawn and smoking. His face wore the hardest expression Rikard had ever seen.

The policeman glanced at him briefly, then holstered his

blaster and went to where Darcy lay in a growing pool of blood.

"Don't move her," Rikard said roughly. He struggled to his feet, recovered the clip that had tripped him, and shoved it into his gun. "I think her ribs are broken."

Polski's hands fluttered over her, but didn't touch her. "How are you doing?" he asked her.

"Not good."

"Who do I call for help?" Rikard asked.

"Nobody," Polski said over his shoulder. "What happened?" he asked Darcy.

"Can't talk," Darcy gasped. Polski stood up.

"That one," Rikard said, indicating the woman, who was still alive but unconscious, "was beating her with this." He kicked at the truncheon. "I'd just left when I saw them come in. I don't know why I came back, but I had to."

"You're doing okay, kid," Polski said. He picked up the truncheon and went over to the unconscious woman.

"If I could turn the recorders off," he said, "for just one minute, I could get a lot of satisfaction right now." He hefted the truncheon, then dropped it on the woman's body.

"What about Darcy?" Rikard asked. "Do we take her to a hospital?"

Polski nodded.

"I heard they take your money or your life," Rikard went on.

"They do, but I've got connections, and so does Darcy, so she'll be all right. And besides, they'll know either you or I will come for them if they hurt her, so that will keep them honest. They can do good work if they want to."

"How do we get her there?"

"I've got a couple of my people coming over now with an ambulance. I'm wired in, remember?"

"I know that. It's just I thought you were working alone."

"In a sense I am, but I've got a support crew of seven. The privilege of rank."

Rikard went over and knelt beside Darcy. He didn't know what was between her and Polski, but he was sure it was close. He hesitated a moment, saw Polski's face tense and then relax. He turned back to Darcy.

"You've got help coming," he told her softly.

"I heard," she whispered, using as little air as possible.

"Want any revenge?"

"I'll get it later." She smiled grimly. "If there's any of them left. Thanks for coming back."

"I shouldn't have left."

"No," she answered, and passed out.

"She'll be all right," Polski said as Rikard stood.

"Yeah, she's tough."

"She only called me because you were leaving her behind," Polski went on.

"I just figured that out."

"We've been friends for a long time."

"I know. It's all right. Neither you nor I have to make any decisions or explanations. And besides, if you hadn't shown up, we'd both be dead."

"Just good police timing."

"Sure. When are your people getting here?"

"They're here now. Want to hear about the Man Who Killed Banatree?"

"After I'm sure she's all right."

"After we're both sure. Then I'll talk your ear off. Neither one of us is going to want to sleep tonight."

And then four Federal police officers came in with the stasis carrier.

# PART SEVEN

## 1.

They got to the hospital within a quarter of an hour. Two of the police support crew stayed with Darcy in the emergency room while Rikard and Polski went to talk to the hospital authorities. They had no difficulty convincing them that Darcy should be given the best of care at the best rates going.

The medical equipment here, like everything else on Kohltri, was badly outdated, but the surgeons were first class, whatever their reasons for being here. Darcy went into emergency surgery at once, and Polski dismissed his officers.

"You look like you could use some treatment yourself," one of the doctors told Rikard, looking at the bruises on his face.

"No thanks. We just want some coffee, and a place to wait until she comes out."

"The waiting room's down the hall. Coffee will cost you."

"Just bring it," Polski said.

There were several other people in the waiting room. Rikard and Polski found a couple of chairs in a corner where they wouldn't be disturbed. After a few moments a young man brought them their coffee. They sat drinking in silence for a while.

"So tell me about the Man Who Killed Banatree," Rikard said at last. "You said it was a long story. I think we'll have plenty of time."

"How much do you know about it?" Polski asked.

"Not much. That was seventeen years ago. I was only nine years old when it happened."

"I was twelve. Well, I guess I'll begin at the beginning."

Telchrome was a world of perpetual spring. Its orbit was nearly circular; its axis did not wobble. Near the poles it was cold enough and snowed enough that skiing and other winter sports went on year round. There were no blizzards. At the equator temperatures varied between sixty at night and ninety during the day, with gentle rainy seasons which were only slightly cooler. In the temperate zones the weather was always perfect. The world was so mild and beautiful that it could be used for nothing other than a paradise vacation planet.

Banatree was one of the poshest resort cities on Telchrome, and hence in the Federation. It had a population of nearly four million, half of whom were employees of the Telchrome Recreation Administration, citizens, or government workers. The other half were tourists who had money to spend. Those on a more limited budget visited other parts of Telchrome. There were even places where you didn't have to spend any money at all once you arrived and proved you had return fare.

A world like Telchrome and a city like Banatree attracted people other than those who just intended to have a good time. Known criminals were turned around at the spaceport. Litterbugs and vandals were fined, made to pay reparations, and deported. The TRA valued its property and made sure the planet was always safe for paying visitors. Nonetheless, occasionally people came who thought they could take advantage of the idyllic planet.

When an unidentified male caller contacted the Banatree city government and demanded a ransom of ten billion, threatening to destroy the city if he was not paid within twenty days, nobody was too worried—until the routine tracing procedures failed to produce the identity of the caller. Even then they were not too concerned, as threats of that nature—though usually much less grandiose—were not all that uncommon. Besides, who could destroy a whole city?

The deadline ran out. A small thermal bomb went off at a racetrack a few kilometers outside Banatree, killing several hundred people. The man contacted the city government again and restated his demands.

This time they decided to take him at his word, though nobody knew how he could carry out his threat. But they stalled and searched, and just when it seemed they might have a lead, with only a day left before the new deadline, a neutron bomb went off in the center of Banatree. Only nine city blocks at the site of the blast were destroyed, but three and a half million people were killed.

At the same time a small freighter at another spaceport on Telchrome was hijacked, though it was over two hours before planetary police took note. When they did, they were certain that the Man Who Killed Banatree, as he was almost instantly called, had taken the ship in order to escape. Police ships followed at once.

But even that small delay had foiled them. Tracking any ship through non-Einsteinian space was more than just tricky. The hijacked ship stopped momentarily at eleven stars on a long, irregular route before the police cruisers caught up with it and blew off its engines.

When they boarded it, the police found the crew all dead. There was evidence that at each of the eleven stops—all primaries of inhabited worlds—an escape pod had been jettisoned. The Man Who Killed Banatree had gotten off somewhere en route, but no one knew where.

The explosion that killed the city of Banatree had completely destroyed the bomb, of course. Nevertheless, by studying the bomb's effects and residual radiations, police investigators were able to determine that it had been a special type, made using a rare alloy catalyst called barodin, at a battery factory on the industrial world of Pieshark.

The factory had specialized in energy-storage devices of from one to one hundred cubic meters in size. These were thermonuclear, fusion, and electrogravitic devices, which also used barodin in their construction. The factory had been destroyed a standard year earlier by the same type of bomb that had gone off at the racetrack just outside Banatree.

Fifty people had died in the factory explosion, including employees, administrators, and visitors. That explosion, the police now reasoned, had been set off to cover the manufacture and theft of the neutron bomb, and to obliterate the identity of its maker, since none of the victims could be identified. The reason for the explosion had been a mystery until the Banatree disaster.

Federal police investigated each of the eleven worlds where the Man Who Killed Banatree might have found refuge. One or two worlds they could eliminate at once, when the wreckage of the escape pods were found. Other worlds took longer, because the pods could not be located immediately, because local authorities interfered with the investigation, or because population records were slackly maintained. It took seventeen years to narrow the list to one out-of-the-way world, the fifth stop on the hijacked freighter's escape flight. Kohltri.

"There's been an awful lot of preliminary work done already," Polski said as he finished the story. It was nearly dawn. "But Kohltri, of course, has presented special problems. Our biggest has been to conduct the investigation without arousing the populace. I'm just the clean-up man, as it were."

"Do you think you'll get him?"

"It's just a matter of time now. The population of Kohltri isn't all that large. And when you eliminate everybody who demonstrably arrived after the Man, or who was probably here before him, that leaves only a few thousand whose presence is not precisely accounted for. And we know he didn't leave. You may be able to drop in on a planet without telling anybody, under just the right circumstances, but you can't leave that way."

"Just a few thousand suspects."

"It's not as bad as it seems. Most of the possibilities are simply too young. They were born here, without records. It's narrowing down fast—at least, in terms of a seventeen-year manhunt it's fast."

"What will you do when you find him?"

"Take him alive, if we can. The government wants to try him publicly. There isn't much doubt he'll be convicted, though, and when he is, he'll be executed. First execution in several hundred years. But the public pressure is too strong to just rehabilitate him."

"I'd say so. There's no way he can get a fair trial."

"Not if what you're trying to prove is that he killed the city. The trial will be to prove that he is in fact the man who fled Telchrome seventeen years ago. There were nine people slaughtered on that freighter. It's the best we can do."

A doctor they hadn't seen before came into the waiting room and looked them over.

"Are you the people who brought Msr. Glemtide in here last night?" he asked.

"We are," Polski said.

"They've just taken her out of surgery. She'll be all right. She'd like to see you now."

They followed the doctor to a fourth-floor ward, where Darcy was lying in a semiprivate room. She looked groggy and her face was puffy, but she was awake, and she smiled when they came in.

"How you doing?" Polski asked, coming up to stand by the head of her bed.

"Seven broken ribs," she said. Her voice was a whisper; her breathing was short and shallow. "Some internal damage, not much, but a lot of bleeding. How am I going to pay for all this?"

"You can owe me," Polski said. "Besides, we convinced them to give us good rates."

"I'll bet you did. Have you been here all night?"

"Sure, nowhere else to go. When can we take you out of here?"

"Ten or twelve days. I'm going to be out of action for a long time. The worst part is"—she looked past Polski at Rikard—"my deal fell through. I won't be able to help pay for your expedition."

"Don't worry about that," Rikard said. "I'll figure something out. You just get yourself well, and then we can all three go looking for whatever's left of that mob."

"Sure thing," she said.

They talked with her a moment more, but she obviously needed rest. Polski arranged for the other bed in the room to be left vacant so that either he or Rikard could stay with Darcy, in case any survivors of the mob that had tried to kill her came back looking for trouble.

Rikard and Polski arranged their schedule to suit the policeman's convenience. Rikard would stay with Darcy until Polski came back from his day's search for the Man Who Killed Banatree, then Rikard would go out, leaving the policeman to sleep in the other bed. Darcy slept most of the time Rikard spent with her, but she seemed glad for his company while she was awake.

When Rikard wasn't sitting with Darcy, he did what he could to prepare an expedition to the ruined Belshpaer city of the Tower of Fives. He moved out of his hideaway into a cheap room to conserve his resources, which were rather depleted by this time. He purchased concentrated food and a collapsible shelter and made arrangements for a jeep, a heavy-duty open-bodied floater, to be available whenever he was ready to go. That took almost his last bill.

Most of his time away from the hospital he spent trying to locate someone to guide him. He needed someone who not only knew where the Tower of Fives was, but who would take the job on speculation. And it had to be somebody he could trust. Meeting this last condition was an almost impossible task. He had no luck finding a suitable guide until the tenth day of Darcy's hospitalization, when Polski came in to take his turn guarding her.

"I ran into somebody who might be who you're looking for," the policeman said. He looked exhausted.

"Who is he?" Rikard asked. He gave Polski his chair.

"His name's Stefan Dobryn. He's one of the people I had to check out as a possible suspect. He was born here. He's a product of his society, of course, but he's proved trustworthy before. He went along as a workman when an archaeological expedition from Zendar went to the Tower about four years ago."

# 2.

Rikard went to see Dobryn at his home that evening. The man wasn't much older than Rikard, and greeted him suspiciously, standing in the door with a drawn gun, a small type of plastic pistol.

"My name's Braeth," Rikard said. "I understand you know where the city of the Tower of Fives is."

"Maybe I do."

"I want somebody to guide me there. Will you do it?"

"Who sent you?"

"Leonid Polski. I have certain information on Belshpaer artifacts."

"So what's in it for me?"

"Five percent. Minimum of a hundred a day after we get back."

"How many people?"

"Just me. I've got the jeep and supplies."

"Small expedition. How about an advance?"

"I have no cash left."

"Real thin, aren't you? What are these artifacts?"

"Would you believe dialithite?"

"Not really. What's your real reason?"

"I think my father is buried somewhere in the Tower of Fives. I want to see his grave. But there may really be dialithite. That's why he went there."

"First time I ever heard of it."

"Me too."

Dobryn stared at him a moment longer, then lowered his gun. "Come on in and let's talk about it."

It was a small but comfortable suite of rooms. Dobryn motioned Rikard into a chair and took one himself.

"So," he said, "you're offering me a hundred a day but you have no money."

"If we find nothing, I'll have the deposit on the jeep, and I'll sell the shelter. That ought to cover it."

"I'd have to lay off at the mines. How about one fifty a day?"

"I can see that."

"You really think there's dialithite there?"

"There was, eleven years ago. I've seen the man who got away. He had a handful."

"No kidding. And you didn't take it from him?"

"You think maybe he gave me the chance? Besides, what I really want is my father. If you find any dialithite, you can have whatever you can carry."

"Generous. And what about you?"

"I have big pockets too."

"Whatever I can carry is more than 5 percent."

"Maybe you could suggest somebody else who could guide me."

"I sure could, but you have to sleep sometime."

"Okay, Dobryn, I've told you what I want. That's the best offer I can make. I can leave tomorrow morning. Will you guide me?"

"Look, man, I just don't know who you are, that's all."

"And I don't know you either. The only person I really know here is Darcy Glemtide, and she's just a visitor herself. I came here to you because Polski said you could be trusted."

"I don't know anybody named Polski. Glemtide? No, that doesn't mean a thing to me. Okay, look, here's what I'll do. I'll guide you out there. You guarantee me a thousand plus one fifty a day and 10 percent or whatever I can carry."

Rikard took the loan agreement on the jeep out of his pocket and handed it to Dobryn.

"You collect the whole remainder of the deposit," he said, "or keep the jeep if you want. It's been paid for. And 10 percent or whatever you can carry, whichever is less."

Dobryn looked over the loan agreement. "Okay, it's a deal." He handed the document back. "Give that to me when we're on the road tomorrow. Pick me up here. I'll be home."

"Thanks." Rikard felt himself relax. He hadn't been aware of being so tense. "I'll see you tomorrow morning, then."

"Sure thing."

Rikard left and went back to the hospital to tell Darcy and Polski what had happened. Then he went home to bed, where he didn't get to sleep until almost dawn.

He woke after two hours, excited and ready to go. He collected the jeep, loaded the supplies and shelter, and drove to Dobryn's place. His guide was waiting for him, seeming a lot more cheerful.

"Sorry about being so short last night," Dobryn said, "but the mines take a lot out of a person, and I was pretty tired."

He got in the jeep, Rikard gave him the loan agreement, and they started off east through the city toward the edge of town. Dobryn gave directions as they went.

After a few blocks Rikard noticed they were being followed. When he had the chance, he slowed and tried to see who it was. It was Emeth Zakroyan.

"What's the trouble?" Dobryn asked.

"That woman behind us. She has a personal grudge against me."

"No kidding. She likely to cause trouble?"

"I hope not." But he loosened the gun in its holster nonetheless. Dobryn, he noticed, still carried the plastic pistol. It was a lightweight weapon, small caliber, short-range, with no real stopping power, but virtually undetectable by most scanning devices. It couldn't penetrate even light armor.

"You're pretty heavily heeled," Dobryn observed.

"Gift from my father."

"Can you use it?"

"Well enough."

"There are some predators farther out from the city."

"I'll show off if we meet any."

They drove through an industrial district. Zakroyan didn't try to close with them, but kept a block back. It made Rikard nervous.

Dobryn didn't seem to pay any attention. "You really looking for your old man?" he asked as they left the city proper.

"I really am," Rikard said and, as they drove through a brief stretch of outlying farms, with their glass roofs ablaze with morning sunlight, told the story of how he'd traced him this far.

"Then you don't really live here?" Dobryn asked when he'd finished.

"This is my twenty-fifth day."

"I would have sworn last night you were either a citizen or a Gesta."

"I'm a citizen now, as of eleven days ago. I've had some real good instruction."

They passed mining domes, dozens of them. Beyond were sparsely wooded hills, through which ran an unpaved track which they followed. Zakroyan was still behind them, about half a kilometer back. She seemed to have no desire to get any closer. Dobryn watched the other car for a while.

"Who is she?" he asked at last.

"Anton Solvay's private murderer."

"God Almighty, you pick good company. You got Solvay on your tail?"

"He's paranoid."

"Doesn't change the shape of the bullet hole."

"If she starts gaining on us, let me know."

"Sure will. Uh, you got other company."

Rikard glanced across Dobryn and saw, a hundred meters to their right, the glowing, ambiguous form of a dragon. It hovered a meter or so above the ground, drifting through the sparse trees, paralleling them and keeping pace. The nodules of light in its transparent body glowed and pulsed.

"Goddamn," Rikard muttered. The hairs all over his body stood up on end.

"That's putting it mildly." Dobryn's voice was unnaturally soft and hoarse. "As long as it stays out there, we're all right, but in an open car, if it comes after us, we're fried. It can outfly us with no trouble at all."

They drove on, the dragon beside them, Zakroyan behind them. It amused Rikard, in a wry sort of way, to note that Solvay's tame killer had dropped back to a full kilometer when the dragon appeared. She was afraid of it too.

"Those things attack often?" he asked, meaning the dragon.

"It isn't an attack, really; it's more like they're curious and just want to kind of feel us out, literally speaking. But if you touch one, it's instant death. You fry."

"So I've heard."


# 3.


They passed an occasional shack and a small mining town or two. The hills continued, as did the small and widely spaced trees. Once they came to a village, similar to Logarth south of the city. Rikard was prepared for another toll-collecting stick-up this time. He drove around the village, and when they got to the other side, the people were there waiting for them. But when the villagers saw the dragon, which was flying higher now, they scattered. Rikard and Dobryn drove on unmolested.

"Looks like those monsters are good for something after all," Dobryn said.

Zakroyan was still behind them, less than half a kilometer back now. She had followed them in their detour around the village. The toll collectors had not bothered her either. Which was a shame, Rikard thought.

A little farther on they entered thicker forest. The track

just faded away. Dobryn guided them as they drove between huge trees, each with a trunk a meter or more in diameter. These trees, too, were widely spaced, twenty or thirty meters apart. Their branches high overhead covered the sky, casting the nearly clear forest floor into cool, green shade.

"If I go off course," Rikard asked, "can you get me back?"

"Sure. What are you going to do?"

"Try to throw our friend back there."

The ground was still hilly, and Rikard waited until Zakroyan's car dipped below a ridge behind them and out of sight. Then he turned the jeep downslope and gunned the engine. Keeping to the low spots, he sped as fast as he dared through the trees, then started to turn back toward the city in a long arc. He couldn't see Zakroyan behind him any more, so he rushed on, then cut sharp and doubled back.

He intended to cross their route about a kilometer or so before the place where they had turned off. Dobryn guided him, and when they passed a familiar spot, he sped on beyond. Then he turned away from the city again to a place farther on their route, where several trees grew more closely together. He stopped the jeep and sat, gun drawn, to see if Zakroyan had managed to follow them. They waited half an hour. She didn't show. And the dragon was gone too.

"Looks like we've lost both of them," he said at last. He put his gun away and started the jeep again.

"Suits me just fine," Dobryn agreed.

They made a short stop for lunch, then drove until dusk, when darkness made driving dangerous. Rikard didn't want to use lights, just in case Zakroyan was still out there somewhere. Dobryn guided him a little farther on until they came to a set of ruins.

Broken hexagonal buildings littered the ground, overgrown by the trees. Nothing stood more than three or four meters above the ground. The ruins, rich terra-cottas and russets, were quite extensive, covering nearly a hundred hectares. Dobryn guided them through the rubble until they came to where a partially intact ceiling offered protection. They stopped the jeep and got out.

"You ever meet any Belshpaer?" Rikard asked as they set up the shelter against an inner wall.

"They're all dead," Dobryn answered.

"I know of at least six who aren't."

"You gotta be kidding. They died out five, ten thousand years ago."

"Well, these six don't know that." He told Dobryn about his meeting with them south of the city.

"That's really bizarre." Dobryn set up the cooker. The shelter let them see out but kept all light in. "I mean, are you sure they weren't just some people playing a trick on you?"

"Now, have you ever met any humans with three legs and six arms apiece?"

"No, I never have." He turned on the cooker. "That's really weird. Boy, if those archaeologists I worked with four years ago had known any Belshpaer were alive, they'd never have left."

"You know a lot about Belshpaer?" Rikard served them their supper.

"A little. I know they had starships. I know there are more ruins of theirs on several other worlds. But this is the most extensive collection ever found anywhere. Why, there are some buildings here that are still intact. The Tower of Fives is one. That's why those archaeologists went there."

"How'd you find the city in the first place?"

"The archaeologists had an aerial survey. Listen, that place is well-known on other worlds. It's been explored before. Of course, this isn't the most popular place for those academic types to visit."

"I can understand that," Rikard said.

They had no trouble during the night. After breakfast the next morning, they packed up and drove on through the ruins and into deeper forest on the other side.

Kohltri was a beautiful world. Forests like the one they were driving through covered most of the planet. There were a very few veldlike areas. Only the poles, and the peaks of a few of the tallest mountains, were bare.

Sixty-five percent of the planet surface was water, forming several large seas and a multitude of smaller ones, all teeming with life. The weather was generally calm, with light rain almost every night and seldom during the day.

It was a warm world, with an F6 primary, three moons, and a fine set of inner rings which glowed in near-white pastels at night. There were no other planets in the system.

There was no native sentient species. The Belshpaer, like the humans and the Atreef, were just settlers. Nobody knew where the Belshpaer home world had been.

Native life on the continents ran the full gamut, lacking only simianoids. The basic form was bilateral, which was also predominant through the rest of the galaxy. There were birds, insects, cold-blooded reptile types, and mammaloids. There were no monsters, just the usual range of predators feeding on a wide variety of herbivores.

Everywhere there were ruins. Dobryn confirmed the theory that if you dug anywhere, you'd find ruins eventually. Those on the surface had just not been buried as deeply, or had perhaps been uncovered by the rather mild weather.

"This whole world was just one city once, I think," Dobryn said. "Except the oceans, of course, and maybe the mountains. I guess they had lots of parkland too, but the place we're going to visit isn't really a separate thing. It just looks that way because everything around it has been buried. It's one of the oldest sets of ruins around, though, at least ten thousand standard years, as far as those archaeologists could figure out."

There was more wildlife this far from the city. On the worlds Rikard knew, there was little left of any native life, and that was mostly on preserves. He was fascinated by the variety. Most species were small, but a few were as big as a human.

They came to a river. Rikard drove out over it to follow it downstream. This was a major landmark, Dobryn explained. Even if they had gotten lost while throwing Zakroyan, they would have come to the river eventually. Now all they had to do was follow it.

"Looks like we've lost Zakroyan for good," Rikard said as they skimmed along over the broad, smooth, wet surface.

"And no more dragons either," Dobryn added.

"Those things can't be native to Kohltri."

"I wouldn't know about that."

"Well, look at it. Whatever the dragons are, they're a very advanced form of life, and there's nothing else at all like them here, is there?"

"Not as I've ever heard."

"Okay. A single species can't exist in isolation, unless it's the original prebiot. Something as advanced as those dragons is the end of a long line of evolution. If they were native here, there should be other life forms similar to them, predecessors and parallels. And they are a pretty bizarre life structure. Where are all the other trials, the ones that succeeded and from which the dragons evolved?"

"Beats me. Are you saying they came here from somewhere else?"

"Either that or were brought. Maybe the Belshpaer brought them when they colonized the world. Or maybe somebody else before or after. I don't know, but I'd bet you almost anything the dragons are from some other planet. And they're rather intelligent too."

"You gotta be kidding."

"No, not at all. Of course, they're so different we can't really tell. Not like dolphins or corvins, perhaps, but not just a superanimal either. They're pretty high up on the scale. I mean, they exhibit curiosity, or what passes for it close enough not to matter. I wonder nobody's come here to study *them*."

They came to a place where the river broadened into a marsh. It was thickly grown with reeds, shrubs, and water trees. The growth was too dense to drive through, and the jeep wouldn't float high enough to go over, so they had to swing around.

They reentered the forest to do so. There was more undergrowth here too. They had to go slowly, no more than thirty kilometers per hour.

Rikard found himself wanting to slow further. The light, though filtered through dense foliage, seemed just a bit too bright. He felt vaguely uneasy at Dobryn's presence. After a while he realized that it reminded him of what he'd experienced down in the tunnel where he'd fallen fleeing the dragon south of town.

"Is there tathas around here?" he asked. His voice sounded sharp and harsh in his ears.

"It's the balktapline." Dobryn, too, seemed to feel uncomfortable and sluggish.

"I was told this feeling was caused by a fungus."

"That may be, but it's the balktapline nevertheless, or at least something that's almost always found with it. See?" He pointed toward the ground.

Rikard slowed and looked over the side of the jeep. The ground was spotted here and there with bits of a dark material, metallically iridescent in a subtle way. It was the same material that had lined the tunnel he'd fallen into. It had not, he now realized, lined the passage to Dzhergriem's secret office.

"Is that balktapline?"

"It's a sure sign there's a lot of it nearby. Anthrace and reserpine too."

"Do you get this effect in the mines?" He wanted to just stop the jeep and crawl in a hole.

"No, we're shielded. If there's trouble, the guys who have to go down to the interface get triple pay."

"How come nobody's mining here?" He had to force himself to drive on.

"It's too far from the city. Look there. Somebody's been digging. You get an occasional prospector who's already crazy, and they'll come out to a place like this and work it for a while. They don't last long. Too much exposure, and they just lie down and die."

"I could use a little hidey-hole myself right about now. How long does this go on?"

"We're almost out of it. Bear left here."

A few hundred meters more and they were away from the influence of the strange stuff and were able to go back to the river again.

In the middle of the morning, they came to a place where the river broke and churned over huge boulders. They left the water here, since it turned and flowed north and they had to continue east. Dobryn was driving now. He turned the jeep toward the bank and entered the forest.

The forest was thick here, and they had to go slowly. The oldest trees, few of which were left, had reached their limit of survival, and most had fallen long ago. Younger trees had grown up in the open ground the fallen ones had left. These were still fairly substantial, though nowhere near the girth of their predecessors. They had not yet weeded themselves out in the struggle for sunlight and air, and grew closely together.

At one point they passed an ancient Belshpaer tower rising six stories through the trees. Its dark brown top was broken off, but it was otherwise intact in spite of the terrible weathering of its surface.

"Oldest datable Belshpaer ruin," Dobryn commented as they drove past. Rikard wanted to stop, but Dobryn told him he'd have plenty of ruins to look through when they got to the Tower of Fives.

At noon the forest thinned suddenly, and they emerged into a broad clearing. They were halfway across it before they saw the dragons. There were three of them on the far side.

The dragons saw them at the same time. Glittery, glowing, golden, glorious, and awful, they climbed into the air, serpentine and transparent, indefinitely outlined with a shimmer of what might be wings, and eyes that were all too real and terrible.

Dobryn jerked the floater into a sharp turn, nearly dumping them. Rikard drew his gun, but even at the accelerated rate of perception the weapon gave him, things were moving awfully fast. He targeted on the head of one of the dragons and fired. The bullet had no effect.

They raced back toward the edge of the clearing from which they had come. Two more dragons came out of the trees in front of them. Dobryn swerved hard left.

Rikard fired again, aiming at a dragon's eye. It wasn't easy. The combined movements of the shifting dragons and the jeep's violent lurching over the ground made it difficult for him to keep his eyes on his target, let alone bring the red spot into the center of the circles long enough to squeeze the trigger. He saw a chance, fired, and saw a terrible eye wink out—and then reappear.

A static discharge made him swing around in his seat. Dobryn was still trying to get to the dubious shelter of the woods. Just a few meters behind them was a dragon, about to close. Rikard screamed and fired at one of the bright points of light in the body of the monster.

He must have hit it, maybe even hurt it, because the dragon shot straight up into the air, leaving a trail of glittering dust motes.

The jeep lurched, swerved, rose up into the air. Then they were careening through the trees. Rikard devoted all his attention to hanging on while Dobryn dodged and swerved.

The jeep never quite hit anything but came close enough to make Rikard want to scream again.

He risked another look behind them. There were no dragons in sight.

"We've lost them," he yelled at Dobryn. The jeep slowed somewhat.

"Keep an eye out," Dobryn said.

"They're gone," Rikard insisted.

"Are you sure?"

"Stop and see for yourself."

Dobryn braked the jeep to a halt. They sat in the silence and looked around. No dragons. They waited. No dragons.

"We've lost them," Rikard said again.

"We've also lost ourselves," Dobryn answered. "I don't know where we are."

"I think the clearing is back that way."

"No, the sun was just to our right, overhead. It's more in that direction."

"You're the guide."

They started back, trying to retrace their mad dash. It took them three hours to find the clearing again. There were no dragons there now. They ate a quick, late lunch, then drove on. At dusk they entered a part of the forest where strange, bent trees grew. It was too dark to go farther, so they stopped there to camp for the night.

# 4.

Their drive the next morning through the strange, twisted trees was uneventful until they came to a place where the forest floor was strewn with gravel. A few of the larger chunks sticking up out of the ground indicated that the stuff was the broken fragments of Belshpaer buildings. As they drove slowly past a larger piece almost as high as a man's shoulder, something about it caught Rikard's eye. He made Dobryn stop while he got out to investigate.

All the Belshpaer ruins Rikard had seen so far had been composed of a plasticlike material, cloudy and opaque, whether the surface was long exposed to the elements or newly broken. The fist-sized chunks around him were no different, nor were most of the larger pieces. But the shoulder-high chunk that had caught his eye was luminous and translucent, a beautiful golden-ocher shade.

He circled the up-jutting stone. On the far side he saw a perfectly preserved stairway leading down into the ground. The substance of the stairs and the walls that surrounded it was a translucent cream color, streaked with a rich Tuscan. There was no rubble or leaf mold on the stairs. The ground in front of the opening was clear and showed odd marks that might have been footprints.

"What is it?" Dobryn called from the jeep.

"Somebody's front door," Rikard called back.

"Some kind of animal?"

"Not unless they use stairs and wear shoes."

"What are you talking about?"

"I think some Belshpaer are living down there."

"You gotta be kidding. Come on, you want to get to that tower or don't you?"

"Okay, don't get impatient. You're getting paid by the day."

"Only as long as your money holds out."

Rikard reluctantly returned to the jeep. He made a plan to come back later, if he had a chance, and investigate this place further.

A few kilometers farther on the forest thinned and became parklike. Huge trees were widely enough spaced to show patches of sky. There was no undergrowth below. Off to the south Rikard saw what he thought was a group of Belshpaer, but Dobryn refused to believe it, even when he saw them for himself. It was true they were a long way off and there were a number of intervening trees, but their rotary mode of locomotion was unmistakable. Rikard didn't press the issue, but he wondered why, with such concrete evidence in front of his eyes, Dobryn persisted in denying that any Belshpaer could be alive.

They stopped for lunch at the edge of the forest. Ahead of them was one of the rare treeless zones, a descending broken slope. It dropped steeply and irregularly down to a veld of considerable extent three or four hundred meters below them.

Navigating the slope was tricky. Dobryn was by far the more experienced driver, so he took over while Rikard just rode and enjoyed the view.

The jeep was a rugged vehicle, but the slope was very steep in places, sometimes presenting a vertical drop of more than the ten-meter maximum lift the jeep could provide. Dobryn had to find gentler ways, or they would have fallen as surely as if their car had been wheeled.

It took them over two hours to get halfway down. Dobryn paused for a moment to rest, then drove the jeep over a crest to a lower shelf. Just as the jeep tipped down, something spanged against its side, followed immediately by the sound of a gunshot from the crest of the slope above them. Dobryn gunned the engine and drove over the next drop. Rikard looked up and back, and saw Zakroyan's car poised at the edge of the slope.

He drew his gun and fired at her, but the lurching of the jeep was too much for him, and the shot went wide. Bullets from Zakroyan's car cracked around them as Dobryn fought to get them down the slope as quickly as possible, yet still in one piece.

Rikard aimed for another shot, but an intervening ridge of rock passed across his line of sight, and the bullet just ricocheted harmlessly away. Dobryn was driving too fast, too erratically. Rikard couldn't keep his sights on the other car long enough to get off a good shot. Even his accelerated perception didn't help. It was small consolation that only about a quarter of Zakroyan's shots passed close enough to them to be heard.

He kept firing to keep Zakroyan jumping. Dobryn, cursing steadily, maneuvered the car over drops he would never have dared otherwise. One time he just sped off the edge of a cliff. The jeep dropped twenty meters before the floatation panel, set at maximum, stopped them just centimeters above the jagged rocks.

It took them only twenty minutes to descend the second half of the slope. They went over a last ledge and hit the veld. Zakroyan, still two-thirds of the way up, let her machine pistol rip. Dobryn screamed; the jeep slammed to a halt.

With a steady rest, Rikard took aim one more time. He could just see the glint of the other car's windshield, and squeezed off a shot that should have gone through it and through Zakroyan's head. But in the fraction of a second between the time the bullet left his gun and when it struck, Zakroyan's car shot forward, and Rikard could see, even at this distance, the great hole suddenly appearing in the under-carriage, right below the engine. The car continued forward over the edge and dropped down into a depression and out of sight.

Rikard found himself counting under his breath. On the count of four, an explosion from the depression above him hurled fragments of the car skyward.

# 5.

Rikard was able to treat Dobryn using the emergency med-ical kit he'd gotten when he'd purchased the shelter. He'd been hit three times by Zakroyan's machine-pistol burst, but none of the wounds was serious. All three bullets had passed through, two in the upper arm and one along the ribs.

Rikard offered to abort the trip and take him home, but Dobryn refused.

"We've come this far," he said. "We'll get to the ruins tomorrow. By the time you got me home, I'd be well enough to start out again, so we might as well keep on from here."

"You don't have to go through with it. There's no clause in our contract that says you have to put up with being shot at."

"No kidding. But look, we're almost there. I don't know if there's any dialithite at the Tower or not, but I'm not about to back out now. Besides, if Old Iron Jaws wanted to stop you that badly, there *must* be something there."

"I really think she was after me for personal reasons."

"Nonsense. I've never had anything to do with any of our beloved Director's watchdogs, but people know who they are, and Solvay doesn't pick them to dash off on personal causes. Maybe you think it's personal, but my guess is there's something at the Tower of Fives they don't want you to see."

So they drove on. Dobryn slept much of the way but was feeling weak and uncomfortable, so they stopped when they came to a sharp outcrop in the veld a hundred kilometers from the base of the slope. Rikard set up the shelter, then changed the dressings on Dobryn's left arm and side.

There was no sign of infection. The wounds had not bled any during the last several hours, and Dobryn was not feeling much pain, but without surgery he would be more or less incapacitated for several days.

The outcrop afforded good shelter, and more important from Dobryn's point of view, a clear view back the way they had come. They'd seen no one else as they had driven across the flat, open veld and from their somewhat elevated position they could see no signs of being followed now. But if Zakroyan had gone to the effort of following them all the way out here, there might be another car coming after her.

As the sun touched the western horizon, a howl broke the silence.

"Caron," Dobryn said.

"What's that?"

"A coursing predator. Hunts alone. Big as a man, twice as mean. It probably smelled my blood back at the slope and has been following us."

"The thing would have to run awfully fast to do that."

"It does. Flexible spine, long legs, it can do sixty kilometers per hour all day long, faster for short bursts. They chase the lopers and bovers. We haven't seen any of *them* all day, so if a caron is out there, it's hungry."

"Have you ever seen one of these things?"

"Last time I was out here. I didn't know what it was, but there was a zoologist on the expedition." The howl came again. "We passed by a herd of bovers, the tall ones with horns, I don't know their regular name, and all of a sudden they started running as fast as the cars. Then this thing came out of nowhere and took one of the calves that was falling behind. Real fast. Clean kill." It howled again, closer. "It's hungry, all right."

"If it hunts alone, we'll have no trouble." Rikard checked his gun to make sure it was working properly.

"I guess not, the way you shoot. No, it will be alone. The adults of the pride quarter their hunting ground during the day and go back to their lair at night. If it's out this late"—howl—"it must live nearby, within ten, twenty kilometers."

"Let's just hope we're not sitting on top of its nest."

"We could be."

Rikard fixed their supper, interrupted at regular intervals by the howls of the caron as it came closer. "Does it always yell like that?" he asked.

"I don't know much about them."

"How about that time before when you saw one? Did it howl then?"

"Before it took the calf, not after."

The sun fell below the western ridge, but there was still enough light in the sky to see when the caron howled again, a small dot moving across the veld toward them. It was moving very fast.

They ate quickly as they watched it approach. It was definitely coming toward their outcrop. Rikard was fascinated by its long, loping stride.

"The shelter won't keep it out," Dobryn reminded him nervously.

"I know. I just don't want to kill it unless I have to."

"I think you have to."

The caron, half a kilometer away, doubled its speed. It streaked toward them like a steel spring let loose. Rikard pulled his gun. Time slowed.

The concentric circles centered on the coursing beast. To Rikard's speeded senses, it seemed to be striding in long, slow-motion bounds. Rikard brought the gun up, and the red spot moved toward the center circle. Spot and circle lined up, but still he waited until there was no mistake. Then he fired.

In midleap the creature curled up and hit the ground like a limp bundle. It lay still. The shot had entered below the throat and come out near the tail.

There were no more howls that night.

They passed several herds of grazing animals the next morning, but heard or saw no carons. The veld continued flat, with occasional solitary trees. Twice they crossed shallow, slow rivers. Rikard drove the whole way.

By noon they could see the eastern mountains at the foot of which lay the city of the Tower of Fives. They had a quick lunch and then went on. Dobryn was much improved, though very stiff. He found moving difficult.

It was nearly dusk before they saw the city itself, still a long way off. Several buildings rose high above the level of the veld. They glinted red in the light of the setting sun.

It was a vast collection of ruins. Dobryn didn't know how many hectares it covered. Long before they came to its nominal edge, where the ancient buildings stood whole or nearly intact, they passed broken pieces and fragments buried in the detritus of millennia.

The transition between rubble and standing buildings, when they came to it, was abrupt. Within a space of just a hundred meters, the ruins stopped being a dense scattering of broken chunks and became upright walls. By then it was dark.

Rikard stopped the jeep in a rubble-strewn street between structures that rose fifteen meters and more. In the light of the jeep's headlamps, he gazed at the remnants of the city ahead of them.

"We've almost made it," Dobryn said. His voice was tired and strained.

"How far to the Tower?"

"About ten kilometers."

"That far?"

"It's a big city. The Tower is more or less in the middle, and it's not easy to get to. You can't see it from here, even in daylight."

"It shouldn't take long to find it. I mean, it's the tallest building standing, isn't it?"

"It is, but you can't drive there. Farther in, the ruins break down again. You'll have to walk most of the way."

# PART EIGHT

## 1.

It rained that night, but they had found a place with an intact roof, and that, along with the shelter, kept them dry. Dobryn was stronger the next day, but stiffer than before.

They drove into the city as far as they could. After half a kilometer or so, the streets became choked with the rubble of the crumbling upper stories. Many of the hexagonal structures were nearly intact, but many more had broken and fallen in.

They spent most of the morning zigzagging back and forth, trying to find a place from which they could see the Tower of Fives. Rikard was fascinated by the ruins. He would have stopped to explore if the goal of his search hadn't been so near.

"You'll see plenty of ruins later," Dobryn reminded him. "I wish I could find the place where we camped before. From there I could give you pretty good directions. But I really don't have any idea where we are. Once we can see the Tower, you'll be able to find your way, though it may take a couple of days."

Shortly after noon they came to a plaza with great avenues leading off in six directions. The street by which they entered was relatively clear, but the other five ways were choked with heaps of broken plastic. Down one of the avenues, leading east, they could see, a long way off, a great towering spire.

"The Tower of Fives," Dobryn said. "That's it."

"Why do they call it that?"

"I don't know. Something to do with some of the things that have been found there, I think. It's been called that as long as I can remember. Hey, I'm no expert. I just came along to clear rubble and like that."

"You still know more than I do. So that's the place."

"It is. I don't know how we can get any closer by jeep."

"We might as well stop here, then. Let's find you a nice place to wait."

"I wish I could go with you. Maybe by tomorrow I'll be loosened up a bit."

"Maybe. And I'd feel better if you came along. But we'll worry about that later. Right now I want to find a place where you can stay and be safe from anything that might live here. And a place to hide the jeep."

"Yeah, just in case Old Iron Jaws didn't come out alone. And if I'm going to be waiting five to ten days, I'd like to be comfortable."

They left the jeep in the middle of the plaza and went to explore the nearby buildings. They didn't bother with any that did not give easy access. That still left them a lot of choices. The first place they tried was one that had had a great window, long since fallen out, through which they could maneuver the jeep if they wanted to.

The first room here was large and empty. Dust lay thick on the bare floor. In the rooms beyond were fragments of furnishings, which crumbled when they were touched. They could find no access to the upper floors. In one small room they found the lair of some carnivorous animal. They decided to try another place.

They went through several buildings. In one, a passageway had the same translucency Rikard had seen in the ruins in the forest. If that meant that living Belshpaer still used this building, then it was no good as a hideout. Rikard didn't think the Belshpaer would be dangerous, but he couldn't trust Dobryn's reactions. He didn't want trouble of any kind while he was gone.

As they explored, Rikard felt more and more a sense of age and strangeness about the place. A trilateral symmetry would give the people who had built this city a completely different outlook from that of any other species he had met. They could have no concept of front or back. Nothing could ever be behind a Belshpaer. There would be no thought of moving forward.

Having six hands gave a whole new meaning to the concept of dexterity, though other peoples had four hands, occasionally six, rarely more. But combined with the Belshpaer's rotating mode of locomotion, they would be equally adept with any hand. Right- and left-handedness to them would be an abstract concept. They would have observed it in plants and crystals and in all the other animals of this world, but it would be an idea they themselves would never have to deal with in any personal sense.

These anatomical and psychological differences were subtly reflected in the structure of their buildings, beyond the obvious six-sidedness. Every room was somehow wrong. Rikard more than once found himself slowly turning in place, trying to orient himself. It made him dizzy.

And the age of the place was oppressive. Five to ten thousand years was not a long time in the overall history of any people, but these ruins were remarkably well preserved, producing a conflicting sense of recentness and age greater than the facts warranted. It made Rikard feel that he was somehow trespassing and at the same time wandering into antiquity beyond reckoning.

Dobryn seemed unaffected by thoughts of that kind, but he was tiring. Rikard left him on a comfortable rock in front of one building while he hurriedly searched through it.

Most of the places they'd looked at had been rejected because of exposure, difficulty of access, presence of animals, or some such. But they had to find a place soon, before Dobryn's strength gave out, even if they had to relax their standards a bit to do it. Rikard would not be able to set out for the Tower this afternoon in any event.

At last he found a place that suited him. Double doors which were still intact opened onto a great foyer. Beyond that were several smaller rooms. There were no signs of animals or Belshpaer. There was a stair going up into the interior darkness, but the dust on the steps was undisturbed.

One of the small rooms off the foyer had windows that looked out onto the plaza. They were no longer glazed, but they could be closed from the inside by ornamental shutters. The room itself was all but bare. The only thing in it was the crumbling remains of what might have been a desk.

Rikard went back to where he'd left Dobryn and found him dozing in the afternoon sun.

"I've got your hideout," he said.

"Good. I could use something more comfortable to lie on."

They drove the jeep in through the double doors and parked it in one corner of the great foyer. Then Rikard carried the shelter into the room he'd chosen. Dobryn wouldn't have to turn it on, except for the cots.

They cleared the desk away from the middle of the room and set up their camp. Then, while Dobryn fixed supper, Rikard went back out to cover over their tracks as much as possible. If someone did come by this way, he didn't want them to know Dobryn was here.

Dusk fell. They ate, and Dobryn told Rikard as much as he could about the city and the Tower. They burned no lights, just to be safe, and tried to sleep as soon as it was too dark to see. Dobryn dropped off right away, but Rikard lay awake for a long time. Excitement made a hard knot in his stomach.

He wasn't sure he could even get to the Tower. Once there, would he find his father's bones, or would wild animals have carried them away? He didn't dare hope that his father, by some miracle, might still be alive. And as for the treasure . . .

He'd take whatever he could find, of course, but that somehow seemed less important now.

The Belshpaer civilization had been great once. No one knew what had caused their fall. Some still lived in the city, doing Rikard had no idea what. Perhaps, he thought, they had found his father and rescued him.

His brain spun, and anxiety clutched at him, but at last he slept.

## 2.

Rikard set out the next morning, carrying food for ten days in a pack. Dobryn wished him luck, assured him he would be all right, and closed the double doors after him.

Rikard crossed the plaza to the avenue that led to the Tower of Fives and climbed over the rubble that closed it off. The street beyond was litter strewn. After a couple of blocks, the ruination of the city became worse. At one point a huge slab that had fallen from a wall blocked the street completely. He had to detour several blocks, and was uneasy until he came back within sight of the Tower.

There were animals in the city, rummaging through the fallen plastic. Plants had taken root where the ruination was worst. There were frequent parks, which were now densely overgrown and well populated with insects, birds, and smaller animals.

Once he saw a tall, stiff-legged creature that stood on a crumbling wall and stared down at him. Apparently it decided he was too big to eat, for after a moment it bounded away.

Once he passed a doorway that was softly translucent instead of dead and opaque. He glanced in cautiously. There was no dust on the floor of the corridor beyond. He passed on quickly.

He ate lunch on a flat slab that had fallen from an otherwise intact building. Ahead of him the Tower of Fives rose into the blue sky, flanked by several other tall buildings. As he ate, a sense of futility came over him.

Eleven years was a long time. Most likely he would find nothing at all, no father, no grave, no bones, no treasure. Even if he came to the very spot where Sed Blakely had abandoned his father, he wouldn't know it.

He almost gave up and turned back.

But if he did that, there would be no certainty in anything. Even if he found nothing at the Tower of Fives, he would at least have tried everything in his power.

He went on.

The way got easier for a while. He was gratified to see the Tower looming closer and closer. By midafternoon the avenue became rubble filled again, and he had to take another detour. The routes back to the original avenue were completely blocked, but he caught sight of the Tower from another direction and went on from there.

When dusk fell, he found a sheltered spot on the second floor of a badly fractured building and made up the best bed he could. He hadn't been able to bring a cot with him. In spite of the hardness of the floor on which he lay, he fell asleep quickly.

He dreamed he had found his father, and they were greeting

each other tearfully, when the sense of a presence nearby broke through his sleep and he awoke.

The room was softly illuminated, not by sun or moonlight, but by something one of the three Belshpaer in the room was holding.

They stood quietly, keeping their distance, watching him. He shoved himself to a sitting position, groping for the gun at his hip. The Belshpaer did not move. They wore no visible weapons.

"What do you want?" Rikard asked, his voice hoarse with sleep and anxiety.

"You are he, then," the middle Belshpaer answered.

"Who were you expecting?" Rikard got to his feet. The Belshpaer stood their ground.

"Harm is not with us," the Belshpaer said. "Come you us we by here a guide to warn at."

"What the hell? Look, I'm sorry if I'm trespassing. I'm just passing through. I'll leave if you like."

"No. Sleep is fine. Our forgiveness, we know it clean and can't talk."

"You can say that again."

"Are you he."

"I'm sorry, I don't understand."

"Rikard Braeth."

"Y-Yes, I'm Rikard Braeth. Your friends in the forest spoke my language much better."

"Smaller word parts. It our end can't break. No. Speak smaller. No training ours then they have."

"Speak smaller? Okay. Short sentences."

"Yes. Short speaking. He you Braeth."

"Yes. I am Rikard Braeth." He slapped his chest with the universal gesture of self-identification.

"Good. Save our quest desire. Help becomes us."

Rikard sighed. He didn't know how these people had learned his language. That was surprising enough, but that they had learned it so badly was almost unbelievable. The Belshpaer he had talked to in the forest must have been some kind of prodigy.

"Help?" he asked.

"Yes," the Belshpaer answered.

"Who?"

"You. Us. Both. All."

"Okay, help you. How?"

"Other worlds."

"I don't understand."

"Importance perative not yet. You first."

"Okay. Help me. How?"

"Tathas guarding."

"The fungus. Yes, I know about that."

"Enter easy. Difficulty come exit out."

"Yes. I know."

One of the other Belshpaer interrupted in its own language. Then the spokesman tried again.

"Come alive and save us," it said. "Must return, no other hope. Finish questing come save us. Tathas gray stone bend all over."

"Let me try," Rikard said. "You want me, after I find my father, to save you?"

"Father questing yes. Come again to assistance remembered. But. Tathas bending all prevention never come."

"Okay, the tathas will be dangerous. I know that."

"Yes. They bundle keep living alone. Mind destroyed and will. Come back must gray stone between."

"Sorry, I missed that. Try again."

"Fire burns. Follow the line. Our times are numbered but. Tathas remembers all gray stones. Return only between. Mark no sky. Exit come brief for two legs."

"I still don't follow—"

"Not beside, anext them, before circles between gray stones."

"Okay." He still didn't understand. "Then what?"

"Return among fevers. No exit. My partners recompense only stars."

"And when I come back?"

"Remember Belshpaer far going when. When help, come again."

"Look, I really don't understand. Do you know where I'm going?"

The three Belshpaer conferred again. Their attempts to communicate had seemed to improve the last time, Rikard hoped they would again.

"I will try," the Belshpaer on his left said, and held up a

hand, a rosette of six multijointed fingers around a central palm. It touched one finger with another hand.

"Rikard Braeth," it said, gesturing at Rikard. It touched another finger. "Parent Braeth." It touched a third finger. "Tathas bundles guard passage." It touched a fourth. "Enter easy exit by two gray stones only with stars mind breaker." A fifth finger. "Talk to us to come to far worlds." The last finger. "Fair trade."

It was making more sense, though it made Rikard's mind hurt to pick the meaning out of their sentences. He held up his own hand and counted off the points.

"I am Rikard Braeth," he said. "I'm looking for my father. The tathas fungus is a danger. It's easy to go in but hard to come out. You want to communicate with people on other worlds. You help me and I help you in fair exchange."

"Yes. Most. Not all. Exit tathas not complete. By two gray stones with only stars. Must be beside next not but before— idea of two sides not three sides."

So that was the problem. The idea they were trying to convey had to do with the fact that they had no working concept that translated from their trilaterality to his bilaterality. He closed his eyes in confusion. His thoughts were becoming as unclear as their words.

"Try again," the Belshpaer said. "Exit mind trap in direction with no sides. See gray stones. Between-ness. Come before them, not with anext. Crossing shorter than passing. Mind stars mind guide between gray stones."

"It's not working," Rikard said. "I'll have to see what you're talking about. Can you take me there?"

"No. Three sides walk other ways. Two sides not after blinding. No contact."

"You can't guide me. Okay, but you know where I'm going?"

"Yes. Parent place. Far deeply."

"Is he alive?"

"I don't know."

One clear sentence, and it was no help at all.

"Okay," Rikard said. "I don't understand your warning, but I won't forget it. I'll try to figure it out when the time comes. Is that all right?"

"Must be. Other not compatible. Fair next trade."

"Yes. If I get back, I'll try to help you. But you'll have to find a better way to communicate."

"Language lost but others now found."

"The one who spoke to me in the forest, can he talk to me again?"

"Earlier questing. That one besides as well also. Far southward but becoming daily."

"If you could just talk more clearly!"

"Our forgiveness become. When ever back, find comer speaking."

"When I come back, you'll have a better speaker?"

"Exactly. Care of tathas. Sleep night." They fell silent, then rotated quietly out of the room.

# 3.

Next morning after breakfast, Rikard followed the tracks of the Belshpaer through the dust to a closed door in the cellar of the building. It was a dead door, showing none of the translucency he associated with the living Belshpaer. It would not open.

He went back to the street. The Tower was very near now. He thought he could reach it by midafternoon.

The way was blocked by a whole building that had fallen into the street. Its foundations were exposed, and rather than backtracking two or three blocks to go around, he went down into the exposed cellars to see if he could find a passage through them.

He clambered down a sloping wall to the floor of the cellar and went two steps when the ramp he'd just descended collapsed into a lower level. The remaining walls were smooth and straight, affording no hand or footholds of any kind.

Since he couldn't go back now if he wanted to, he went on. He clambered over broken slabs of plastic, which he thought he might be able to build into a stair back to the street if he found no other way. The buildings on the other side of him still stood, though the outer walls had gone. He could see into the hexagonal rooms thus revealed.

He came to a stairway leading down to a lower level. It was clear of rubble. The way above was badly choked, so he went down. If this turned into a dead end, he'd have to retrace his steps, build the stair, and take the long detour he'd hoped to avoid. That would cost him half a day.

At the bottom of the stair was a passage that led in the direction he wanted to go. Doors opened off both sides, all tightly shut. He lit his torch and went on.

At the end of the corridor, he came to a series of rooms connected by open archways. He made a guess as to the best direction and tried every arch he came to, looking for a way up.

Something was following him. He flashed his light back the way he had come, but saw nothing. But he could hear a soft slithering, not exactly like tiny feet, more like a snake.

He went on, and the sound came again, not like one snake but a hundred. The noise was too soft to be that of scales on the hard plastic floor. It was more like insects flying. Still, he saw nothing when he looked back. He walked a little faster.

He entered a large room where machines lay in ruins. The walls and floor were deeply etched, as if by acid. He flashed his light over the uneven surface. It reflected darkly metallic and iridescent.

It was the mark of the tathas. It was the fungus that had corroded the walls. He checked himself for the first signs of tathas intoxication. Yes, his light did seem a little too bright. The closeness of the cellar did seem a little too comforting. The effects weren't strong, but they were definitely there. The tathas was alive down here, but it hadn't been for long or the psychedelic effects would have been stronger. They were noticeable only if he thought about it.

That meant that this couldn't be the particular tathas the Belshpaer had warned him about. They had had no way of knowing he would be taking this route, and he was still a long way from the Tower of Fives. But if the effects became stronger, he'd have to turn back, even if there was an exit down here somewhere. He didn't want to run the risk of

succumbing to the as yet subtle desire to just sit down and
wait.

The slithery sounds came from behind him, very close
now. He turned his light on the source of the noise. There
was a bundle of coarse fibers sliding wormily across the floor.
It stopped when the light hit it, pale and gray, a tangle of
thick hairs that twisted slowly and waved branching ends at
him. Its volume was about the same as that of a man, though
its bulk would be much less.

Rikard felt a thrill run up his spine as the tangled mass
rolled oozily toward him a few centimeters. From it came a
subtle wave of sensation, as if he were telepathically per-
ceiving through its senses, a confusion of all senses into one.
No, that wasn't right. Sight and sound and smell were one
sense, taste and touch was another. Both were altered and
modified.

The hair all over his body stood up. This mat of coarse
fibers was the tathas. He could feel it, a soft and subtle thing,
disturbed at his presence, unhappy with the light, desiring
peace and solitude, craving emptiness. This was the fungus,
a huge, naked mycelium. It was a sentient being, or once
had been. The Tathas—and now he capitalized its name.
Beyond this one were others.

He drew his gun and fired at the Tathas. The noise was
deafening. The bullet slashed through the weebly creature,
ricocheted off the floor, then the ceiling farther away, and
into the floor again farther yet. The Tathas writhed in pain,
but a moment later Rikard could sense that the pain was gone.

It had no vital organs. It was homogenous, one part as
good as another. He fired again, but it only made the Tathas
angry. The others beyond it hurried closer, and not at a snail's
pace.

Something touched his ankle. He jumped away and flashed
the light down. A fiber bundle at this feet twisted tendrils at
the place where he had been. His skin crawled.

One long tendril stretched out from somewhere and touched
his cheek. It was like fire. He jerked away, kicking at the
bundle near his feet. His clothing and armor protected him
from their touch, but their psychic presence was becoming
stronger. His feeling of revulsion countered it, but it wouldn't
for long.

He stomped on another Tathas, then flashed his light around the chamber. The way he had come was thick with the mobile fungus. He jumped away from two that had risen up almost as tall as he, one on either side. His fear of them did not completely block his involuntary perception of their thoughts. They wanted to eat him because he was violating their privacy and solitude.

He dashed for a doorway where the Tathas were less numerous and slammed the door behind him. They came through the cracks around the jamb.

His gun was useless. What he needed was a knife, or fire. But anything combustible had long since rotted away or been eaten by the Tathas. He backed from the opening door. Several Tathas were piled on top of each other, working the catch.

He fled without regard for where he went. He ran up one hall, down another, through rooms, down a flight of stairs. The walls here were clean, unsullied by the corrosive juices of the Tathas. He stopped to catch his breath. He was trapped. The only exit he knew was filled with the sentient fungi.

Rikard had heard of other races of a fungoid nature. That type of sentient life was among the rarest in the galaxy. These Tathas, no matter how evolved, were as advanced beyond a common toadstool as a man was beyond an amoeba. Their psychic residue was evidence that they had once been sentient, but they were not any more. They were the essence of insanity, the epitome of madness.

There were none in this room with him now, but they were out there. This was their habitat. If they wanted him, they could find him. Once their tendrils got to his bare flesh, they would kill him. It would be painful. He touched the mark on his cheek. He could feel a long, thin welt blistering and still burning.

He could hear them. They were no longer stealthy in their pursuit of him. He could outrun them, but not forever. Sooner or later, if he didn't find a way out, they would trap him in some dead end, and then it would be all over but the screaming. He retreated farther.

He came to a place where a wall of crystal had broken and shattered. His light glinted off long, bright shards.

He picked up a piece. Its edges were very sharp. He kicked among the fragments. There was one piece a meter or so long and five or six centimeters wide that he could use as a sword. But he'd cut his hands to ribbons if he tried to wield it.

The sounds of the Tathas were closer. He took the belt from his jacket and wrapped it around the end he wanted to use for a handle. The pseudo-leather was strong, designed to resist cutting edges. It withstood the sharpness of the crystal shard.

The door of the room creaked. The Tathas flowed through in a wave. Rikard slashed, trying not to strike the floor with his brittle weapon. He cut the Tathas in two, and they recoiled.

He slashed again and again, cutting them up. Once his sword struck the floor, but it only sang; it didn't break. And the Tathas were afraid of him now, he could feel it. He kept on slashing, striding back the way he had come, leaving writhing fragments of fungus. The Tathas retreated.

The wounded Tathas did not die. In time they would regrow like amoebas, becoming two or more individuals as each fragment regenerated the missing parts. But for now they were out of the fight. Their pain, which Rikard could telepathically feel, prevented their continued participation. And their minds, as degenerate and degraded as they were, were a product of the whole body, not just a localized brain. As they were cut apart, their intellectual capacity was accordingly reduced.

He felt every blow he struck. His involuntary telepathic reception of their thoughts and feelings brought him their every sensation. Only his hatred, disgust, and fear kept him slashing.

That and the realization that this was what Sed Blakely had left his father to face. He wished now that he'd killed the old hermit, or better yet, could bring the lunatic here to throw to these monsters.

The effort was exhausting, and he was still surrounded by the violently wriggling fungoid beings, but at last he regained the chamber where he'd first been attacked. He could go back now to the collapsed cellar.

Instead, he went on in the way he had been going before the Tathas had come upon him, fighting the fungi every step of the way. He could not have much farther to go. The Belshaer had not built these cellars as a maze, but to serve some useful purpose. However much they differed from humans, they were virtual brothers compared to the Tathas.

In that light, their behavior made perfect sense. However strange they might seem at first, they could be understood, given time. Between humans and Tathas, however, there could never be common ground.

There had to be a way up and out, and soon. Because, in a larger sense, the Belshpaer *were* like humans. They would not have built these cellars without handy and easy means of access. That Rikard had not found a way out so far was merely accident, and the result of ruination.

He caught his breath, then continued forward. He fought with renewed vigor and determination. The Tathas gave way, fell back, retreated, broke, fled, and were gone. Ahead of him was an empty corridor. At its end the light of his torch revealed a stairway going up.

# 4.

The sunlight, when he came to it, looked so good that for a moment he had to blink his eyes to keep the tears from blinding him. He was in another ruined cellar, but only a meter or so below street level. There were piles of rubble handy for climbing. He wiped his eyes and clambered up onto the road.

He decided to keep the crystal sword. He was sure to meet more Tathas later, and it would come in handy. The juices of the Tathas had stained the transparent blade blue-black. It shimmered darkly iridescent in the sunlight, a fantastic and poisoned sword. Feeling like some ancient warrior, Rikard strapped it carefully to his waist with his belt.

Now he had to find out where he was relative to the Tower of Fives. He didn't know how far he had wandered from his course while underground. It had seemed a long way, but anxiety, fear, and excitement had magnified things. He would have to scout until he saw the Tower again, and not make any assumptions as to his position or the distance from his starting point.

As it turned out, the assumptions he did have were all wrong. He had gone a very long way underground. The Tower was no longer ahead of him, but 120 degrees to his right.

He was able to keep it in sight the rest of the day. Toward dusk, climbing over one last pile of rubble, he came to a plaza across from which stood the Tower itself.

It was a tall building, as tall as anything elsewhere in the Federation. Its base occupied several hectares. Its walls were smooth and straight and unbroken for at least fifty meters. He could see no doors.

There had to be access. It would be around one of the other sides. Rikard chose left, and started to circle.

The sun was sinking. The side of the Tower he had first approached was the only one clear of rubble. His progress was further slowed by the deepening shadows on the piles of debris. He could wait until morning, but he was determined to find a way in tonight. In spite of his fatigue, he could not rest until he had entered the Tower.

Had he gone right instead of left, he would have come to the door sooner, but he did find it. Rubble had fallen in front of it, but the expedition of four years ago had moved much of it away. He stepped down into the cleared pavement and approached the door. It was latched but not locked. He swung the portal open and stepped in.

The foyer was dark but not empty. He switched on his torch. Piles of broken furnishings lay on the floor. Three statues of Belshpaer in various forms of dress stood on low pedestals. Thinking of the live Belshpaer he'd seen, Rikard thought these statues were commemorative rather than representative.

There was plenty of evidence of the expedition's presence. Footprints in the dust went everywhere. If his father had left tracks eleven years ago, they had been obliterated.

He went from chamber to chamber, examining the floor for tracks that might have been laid down earlier than four years ago. Most of the prints were thinly overlaid with new dust. Older ones should be distinguishable.

Near the center of the building, as far as he could judge, was a bank of five great elevators, which no longer functioned. Maybe it was this which had given the Tower its name.

There were also at least three sets of stairways, leading upward only. One of these was a utilitarian service stair near the central elevator bank. The treads were strange, to accommodate the Belshpaer's rotating mode of locomotion. Another was formal and ornamental, rising from what might have been a ballroom, looking like other such stairways Rikard had seen. The third was a narrow back stair off in a corner of the building.

The marks in the dust indicated that the archaeological expedition had concentrated its efforts on the upper floors. But Sed Blakely had implied that he had abandoned Rikard's father to the Tathas, and they dwelt belowground. The Belshpaer, too, had said that the "parent place" was "far deeply." Rikard looked for a way down. He entered a large chamber, illuminated by the golden light of a dragon.

He froze for a moment, then drew his gun. A thrill of fear ran through him. But it wasn't the same fear he'd felt in the presence of the Tathas. In fact, the sensation wasn't really fear at all. It was simply his perception of a huge, static field. It was the dragon itself he was feeling. The physiological sensations were so similar to fear that that was the way he—and everybody else—interpreted it.

The dragon was dangerous nonetheless. If he touched it, or if it touched him, Rikard would be killed. A static field that large couldn't help but be fatal if grounded through a human body. It would be like being struck by lightning.

He stood motionless, gazing at the dragon, feeling that he'd achieved some kind of new understanding of what dragons were. It was a living thunderbolt. It still gave him the impression of being serpentine, but it wasn't really that. It was a spherical field of energy, yellow-orange, with no hard edges. It was immaterial, and therefore transparent. It was highly energetic, and therefore it glowed.

The points of light tumbling over each other in its middle were its version of bones, its real body. The rest was merely an envelope which it could extend as pseudopods in any direction. The shimmering above and behind it, which were seen as wings, was a diffraction and reflection of the light emitted by the creature itself.

Only the eyes were material. This creature would not normally perceive the world in any fashion analogous to the senses of humans. Even the Tathas had physical senses.

The dragons, however, would be aware of a different order of energies. Its eyes had been created solely to enable it to deal with the sense of sight, which perhaps was not natural to it. In their own world, of energies rather than objects, the dragons would have no need for sight. But this was not their own world. However long they had been here, the dragons were only visitors.

The eyes looking at Rikard hinted at the possibility of intelligence and sentience. Then the dragon moved.

It came toward Rikard slowly. Maybe the presence of a dragon didn't automatically strike fear, though that might be the usual interpretation of the sensation of its static field, but that did not mean Rikard could afford to be casual in the dragon's presence. One touch would kill him regardless of the dragon's intelligence or intentions.

He backed away out of the hall. He tried to retrace his steps toward the front of the building, but the dragon moved quickly between him and the door. It forced him to take another way. It was herding him, guiding him. Rikard wondered if it knew its touch meant death to him, or cared.

He went, perforce, where the dragon seemed to want him to go. He went down a corridor, through several large rooms, across a large hall, and up another corridor. At last he came to the head of a stair going down.

He started to descend, then noticed the footprints in the dust. He forgot about the dragon and bent to shine his light on the marks.

They were older prints than those elsewhere in the building. They had twice as much dust in them as those made by the archaeological expedition of four years ago. There were three sets, two leading down, one coming back up.

He remembered the dragon then, and looked up to see how near it was. The dragon was gone.

# 5.

He had been asking the wrong people all along. The dragon had guided him here and then left him. It had known where Rikard wanted to go. A new kind of fear touched him. How had the dragon known?

The tracks in the dust on the stairs were very plain. The story they told was every bit as clear. He followed the prints down to a cellar, through a vaulted room, to another stair, then down again, and yet again, deep into the earth under the Tower of Fives.

Seven levels down were all Belshpaer cellars, but the footprints went on into an irregularly circular tunnel that sloped still deeper. The walls were dark and metallically iridescent.

He stepped into the tunnel. He felt, very strongly, the pain of the light, the need to be alone, the desire to wait forever. He hurried. He got a mental image of strange monoliths off on the sides, but there were only the walls of the tunnel, which frequently branched. He felt a dark sky overhead, but it was only the roof of the tunnel. The footprints went on.

Suddenly the walls of the passage became white. The oppressive sensations ceased. He was in a lower Belshpaer chamber, maybe part of the Tower, maybe part of an adjacent building. He no longer felt an aching loneliness. Instead he felt a subtle sense of competency and calmness. It was oddly reminiscent of what he had felt in the presence of the dragon— once he had realized that the "fear" was really only static electricity.

These cellars, though of Belshpaer construction, were much older than anything Rikard had seen before. The walls were bleached bone, coarse and porous and stark white. These were ruins below ruins, a lost place buried by the lost civilization that had risen above it.

All three sets of footprints went on. The feeling of competence and calm slowly faded as he followed them. He went down a level, wondering how his father had found this place. Rikard had no doubt that it was his father's tracks he was following.

He knelt to examine the tracks more closely. The two men had worn different kinds of boots, and their marks were easily distinguishable. One kind of track went both down and back. The other kind went down only. The man who'd come back had been in the lead going down. His prints were overlaid by the prints that did not return.

And then Rikard saw that there were other sets of tracks under these, obscured by them and the dust of at least a century. He couldn't tell how many sets there were, but some were going in each direction.

Blakely had returned, and Blakely had led Rikard's father here. He must have heard a story from some old prospector. With Arin Braeth's information and encouragement, he had remembered that story and led him here. Someone else, long since dead, had stumbled on this place by accident and had lived to tell about it, though he might not have understood the true significance of his find, nor have been believed when he told his tale.

Rikard stood up, and a wave of exhaustion swept over him. It was long past nightfall. His watch read one. But he could not stop now. He followed the tracks on down to yet a lower level, across a room, and up a short hall. He came to a huge chamber with a high ceiling. It was filled with dead machines which cast shadows so thick he couldn't see the far wall.

The Tathas effect was strong again. The dark metallic marks of their presence lay on everything. Even the footprints had been wiped away. But Rikard could see that Blakely's footprints did not cross that chamber. He had waited here before turning back.

Rikard took off his belt and wrapped it around the handle of his crystal sword. Then he stepped into the machine room. He saw, superimposed over the machines and hulks, a gray and plastic plane, plastic monoliths standing at odd angles, strangely apertured heaps of gray stone, wire trees made of plates and bars, artifacts of indecipherable form and function.

There were no Tathas here now, which suited Rikard just fine. He wanted to be alone. He gripped his crystal sword and shone the light ahead of him. It hurt his eyes and skin and smelled acrid. He worked his way across the chamber, past the illusory landscape of gray emptiness.

He dreaded contact with anything—Tathas, human, dragon. The light struck a far wall. He wanted to slow down and wait, not hurry so. He forced his feet to move.

A Tathas stood at his left, as tall as he, its gray-white fibers a loosely tangled basket weave in imitation of a man. Rikard pointed his sword at it and hurried to the wall. The Tathas did not follow; the sensations eased a trifle.

There was a door in the wall just to his left. He went to it and stepped through. The superimposed Tathas world faded away.

He flashed his light back across the machine room. From here he could see the door at the other side. A person could toss something across the room from here to the door at the other side if they tried.

He turned away from the Tathas place. He was in a short corridor. The floor was free of dust, except at the edges. Someone walked here almost every day.

His excitement nearly choked him. He went up the short hall to the door at its end and opened it into light.

Someone was living here. There was furniture, knocked together out of scrap and ruin. Lights burned in the ceiling, from what power source Rikard could not guess. A door on the other side of the room opened, and a man stepped out.

# PART NINE

## 1.

The old man froze when he saw Rikard. He was old more with hardship than with time. His hair was white, his beard full and gray. But Rikard knew his father's face, even after thirteen and a half years.

Rikard tried to speak, but his voice wouldn't work. There were too many conflicting emotions—anger, relief, exhaustion, hatred, joy. His vision blurred. His father was staring at him, afraid, surprised, wondering.

"Rikky?" the old man asked. His voice was choked. "Is that really you?"

"It's me Father," Rikard said.

Then suddenly they were in each other's arms, hugging, crying, slapping, shouting, laughing, kissing, all tangled up in each other.

"Oh, my God, Rikard," his father said, holding him at arm's length. "It is you. It really is."

"Father, are you all right?"

"Well, under the circumstances, yes."

They laughed and cried and hugged some more. When the first shock wore off at last, they sat and told each other how they had each gotten here.

Arin Braeth was deeply saddened, but not surprised at the news of his wife's death.

"I hadn't intended to be gone so long," he said. "It took me longer than I had planned to track this place down, but I could have come home in a month if it hadn't been for Blakely. He was going to pull me out with a rope, but he left instead."

"He's still alive," Rikard said, "and I know where he is. I'll take you to him when we get back."

"Yes, I'd like that. Who's your partner?"

"A guy named Stefan Dobryn. He got hurt on our way here. I left him camped in the ruins."

"There's nobody else with you?"

"Not here, no."

"Then you're trapped too."

"Maybe not. Some friendly Belshpaer tried to give me advice on how to get out of here. I'll have to try it once or twice before I figure out what they meant."

"But the Belshpaer, aren't they extinct?"

"Apparently not. I've met several. They know who I am, and who you are too, for that matter. They seem to think I'm some kind of savior. I don't know what they've been doing with themselves for all these years, but I think they finally want to come out of hiding.

"But that will have to wait until *we* get out of here, and I'm not going to try for our escape right now. I'm exhausted. And we have too many things to talk about."

That talking, covering only the high points, took until six in the morning. His father told of how he had deduced the existence and presence of the dialithite and had traced it here, but the last eleven years had been spent in simple survival.

"And the dialithite made that possible," Arin explained. "You've seen it? You've touched it? Then you know that feeling of peace and power it gives. That, and only that, kept me from losing my mind, kept me from giving up."

"But how did you live? I mean, power and food?"

"The Taarshome. No, I'm not crazy. There are none here now, but later there will be. Their time sense is different from ours. I'll show you one. And if you tell me then that I'm crazy, I'll believe you. But withhold your judgment until I have a chance to prove myself."

Rikard's story took most of the time. Arin wanted to know everything, how his son had gotten on after his departure, how Sigra had died, Rikard's education, his trip as an exploiter, how he'd traced Arin's movements here, and all that had happened since his arrival on Kohltri.

"You know I always wanted you to be a Gesta," Arin said, "and by God, you sure have the makings of one."

"I don't know how long it will last."

"What does it matter? Be what you want. Then you *will* be a Gesta, in the truest sense of the word, though there are few who will understand that. I've had a lot of time for meditation, Rikky, and rightly or wrongly, I see things a bit differently these days."

At last Rikard could stay awake no longer. Arin made up a bed for him in another room, and Rikard fell asleep at once. He dreamed he was in his backyard on Pelgrane.

He awoke with his father's hand on his shoulder.

"A Taarshome is here," Arin said. "Come talk with him."

Rikard got up. He'd slept about five hours; it was enough. He followed his father into the main room and then up a side corridor to another, larger chamber. In the middle was a great golden glowing dragon.

"This," Arin Braeth said, "is a Taarshome."

# 2.

The dragon floated quietly in the middle of the chamber.

"Don't touch it," Arin said, "or you'll fry."

"I know that much. I've seen them up on the surface. One of them guided me to the stairs down to here. But how do you know it's a Taarshome? They were supposed to have disappeared from the galaxy millions of years ago or more."

"They have come back. You can learn to talk with them if you have patience and time. I have had plenty of both. I could probably teach you a lot faster than it took me to learn."

"And they provide you with food and power?"

"Yes. I can't explain how. All I know is they found me down here about ten days after Blakely ran off. He'd taken all the food, and I was in pretty poor shape.

"And I was lucky. Taarshome don't see the way we do, even with eyes, and have trouble knowing just exactly where we are. Apparently, our energy envelope is very weak and small. This one here has learned to perceive our physical shape, but it's as hard for him to see us as it is for us to see him."

"Him?"

"Well, I call him that. Actually, they're neuter. Parthenogenesis when it's necessary. Anyway, the dragon didn't touch me. Which was lucky. But it perceived that I was dying and figured out a way to get food to me. It's quite nourishing, but I'm sure glad you brought some human food with you."

"Couldn't they help you get out?"

"Not the way they come in. They follow the electrical wiring down from aboveground."

"Eyes and all?"

"The eyes have to be remade each time."

"How about leading you across the Tathas chamber?"

"They could only do that by touch, and that would kill me instantly. They don't handle physical matter much. They can, but it's an advanced technology for them. Something like pulling on a rope requires as much ingenuity and effort for them as constructing a plasma bottle would for us. And there are few of them here who have any interest in me personally, though they are very interested in humankind— and in the Belshpaer too, for that matter."

"So you were stuck."

"As you see. But life hasn't been a total bore. Not quite. Learning to talk with the Taarshome took much of my time after I recovered my strength. I lived in darkness for, I guess, two years before I got across to them that I wanted light. Food they understand. They have a direct analog. But light to see by is totally alien to them. They always see, in some sense or other, regardless of the surrounding medium or energy field.

"But I learned something else. I came here for the dialithite, and I found it. Lots of it. What Blakely didn't know was that the bag full I threw out to him was only the first installment. He didn't wait around long enough for the other twenty-some bags."

"My God!"

"And I stopped at that only because I'd run out of bags. There's enough dialithite here to bring the value down to around a hundred thousand a gram, if it were all taken out. I wouldn't do that, of course.

"And the thing is, I know how dialithite is made. If you can bring a mass into contact with one of those central glowing spots in the middle of a Taarshome's body, you produce a bit of dialithite, provided the material is a nonconductor, relatively dense, and has the energy to penetrate their body."

"Does it hurt them?"

"God, no, they love it. Why?"

Rikard told them about shooting a dragon in the clearing in the woods, and the sparkling dust that had fallen from it.

"Probably tickled it silly," Arin said. "Come on, I'll show you the dialithite mine." He crossed the room to a far door. The dragon followed.

Beyond the door was a hallway, broken by some shifting of the earth. Where the hallway came to an abrupt end, a rough cavern opened out. It was not very large, only forty meters wide and thirty meters across and about three meters deep.

Across the bottom of the cavern was a fissure, glowing with its own light. On the rough floor, on either side of the fissure, were piles of dialithite stones, heaps and mounds, glinting and shimmering.

"All the treasure anyone could want," Arin said softly. There was no trace of avarice in his voice.

The dragon came out of the hall behind them. It carefully avoided them, flew out into the cavern, and hovered a moment over the fissure in the floor. Then it plunged down into the volcanic recess. A moment later it came up again, brilliant, glowing, huge. Several sparkling dialithite crystals fell from it to the cavern floor. They dislodged others, which fell into the crevice and were gone.

"They've been doing this ever since they came back two thousand years ago or so. The stones there represent only a fraction of what they've produced, inadvertently, over that period of time."

Rikard gazed at the treasure and was overwhelmed. He had to take his mind off it. "You say I could learn to speak with them?"

"The Taarshome? Yes. They've learned the trick now, so it shouldn't take too long to teach you the method."

They went back to the chamber where they'd first met the Taarshome. It followed them. Arin stood in the middle of the room, facing the Taarshome. He seemed to flicker. Then he turned to Rikard and held out a hand.

"Come here," he said, "and I'll teach you."

Rikard stood beside his father, took his hand, and turned to face the Taarshome. Its tremendous static charge made all his hair stand on end.

He felt a sense of competence and calmness.

"It's this spot," Arin said, as if reading his mind. "You passed another such spot to get here. It was white and porous, like bleached bone. Such places are rare in the upper world. They are where the original power grid of the Taarshome still functions, although weakly, and it's that that lets you talk to them."

Rikard stood, waiting for something to happen. He felt a lightness and a brightness, an effervescence, rainbowed and prismatic. The creature before him became more solid seeming, more real.

Rikard knew that what he was seeing was only illusion. The Taarshome took on the form of a classical dragon, with a strong body, clawed legs, serpentine tail and neck, great head filled with teeth, and webbed wings.

As he watched, the ancient power-web in which he was enmeshed grew stronger, fed by the energy in the Taarshome. The brilliance and color and effervescence of his surroundings became stronger. The calmness became peace and the competence became power.

He floated in the heart of an ever-expanding crystal, the heart of a dialithite crystal, with planes and facets passing through each other, level upon level, in more than three dimensions, more than four.

The dragon shape before him stood on its hind legs. Without any further change in form, it was no longer an animal but an angel. It was bright, white, iridescent, metallic, huge. It filled the crystal in which Rikard floated, a crystal which expanded beyond the intangible surface of the planet to spark on stars and suns. It provided the fabric and the substance of the universe itself.

˜We were the first,˜ the Taarshome said. ˜We have been away, visiting distant relations. Now we have returned, and find this one park the only remnant of what once was ours.˜

They had first come to Kohltri a very long time ago, when the planet had just formed and was still hot. Their first home and birthplace was somewhere else, which even the intelligence and wisdom of the Taarshome could not make clear to Rikard's human mind.

They had always been semicorporeal beings. Theirs was the first species in the galaxy to achieve sentience. In those early years they had not yet transcended the bounds of mortality. Their history before coming to Kohltri was longer than their history since. They were a space-faring, technological species, alone at that time in the all-but-empty galaxy. There had been little life of any kind then, and only a handful of sentients.

They came, and they found this world good, by their standards at that time. They grew and prospered and perfected certain technologies. They built an empire, which they shared with the six or seven other sentient species, only one of which, the Keltharin, were corporeal. They filled the galaxy.

They changed Kohltri to fit their needs. As they reached the peak of their earlier mortal existence, life began on Kohltri. It was no doing of the Taarshome. It was the perfectly natural course of events.

But the presence of the Taarshome had an influence on some of that life after it had formed. One species in particular developed intelligence, though biologically it was surpassed by other species. That was the Tathas.

The Taarshome transcended their mortality, just as the Tathas, slower to evolve than purely animal life, finally developed a nuclear technology. The Taarshome left. The Tathas inherited the world.

The Taarshome knew little of what had transpired on Kohltri after their departure. What they did know was only by inference from what they had found on their return a bare two thousand years ago.

The story ended. Rikard blinked. He still held his father's hand. The Taarshome floated in front of him, glowing and golden. He felt as though hours had passed. He looked at his watch. The long conversation had taken less than a minute.

"They gave you the full treatment," Arin said.

Rikard turned and saw that there were two other Taarshome in the room with them.

"Well," Arin asked, "am I crazy or not?"

"Not unless I am too."

˜You understand us now,˜ one of the Taarshome said in his mind. ˜And now we see you more clearly than before.˜

"I am overwhelmed," Rikard told it.

˜Not many mortals would allow us to talk to them,˜ the Taarshome went on. ˜You have the ability to hear, the willingness to listen. We would ask a favor of you.˜

"What is it? I'll be glad to do whatever I can. If we can ever get out of here."

˜The Belshpaer, at our request, have already given you the key to escape the Tathas. We could not give it to your parent without the Belshpaer as intermediary. You need but try it to learn its working.

˜And they, too, the Belshpaer, would ask a favor of you. We know this because we have spoken with them, and their desire is similar to ours.˜

"I'll do what I can," Rikard repeated.

˜What we desire, both the Belshpaer and ourselves, is to establish meaningful contact with the peoples of the galaxy. The Belshpaer need to be brought from their lairs, where they have hidden for the last *vor-splatz-verng-relpank-lothik*—your time sense is different from ours. We can't express ourselves. But their needs are simple. Select representatives to your governments will accomplish all they desire.

˜We, too, would become a part of your greater culture. Believe that we do not look down on you, though we transcended your life level long ago, even in our terms. This is because we once were like you in certain ways, and we can see you, in a certain sense, more clearly than you can see yourselves. All you lack is time. Given that, there is no downness to look at all.

˜But to introduce us into your society will be a much greater task. We ask. Will you help us?˜

"I'm willing, yes, but I have no knowledge of such things. I don't know if my help would do you any good."

˜You have the ability—this we know—even more than your father has. Are you willing?˜

"Yes, I am."

# 3.

They started packing right away. Arin didn't have much that he wanted to take with him, and Rikard only what he'd brought, but there were the dialithite crystals.

They spent an hour down in the crystal cavern in a constant state of near ecstasy, selecting only the largest and the best of the stones. They took over five thousand of them, which they planned to sell a few at a time over a period of many years.

When they were ready, they went to the short passage leading to the machine room—the Tathas chamber. Standing at its edge, they both could feel its influence, the desire for darkness and solitude.

"We go together," Arin said. "If anything happens to you, I won't want to live anyway."

"We'll make it," Rikard told him. He took a good grip on the crystal sword. Together, they stepped forward.

This time there was no overlay, no superimposition. The world of the Tathas completely replaced everything else.

It was singularly amorphous and asymmetric, and yet there were shapes within it, and zones. Everything was darkly metallic, with an iridescent sheen that, under the Tathas influence, was sinisterly comforting. In the Tathas world one could not help but view that world as the Tathas would. That was its greatest danger, that one forgot one's original being and became lost in the psyche of the Tathas.

"I think this is the way it used to be," Arin said. His voice was thin and metallic.

"They can't accept change," Rikard said.

"No. As a species, they are psychotic. I don't think they are even conscious any more, as we know that term."

"They couldn't always have been like this."

"They weren't, I don't think. I don't know, but I think something broke their spirit a long time ago."

241

They took another step forward. They stood on an empty plain, with a dark and starless sky overhead. There were dim auroras to the north and south, but for the most part the sky was black. The colors of the shifting auroras, though dim, were painfully clear. Another step.

They stood on a moorland. The ground was jumbled, with boulders scattered over it. Hollows held still, black water. There were scraggly bushes and strange fungus growths. But it was all surrealistic and plastic. None of it was natural. This was the way the Tathas had made their world. This was how, nearing the height of their culture, they had rebuilt the surface of their planet to provide them with the most comfortable life.

Or rather, this was their psychotic memory of it.

Rikard and Arin walked on. In a back corner of their minds they knew they were really in an abandoned Belshpaer machine room.

The place that they *seemed* to be in had its fascinations. Everything had been made the way it was in order to satisfy the Tathas' totally alien sense of aesthetics and utility. Everything was artificial, and looked it. The Tathas had no true sense of sight. The visual appearance of things would make little difference to them. To human eyes, however, the artificiality was obvious.

They passed a tree. It was no living thing but a construct of rods, wires, bolts, plates. It had a plastic, unrealistic, artistic style. A nearby bush had square leaves of foil; its branches were a network of rods. Its base was bolted to the ground.

It had style, a highly evolved technique, and showed a thoroughly developed aesthetic sense. But the horizon was frighteningly, impossibly near. Strangely carved monoliths stood here and there, proof of the total alienness of the minds that had created them.

Most unsettling of all were the strangely apertured heaps of small stones, reminiscent of tiny huts. They passed near one, taller than they, its structure defying gravity. Its openings were irregular and dark. Did something move within?

They hurried on.

Three Tathas stood in front of them, or seemed to stand,

aller than broad, tangled basket weaves of shapes parodying human structure. They were people.

Or they had been once. They retained intellect. They were aware of the world around them, both the true world and that of their memories. They remembered.

But there was no spark of self-consciousness. They had lost self-awareness. They were intelligent, unconscious, awake, insane, like biological computers misprogrammed. Their desires were only vegetable desires.

Without regret or compunction, Rikard struck at the three in front of him. The crystal blade sheared through their fibrous bodies. They fell, writhing, crawled away, and left them alone.

"How do we get out of here?" Arin cried. His voice was a chalk-squeak across the blackboard sky.

"Not beside, but before," Rikard said. There were Tathas just over the terribly close horizon. "Between the gray stones, and with the stars." They stepped forward. The whole scene shifted, as if they had gone a hundred meters instead of one.

"There are no stars," Arin said.

There were no stars. There were no gray stones. There was only between.

"We're trapped forever," Arin cried. The sound of something wet slapping came from a nearby heap of small stones. At the horizon to their left they could see a not-distant-enough gathering of fiber bundles.

Rikard looked at his father. The psychic overlay tried to make him see his father as a Tathas would "see" him: colorless, textured, a form more felt than seen. But Rikard still had eyes, and though the face in front of him withered, it was his father's face.

It was gray. He looked at his hands. They were gray. A sticky tendril groped out from the stone heap.

"The dialithite," he said. He groped in his father's pack for one of the stones and brought it out. It was gray, dull, dead, lifeless. But there was a flicker of light elsewhere round the landscape. He took another stone out of the pack and held one in each hand, out to the sides.

The Tathas world shimmered. He was between the gray stones. No, not beside; "anext" as the Belshpaer had said, but also before, in front. He didn't know what that meant yet.

"Put your hand on my shoulder," he told his father, "and follow me as closely as you can." Where were the stars?

The stones in his hands warmed. He could feel a subtle pulse of competency and calmness. The full effect of the stones could not be felt unless he looked at them. But then he wouldn't be between them. And besides, the stones here were gray and opaque. Where were the stars?

They were in his mind, "mind stars," in his own memory.

He fought to visualize the stars, to see them as he had seen them countless nights where city lights didn't wash them out. Bright white sparks in an onyx sky. The Tathas screamed soundlessly around him. He stumbled forward, with his father clutching his shoulders with both hands. The Tathas world crumbled like melting ice. They stepped out of the machine room into the corridor on the other side.

"Look out," Arin cried.

Rikard turned to see several Tathas grabbing at him. He dropped a stone, swung his glass shard, and sliced through them. He could feel their unselfconscious hatred of him. They feared him as much as he feared them. He shoved his father ahead of him up the corridor while he covered their rear, cutting at the fungus Tathas until they stopped coming.

His father was laughing.

"We made it," Arin said. "My God, Rikky, do you know how long I've *been* in there?"

"Eleven years."

"Eleven years. Alone with only the Taarshome for company. Nothing to do but stare across the Tathas chamber and survive. Nothing to think about but that there was no way out, and how much I wanted Sigra, and how I hoped you didn't hate me." His face twisted and suddenly he was sobbing, clinging to Rikard. Rikard held him and comforted him as best he could. After a while the fit passed. Arin straightened, wiping his face with his hands.

"I think I'm glad I came and found you," Rikard said.

"By God, I'm glad you did. I'm so glad to see you."

They hugged again and then started the long trek back to the surface.

Something dripped fire in the darkness ahead of them.

Before Rikard could bring his light up to see what it was, a bolt of flame came from the darkness. It enveloped his father, who leaped once and fell.

"No!" Rikard screamed. He raised his light, but the flames of his burning father were between him and the assassin. He threw the crystal sword at the still-dripping fire, then drew his own gun. The assassin shot again, but the weapon was defective; the gout of flame was small and fell short. Rikard fired blindly through the flames, heard retreating footsteps, then sat down on the floor beside his father, and waited for the fire to go out.

# PART TEN

## 1.

The last sparks died and went out, leaving only bones, ash, charred floor, and a pile of dialithite stones glittering in the reflected light of Rikard's torch.

It was all over. His father had gotten what he had sought. Rikard had found his father. Revenge, vindication, justification—it all came to nothing.

There was no sense picking the dragongems from his father's ashes. Rikard had three thousand or more in his own pack, nothing else to carry any more in, and after all, those stones were what his father had come here for.

There was no need to bury the remains. They were suitably entombed as they were, the pile of dragongems a fitting monument. If somebody came later and found the stones, so be it.

He felt nothing. It was as if he had never found his father at all. Somewhere in his mind he knew he was suffering from shock, but he couldn't be bothered to think of anything to do about it. He stood, retrieved his dropped torch, and started to find his way out of the cellars. He knew he would have to grieve sometime, but not now. First he had to get back to the city and find his father's killer.

The assassin's footprints were plain in the dust of the cellar floor. They followed his own prints down and went back the same way.

Who could have done it? he wondered, unnaturally calm. The only people who knew where he was, even approximately, were Darcy, Polski, Arshaud—and Dobryn. Rikard had seen no weapon among Dobryn's belongings that could have produced fire like that. Still . . .

Darcy had been too badly hurt and would have used her laser in any event. Murder wasn't like Polski, and he didn't have a motive. Arshaud had been—not exactly a friend of his father's, but had respected him. Dobryn, of the four, was the only one who knew exactly where the Tower of Fives was, how to get in, and how to find his way down. Greed was an excellent motive.

When Rikard finally left the Tower of Fives, it was mid-afternoon. The assassin had left no trail outdoors, of course. That didn't really matter. Rikard knew where he was going. He retraced his route of just the day before.

He stopped to sleep for a couple of hours before going down into the cellars where the Tathas had first ambushed him. Then he entered their lair boldly. Even though he no longer had his crystal sword, he did not fear these creatures, however evil and insane they might be. He held two dialithite crystals as he traversed the cellars, and had no trouble.

He arrived back at the plaza where he'd left Dobryn just as the sun was setting the next day. He didn't know for sure that Dobryn was the assassin, but he didn't dare take any chances. He drew his gun, to give him the time-compression advantage, and warily approached the doors of the hideout.

"I'm back," he called out. His voice sounded slowed and distorted by the time-compression effect. There was no response. He carefully crossed in front of the shuttered windows, watchful lest they open to allow Dobryn a shot at him. They didn't. He pushed one-half of the double door open and slipped into the foyer.

The jeep was where he had left it. If Dobryn had been the assassin, he would have taken it and gone back to the city—unless he had gotten lost in the Belshpaer ruins somewhere.

"Dobryn?" he called again. "It's me." There was still no answer. He crossed to the door of Dobryn's camp room and knocked loudly. There was only silence.

He stepped back from the door, then noticed a spot of char on the floor near his feet. There had been—he remembered now—similar spots on the floor of the cellars where the assassin had stood before shooting his father. Rikard moved to the wall beside the door, pushed it open, and peered in.

Bones and ashes were mingled with the melted plastic of the cot on which Dobryn had lain. Rikard went in cautiously, but there was no one else there. He went over to the charred remains.

He couldn't know for sure that it was Dobryn, but the skeleton was the right size, and one of the ribs bore a scar in the right place, where Zakroyan's bullet had grazed him. Rikard took a dragongem from his pack, placed it gently among the ashes. Then he left the room, closed the door, got in the jeep, and went to sleep.

He awoke before dawn. He drove out of the foyer and out of the ruins. He knew his way only approximately, and had no radio equipment to call for help.

The next morning he came to the steep, irregular slope where Zakroyan had overtaken him. He worked his way to the top and took the time to cast back and forth along the summit until he found the wreck of Zakroyan's car below him. Partly, that was to help him get his bearings, and partly he wanted to make sure Zakroyan was dead. He drove his jeep down to the wreck.

Nightly rains had washed away much of the lighter detritus around the demolished car, but he thought he could see marks of padded, clawed feet, like those of a caron. There was no sign of Zakroyan's body. That would make sense, if this was the hunting range of a pride of carons. He drove back up the slope and headed toward the city.


## 2.


He parked the jeep in the courtyard of his building and went to his room. He stashed the pack of dragongems under his bed, then called the hospital to find out how Darcy was doing. They informed him that she had been released the day after he left for the Tower of Fives.

He called over to her place, but the phone was disconnected. He had no idea how to get hold of Polski. He drove over to Darcy's building, only to find that her whole floor was uninhabited. The damage caused by Polski's blaster fire had not yet been repaired.

On a hunch he went to the place Darcy had found for him to hide out in. As he entered Mendel's sitting room, the man came out, shotgun in hand.

"Hey, Rik," Mendel said. "Darcy said you might be by. She's in your old room. Go on in."

"Thanks," Rikard said. He followed the hallway to his door and knocked. After a moment, Darcy answered it.

"Rik, you're back," she said, smiling and surprised. "Come on in. Did you..." She hesitated, searching his face.

"I found him," he said, and told her briefly what had happened.

"Oh, Rik, I'm sorry. To have come so close. What are you going to do now?"

"I don't know, try to find the killer, but I don't know where to begin."

"The weapon used is a good start. From what you said that sounds like a flamer instead of a blaster, and a defective one at that. They're not very common."

"You think anybody's going to tell me anything about this? After all the trouble we had before?"

"Rik, that was in large part because people wanted to defend your father. If they know he's been killed, they may very well want to avenge him."

"Unless they think I did it."

"Somebody will know the truth. You'll have to start asking around again."

"Just ask, I suppose, who's got a defective flamer. Hell, I don't even know what one looks like."

"You can't mistake it for anything else. It's got a regular pistol grip, a spherical frame, the pressure chamber extends back over the hand, and the barrel is a nozzle, slightly flared, with a—"

"I've seen one," Rikard said. "Sed Blakely, the man who abandoned my father to the Tathas in the first place, he had a gun like that. He said he couldn't remember where he'd left my father. I'll bet he remembered after I left. He was crazy, I know, but that was because of his guilt. I'll bet you he's the one."

"So then what are we waiting for? Let's go talk to him."

They left at once, got in Rikard's jeep, and drove south through the city. They reached Blakely's hideout shortly after sunset. Rikard parked the jeep out of sight of the repaired ruin, and he and Darcy approached the makeshift door with guns drawn.

"Braeth!" Rikard called. He felt funny using his father's name, but he didn't want Blakely to know he'd been found out. "It's me," he said. "I visited you a few days ago." There was no answer. He put his hand on the door, then smelled something foul and drew back.

"What's the matter?" Darcy asked from behind him. Then she smelled it too. Rotting flesh.

Rikard opened the door cautiously, not fearing a shot but anticipating the wave of stench that billowed out. Flies buzzed loudly. On Blakely's bed lay a putrefying corpse. Darcy, behind him, gagged.

"Is that him?" she asked from behind a hand that protected her mouth and nose as she peered into the darkened chamber.

"I don't know. Let's give it a minute to air out." He went back to the jeep and returned with his torch. There was no artificial light in Blakely's hideout. The stench of decay had abated somewhat. He went inside.

It was Blakely. His bloated body had burst from the pressure of the gases of putrefaction. Insects had burrowed through the flesh, speeding the processes of decay. But that did not conceal the fact that his arms and legs had been broken in several places. Parts of his naked body looked as if they had been burned.

"So we guessed wrong again," Rikard said, trying to keep his stomach down. "At first I thought it was Dobryn, but he'd been burned with a flamer." He flashed his light around the disheveled room, saw the crudely tanned leather clothes Blakely had worn piled in a corner. He went over and prodded them with his foot. No gun. He quickly kicked through the scattered junk. There wasn't much. The strange gun was not there.

"Who knew Blakely was here besides you and Aben Arshaud?" Darcy asked from the door. She refused to look at the corpse.

"At least one farmer, and probably several of the people we talked to. Arshaud will know for sure. Whoever it was tortured Blakely to find out where he'd left my father, and then took his gun and came down to kill us. Dzhergriem? Davinis? One of Avam Nikols's friends?"

"Arshaud's the one to talk to in any event," Darcy said. "He was the most helpful before. But he's a dangerous man."

"So am I."

Rikard went into the storeroom where Blakely had kept all his skins. They were untouched. He was just about to leave when he noticed a small, handmade leather bag on top of the farthest stack. He reached over and picked it up. The dragongems were still inside. He brought the bag out of the building to where Darcy was waiting in the twilight.

"Whoever it was," he said, showing her the gems, "they didn't know about these."

Her eyes widened as she recognized the dialithite in the fading sky light.

"Rikard," she said, taking one of the stones from the bag, "there's enough treasure here to make us both rich for life."

"You want them? You can have them if you want. I have more."

"How many?"

"Over three thousand. My father found the treasure he was looking for. These were only to be the first installment."

Darcy looked down at the gem in her hand, then put it back in the bag. "Are there more?"

"About two thousand lying in my father's ashes. And I don't know how many more we left behind."

"God. If we dumped just these here on the market right now, the price would plummet."

"It would. And if the prime cache were discovered, it would destroy the market altogether. It's there for anybody who can find it—but I'm not going to tell."

"I think you're right." She reached for the bag, then hesitated. "No, not these. We made a deal, remember?"

"I do. It still holds."

"Even though I couldn't fulfill my end of the bargain?"

"Even though."

She looked at the closed door of the hovel behind Rikard. "Let's leave these here then," she said.

"Suits me." He reentered the death chamber, put the bag back where he'd found it, and rejoined Darcy outside.

"After you find your father's killer," she said as they got back in the jeep, "then what?"

"I've got some other things to do." He told her about his promise to the Belshpaer and the Taarshome as they drove back to the city.

# 3.

It was too late to visit Arshaud by the time they got back to the city, and Rikard was running on the ragged edge of exhaustion. He dropped Darcy off at her place, drove back to his own rooms, and fell into an instant sleep. When he woke it was midmorning, and Darcy was sitting in his room.

"No ice water?" he asked wryly as he peered through gummy eyelids.

"Didn't have the heart. I wasn't sure you were going to make it home last night."

"The last few days haven't been the easiest," he admitted. He got out of bed and dressed, only marginally aware that Darcy was watching him. He was rested, but his thoughts were primarily concerned with what he was going to say to Arshaud.

Darcy made breakfast as he dressed. They ate quickly, then went to the hardware store. They found Arshaud in his office doing paperwork.

"Rikard," he said brightly as they entered. "Good to see you, boy." He got to his feet and shook hands warmly. "And you, too, Msr. Glemtide. But where have you been? My God, boy, but it's been a long time. I've been worried about you. Somebody heard that you'd been out looking for Sed Blakely, and apparently took offense, came by here a couple of times, wanted to know who you were, what you were up to. You can bet I talked a lot and didn't tell him anything, but apparently you've made some enemies. When you dropped out of sight, I thought they'd gotten to you. Hah, but you're just like your old man. You're too tough for them, too smart, just like he was—hey, I'm sorry, I shouldn't talk about him like that."

"That's okay," Rikard said when he had the chance. "Who was looking for me?"

"An old-timer named Dorong. I don't know him, but he's

been around here for sixteen, seventeen years or so. Got the distinct impression he had a grudge against you, was out for revenge of some kind. But now that you know about it, I'm sure you can take care of yourself. Where have you been?"

"Tracing down my father."

"But—but you found your father in his hideout south of town, didn't you?"

"No, Aben, that wasn't my father. That was Sed Blakely. I'm sorry I misled you, but I had to be careful. I found Pedar Gorshik, and he told me about the Tower of Fives. I got a guide to take me there and found my father alive, underground, where he'd been trapped by the Tathas for eleven years. The dragons had kept him alive. And he had found his treasure, more than he could carry. We brought it out, and someone shot him down with a flamer. At first I thought it was my guide, then that it was Blakely, but somebody else got to Blakely and tortured him to make him tell where he'd left my father."

"Damn, damn, I knew I should have done something about Dorong. The man's crazy, drunk most of the time. I didn't think he was any threat."

"Is that the same Dorong," Darcy asked, "that hangs around at the Troishla?"

"Yes, you've met him? No good sonofabitch. Hell, Rikard, what can I say? I should have fried him when he came in the first time, let alone the second. I knew he was up to no good. What I can't imagine is why."

"I embarrassed him in front of people at the Troishla." Rikard told Arshaud of the incident. "That was why Darcy had me hide out in the first place. Dorong couldn't have known anything about my father or why he'd gone there. He just wanted me, I think. Otherwise he would have had a more effective weapon, and stayed to get the dialithite."

"What? There was dialithite there?"

"Yes, lots. There was dialithite at Blakely's place too, and Dorong missed that."

"Damn! I think maybe we ought to go over to the Troishla and talk with our friend Dorong a minute."

"Just the three of us?" Darcy asked.

"Nothing to worry about." Arshaud's voice was grimly satisfied. "I'm part owner. Even Gareth has to listen to me."

"That's as may be," Darcy said, "but I'd feel happier with a little more weight on our side. I'm going to call Leo."

"If you want," Arshaud said. "The phone's out front." Darcy left. "Who's Leo?"

"Leonid Polski taught me to shoot," Rikard told him.

"Good enough for me." Arshaud opened a drawer in his desk and took out a laser pistol, larger and heavier than Darcy's. Rikard could see something else in the drawer as Arshaud pulled the power pack from the butt of the laser to check the charge.

"What's that?" he said, stepping closer to take a look.

"Hah?" Arshaud looked down at the battered flamer in his desk drawer. "Just an old gun," he said, fumbling the pack back into his own pistol.

Rikard felt time slow and was almost startled to see his hand come up with the megatron in it, sighting on the bridge of Arshaud's nose. He watched the surprise slowly register on Arshaud's face, his hands slip on the pistol, the power pack drop to the floor.

"Let's take a look at it," Rikard said. His voice sounded like a greatly slowed recording.

"Now, Rikard, wait," Arshaud protested. But his hands went up. Rikard stepped forward and hooked the flamer out of the drawer with his left hand. He couldn't tell without taking his eyes off Arshaud's face, but in his peripheral vision the gun looked an awful lot like the one Sed Blakely had had in his hovel. He backed away from Arshaud until he came up against the shelves beside the desk.

"Why?" was all he said.

Arshaud licked his lips, glanced down at the flamer, back up at Rikard's eyes.

"Because your father could connect me with the barodin," he said. "As long as he was hiding out down south—or trapped under the Tower of Fives—it didn't matter. But if you brought him out alive, there'd have been more trouble than I cared to face. I didn't want to do it. You've got to believe me."

"I think I do, but that doesn't help much. Especially after what you did to Blakely." Only his speeded-up senses let him see the tiny twitch in Arshaud's cheek when he said that. "What about Dorong? Another handy lie?"

"No, it's true, he did come here, told me the whole story. I would have killed him before you had a chance to talk to him, though, because he's of no account and would have given the lie away."

"You tried to kill me too down there under the tower. Why didn't you use your laser instead of this thing?"

"To cover up every chance I could get. You've gotten a lot of people stirred up since you came here, Rikard." He sat down slowly at his desk, still keeping his hands high. "People like Boss Bedik, Dzhergriem, Mareth Davinis. Other people were asking questions too."

"I think I want you to stand up against that far wall," Rikard said, suddenly uncomfortable at Arshaud's calmness.

"Sure thing, Rikard," Arshaud said, starting to rise. Voices spoke just beyond the office door. Rikard tried to hear what they were saying, prepared to move if they were Arshaud's clerks coming in. Arshaud seemed to slip ever so slightly, his foot sliding out from under him. Then the rack of hardware behind Rikard came down, his gun went off, and he was buried under the falling shelves of tools.

# 4.

He never quite lost consciousness. He was aware that he had dropped his gun. He could hear voices shouting. But he didn't know whether it was several minutes or just a few seconds before he recognized Polski's voice ordering other people to lift the heavy steel shelving off him. He returned to full awareness as the crushing weight was removed. Then wrenches and sockets and hammers were scooped from his body. He could recognize Darcy's boots near his face.

"Are you all right?" he heard her ask.

"I think so," he said, and then he was free to move. He pushed himself to his knees, feeling bruised. His left elbow was wrenched, there was a throb over his right ear, and his back and the backs of his legs felt as if they had been pounded on. Polski, with blaster drawn, was directing the clerks, who had freed Rikard from the shelving and hardware.

"What happened?" Polski asked as Rikard staggered to his feet.

"That shelf was booby-trapped. Arshaud sprang it on me. Where is he?"

"He didn't come out past us. We were just outside the door when we heard the crash."

"Then he's got some secret exit. He's the one who killed my father." He retrieved the megatron, then started kicking through the hardware jumbled on the floor until he found the flamer.

"Are you sure?" Darcy asked.

"Yes. He had this in his desk." He showed Darcy the flamer. "It's Blakely's gun. See the way the grip is burned? I got the drop on him, and he admitted it."

"But why?" Darcy asked.

"I don't know, except he said that my father knew about the barodin, whatever that means."

"What about barodin?" Polski's tone was one that made both Rikard and Darcy look at him sharply and made the three clerks by the door stop their murmuring.

"I can't quote him," Rikard said carefully, trying to remember where he'd heard the word before. "It was something like, my father could connect him with it. As long as Father was trapped or hiding, that didn't matter, but if he came back alive, Arshaud would have more trouble than he wanted to face. Something like that. Why?"

"The bomb that destroyed Banatree had a barodin catalyst, remember? It's rare and expensive and a controlled substance, and every gram is accounted for, except for what was in the battery factory on Pieshark when it was blown up the year before Banatree. If Aben Arshaud had barodin, or could be connected to it in some way, that's a strong indication that either he knew the Man Who Killed Banatree or is the Man himself."

"I understood he'd been here twenty years," Darcy said.

"Just a minute." Polski's eyes turned aside as if he were listening to something. "I've just been in communication with my liaison on the station," he said after a long moment. "Arshaud is not on my list of suspects, because, as you said,

he'd demonstrably arrived here long before the Banatree incident, so he couldn't be the Man himself."

"Are you sure?" Rikard asked. "Couldn't he have come,
gone away again, and then come back on one of those escape
pods from the hijacked freighter?"

"I've checked the records up on the station myself. He
couldn't get off Kohltri except through the station, though
the pod could have brought him in undetected—just a moment." His eyes turned inward again. "No, no record of his
ever having departed. But he knows something, and I mean
to find it out."

"Your people up there must be awfully fast," Rikard said.

"What do you mean?"

"You were in contact with them for only a moment. There
are at least three sets of records, and it would take longer
than we've been talking to check them all."

"What do you mean?" he repeated.

"You know, the plain text, the coded sets, the alternate
records."

"No, I don't know anything about that." Polski was obviously upset.

Rikard told him how he'd uncovered the secret records of
transport, shipping, and passenger movements while looking
for information on his father. Polski stared at him in disbelief,
but occasionally his eyes would flicker, as if he were getting
information from his station liaison.

"All right," Polski said when Rikard had finished, "I've
got confirmation that those records exist, but the ones in code
will take a while to break. How the hell did you find them?"

"I'm a Local Historian. As such, I never assume that the
visible record is the only record. How did you *miss* them?"

"I'm a Federal Police Officer. As such, I assumed that
any Federal office keeps its records according to protocol.
Damn stupid thing to do. It may give you some satisfaction
to know that this will warrant a full investigation of Director
Solvay's activities during his term of office. I think we'll find
some very interesting things. He—wait—got it. Aben Arshaud arrived twenty years, one hundred forty-three days ago,
according to the open record. One of those secret records has
him departing for Pieshark just fifty days before the battery

factory was destroyed. No record of his having ever returned. Yet here he is. Interesting."

"You've got your man," Rikard said, "except he's also the man who killed my father."

"Are you going to give me any trouble? Arshaud owes more to the Federation than he does to you."

"I know that, but I'm coming along."

"Good enough. Now all we have to do is find out where he got to."

"Well," Darcy said, "while you two have been chatting, I've been finding his escape hatch." She pointed to a low panel on the other side of the desk.

"We've lost too much time as it is," Polski said. He went to the open panel and went through. Rikard glanced once at the three clerks, then followed Darcy through the hatch.

A narrow corridor ran parallel to the wall for a way, then turned to the left. Stairs spiraled up, and they mounted them quickly but not hurriedly. They came out on the roof of the building, four floors above the street. To one side was an Atreef enclave. Polski stared at it for a moment.

"I'll tell you about that later," Darcy said. "This is what we're looking for." She pointed to a power box set near the stair door. It was the kind used to recharge a ground-fan flier.

"Damn," Polski said. "This is a big city. If we're going to comb it, I'll have to call in people from Kylesplanet. That will take a couple of days at best." He looked back at the white Atreef street nestled within the human block. "And as if trying to deal with Kohltri wasn't bad enough, it looks like I've got another whole population to deal with."

"I'm afraid so," Darcy said. "You want to hear about it now?"

"If you know what all that means, you can brief me when my crew comes in."

"I don't think you can afford to wait that long," Rikard said. "It's funny but Arshaud never believed in the treasure my father was looking for, but he sure reacted when I told him what it was and that he'd found it."

"What was it?"

"Dialithite, all a man could carry."

Polski stared at him in sudden dismay. "But . . . but, are you sure?"

Rikard took the stones he'd used to get past the Tathas from his pocket and held them out to the policeman. Polski didn't touch them.

"That means," Polski said, "he can buy his way off here, even going through the station."

"Not if we get to him first. I know where the dialithite is. That's where he's gone, I'm sure."

"Okay, kid, we'll have to take the chance. Just a moment." He communicated with his people again, taking several moments this time.

"I've done what I can about securing the station," he said at last. "Without having all the proper warrants, that isn't much. A copter will be here shortly. I suppose you'd like to come along," he said to Darcy.

"You couldn't keep me away, Leo," she said without humor.

"I wouldn't try." He walked over to the interface between the human and Atreef worlds. "Why don't you tell me about all this," he said, gesturing at the rounded white buildings below him. "We might have to comb the city after all."

The copter, with six Federal officers, arrived before she finished. Polski had one man go below to search and hold Arshaud's office. Then he, Rikard, Darcy, and the other five took off, heading east toward the Tower of Fives.

With a police copter flying well above the ground, it took them only four hours to make the trip. But the ground-fan flier was already in the plaza by the Tower when they got there.

"At least I guessed right," Rikard said as they all got out.

Polski left another officer at the copter to guard the flier and told the woman to take Arshaud alive if at all possible, if he should come back before they did, but to take him at all costs. As Rikard led the rest of them to the Tower's entrance, the officer moved the copter so it would be out of sight from the ground.

Rikard led the way through the Tower to the stairs going down. This time, as they passed through the first cellar to the second, he was aware of the complexity of the architecture; the rooms, branching corridors, odd passages. He'd ignored it all on his first trip, being concerned only with following the trail down, not exploring.

They paused at the stairs to the third level, and Polski left one of the four remaining officers to set up a guard post in case Arshaud came back by a route other than the one by which he descended.

"If Arshaud gets the dialithite," he said, "and manages to lose us down here, we'll never find him before he gets back to the surface. There's too much of a maze to cover completely, but there's no sense all of us being in one bunch."

Polski left another officer at the seventh level, at the mouth of the Tathas tunnel, with instructions to check for other similar tunnels but not to go too far.

The psychic effects of the Tathas tunnel were a surprise to everyone but Rikard. He explained them quickly and hurried the others on, past the hallucinatory monoliths and pseudoplants. There were more side passages than Polski liked. When they came to the lower Belshpaer chambers, with their bonelike white walls, Polski left another officer. The four went on down.

## 5.

They reached the lowest level, crossed the room, and entered the short hall just before the major Tathas chamber. The floor of the hall was strewn with charred and shattered bones.

"Goddamn," Rikard said in a choked voice, looking at the desecrated remains. "He didn't have to do that."

"Your father?" Darcy asked gently.

"Yes. I left him here just as he'd died. Arshaud's taken all the dialithite too." His eyes stung. His chest felt as if someone were sitting on it.

"You left the dialithite down here with your father?" Polski was unbelieving. "Why didn't you bring it out?"

"Dammit, Leonid, I don't care about the goddamn treasure. I care about my father. I didn't need what he was carrying so I let him keep it."

"Sorry, kid. Let me have your gun."

"What? Why?"

"I want to take Arshaud alive if he's still here. I don't want to take any chances that you'll shoot him first."

Rikard stared at him a moment, than handed him his megatron and the flamer, which he'd carried stuck in his belt.

"I understand," Polski said, "how much this means to you, but you have to understand my position too."

Rikard didn't say anything. He just turned up the passage toward the Tathas chamber.

The sound of a curse came from up ahead. Rikard ran to the edge of the chamber, feeling the Tathas psyche, and stopped, shining his torch in among the dead machines, slickly coated with the dark metallic residue of the fungus.

The other three came up just as his light picked out movement across the chamber, not far from the door to where his father had lived for eleven years. As the light struck, a moaning cry came from the writhing shape, then sobbing screams. It was Aben Arshaud, legs widespread, arms flailing, covered with a sickly white basket weave of coarse Tathas fibers.

"Oh, my God!" Darcy said. Arshaud cried out as the Tathas slowly dissolved his flesh. Rikard remembered the single touch he'd suffered, and felt sick.

"Put him out of his misery," the last officer said in a choking voice, raising his blaster.

"No!" Polski snapped. The officer hesitated. Arshaud screamed, staggered, spilling dialithite gems all over the floor.

"But Leo," Darcy protested as the officer turned away to vomit in a corner. "You can't just let him suffer."

"He killed three and a half million people." Polski's voice was tight and harsh.

"You don't *know* that."

"All right, then," Polski snarled, turning on her, "he killed Rikard's father. So what should we do, walk in there"—he indicated the chamber, where other Tathas were congregating—"and get eaten too?"

"Just put him out of his misery," Rikard said. He could no longer see Arshaud, just a towering mass of fibers which moved blindly this way and that. The screaming rose in pitch.

"Here, then," Polski said, and handed him back his gun.

Rikard fired into the center of the mass of writhing Tathas. The screaming went on. He fired until his gun was empty.

He could feel the Tathas' pain, but he was unable to see or hit Aben Arshaud.

Even Polski couldn't stand it any more. He took Sed Blakely's flamer and shot it across the chamber at the nightmare, but the gun was defective; the flame went only five or six meters. He pulled his blaster.

And then, from the doorway across the chamber, from the place where Rikard's father had lived, came a golden glow and the nebulous form of a dragon. Polski's hand froze, the dragon floated over to the huge bundle of Tathas, and touched it briefly. There was a flash and a flare and acrid smoke—and blessed silence as the whole mass charred to instant ash.

Then the dragon went back the way it had come.

"Let's get out of here," Polski said, his voice choked.

"What about the dialithite?" the white-faced officer asked.

"You want it? You go get it."

"Ah—no thanks," the man said. He looked at the dozens of other still-living though stunned and shocked Tathas squirming across the floor of the chamber. "I guess I can live without it."

They returned to the surface, retrieving the other officers as they went. None of them had to be told what had happened. Their implanted communicators had informed them of the events.

The copter settled down into the plaza by the Tower of Fives as they emerged.

"I'm going to assume," Polski said as they entered the copter, "unless instructed otherwise that Aben Arshaud was in fact the Man Who Killed Banatree. And if the public wants justice, the monitor has what we saw recorded. So as far as I'm concerned, I'm through here."

"Me too," Rikard said. "That was a bit more revenge than I had in mind."

"So what will you do now?" Polski asked.

Rikard looked around at the other police officers, not sure of just how much he should say in front of them.

"I did bring out a few stones," he said quietly. "They'll keep me going for quite a while. And I made some promises that I'm going to have to keep."

He looked out the window of the copter at the ruins, then at the wilderness passing below. In his mind he had a brief image of his father enveloped in flames in the dark tunnel under the Tower of Fives. Then he felt someone touch his hand. It was Darcy.

"You owe me a couple of those stones," she said softly.

"I sure do," he told her. Polski was studiously looking somewhere else. "You want to help me find a good market for them?"

"Nothing I'd like better."

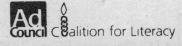